A PLACE TO START OVER

BARRINGTON BOOK TWO

SUSAN MACKIE

For Bloke

For telling me you're my Trophy Boyfriend.
Still laughing.

Susan Mackie

Dusk descended as Harriet drove through Stroud. She yawned. Only four hours from Sydney's lower north shore, but the events of the last few days had left her exhausted. The GPS indicated it was forty-five minutes to her accommodation at Barrington Homestead. She'd planned to leave earlier, should have stopped for the night already, but it seemed so close on google maps.

Dark now, a vehicle travelling behind her sped up and turned their lights to full beam, almost blinding her in the rear-view mirror. Bloody idiot. Driving too fast and lights on full. Harriet slowed, hoping the faster driver would pass her.

Instead, he flashed his lights. Once. Twice. While simultaneously blaring the horn. Then Harriet saw them. A large mob of kangaroos bounding along the other side of the road. One very large 'roo veered across the road in front of her. She wrenched the wheel to the left and slammed her foot on the brake. Almost stationary, her car hit the 'roo with a sickening thud, although it seemed to bounce right off the bonnet. With one wheel in the ditch at the side of the road, her engine revving furiously, Harriet sat in shock, breathing hard.

The seatbelt was digging in painfully, so she released it quickly. The other vehicle, a large Range Rover, stopped behind her, lights now dimmed. Glancing at her side mirror, Harriet saw the driver striding toward her. He yanked her door open and dropped to his haunches, peering at her in the evening gloom.

'Are you hurt? Can you move?' He put his arms in to help her out of the car.

'Stop it. Don't touch me!' Harriet fought down panic. She just needed to get out of the car slowly and assess how she felt, without this man-giant grabbing at her. She registered pain in her right elbow, and across her chest from the seatbelt.

He stood up and stepped back. 'Of course. Forgive me. Take your time.' He spoke in a deep, modulated tone, which surprised Harriet. More 'Melbourne' than country, she thought to herself.

Harriet turned in her seat, gingerly swinging her legs out first, before carefully standing up. Her elbow was tender, but she felt otherwise intact. Her car, on the other hand, looked like it would need a tow to get it out of the ditch. The bonnet was pushed back several inches and the bumper was hanging off one side. Her heart sank. This was all she needed.

'Drummond Murray.' He held out his hand. Hesitating for a few seconds before placing her slender hand in his massive paw, she shook firmly. 'Harriet Russell.' She clenched her jaw as he looked her over, watching his eyes rove from her too-thin face to the way she was holding her right elbow, supporting it with her left hand.

Harriet tried to hide her annoyance. She knew he was checking her for injury, but his scrutiny made her uncomfortable. She was on the side of the road, with a car requiring repairs just a half hour from her destination. Taking a deep breath, she returned his gaze.

Drummond Murray was extremely tall. Broad shouldered. A man-mountain. She blinked. Mid-thirties, well-dressed in mole-skins, boots and buttoned shirt. Harriet realized, rather belatedly, he was quite good looking with a strong face, dark hair and ginger chin stubble. With a name like Drummond Murray, she wasn't surprised, the area had been settled by the Scots more than a century ago.

'I am uninjured Drummond. Perhaps you would rather assess my car? I fear I'll need a tow into Barrington.'

Drummond looked momentarily surprised, before turning to her red Alfa Romeo Giulietta. After starting it and checking under the hood, he nodded. 'You're right, it's not drivable. It's not really suited to country roads. Too low slung.'

Harriet bristled at his words. 'This car is perfectly suited to country driving. This is not a dirt road, but a main road, and had you not blinded me by flashing your lights I would not be having this conversation with you.'

She saw him frown as he glanced at the kangaroo lying in the ditch. 'This is why I had my lights on full, your lower lights would not have registered the mob in time. I'll call the local mechanic to see if he can pick it up tonight.' He quickly made the call and Harriet could hear that it would be a job for tomorrow.

Sighing, she retrieved her phone from her bag on the passenger seat. It was unlikely she would get a taxi out here, but she had no option, other than to call her host, Rose Gordon at Barrington Homestead.

While she scrolled through her contacts, Drummond asked 'Where are you headed?'

'Barrington Homestead. I'm staying there for a few days.' Harriet found the Homestead number and glanced up.

He looked again at the kangaroo. 'As I am responsible for your car leaving the road …' he paused, and Harriet blushed slightly. 'I will deliver you to your destination. I live just beyond the Homestead myself. Would you like to retrieve your personal items from your car?'

Harriet had to admit Drummond was a gentleman as he assisted her with her bags, placing them on the back seat. He held the passenger door open and waited while she secured the seatbelt, before walking to the rear of the car. Harriet couldn't see what he was doing, and the sound of the rifle retort somewhere behind the vehicle caused her to jump in her seat. In the rear mirror she saw him drag the carcass of the kangaroo further off the road. She had assumed it was killed by the initial impact. She shuddered.

They drove in silence for a few minutes. Harriet had time to consider the accident and knew the damage to the car, and herself, would have been far worse if she'd hit the mob at full speed.

'Thank you. I could have encountered a kangaroo at any time after dusk. I had planned to leave earlier. I was just so close.' Hesitating for a moment, she continued, 'I didn't see them until you forced me to stop.'

Harriet looked at the road ahead as she spoke, hoping he couldn't see the tension in her jawline and darkness beneath her eyes. She was exhausted and not in the mood for conversation. Glancing at him, she was pleased when he nodded and drove on.

They drove slowly along the poplar lined driveway of the homestead. Night had fallen, but a half moon and the headlights lit up the magnificent old house. Harriet drew a breath. She had seen the pictures on Airbnb of course, but they did not do it justice. How she would love to own a home like this.

A half-grown cattle dog barked from the house yard as they pulled up. The lights were on, and a woman strode out to meet them. This must be her host, Rose Gordon. She seemed surprised to see Drummond, even more so when Harriet climbed awkwardly from the passenger seat.

'Drum, hello. I wasn't expecting you.' She looked from him to Harriet.

Before Harriet could introduce herself, Drummond stepped forward. 'Hello Rose. This is Harriet Russell, your guest I understand. She hit a kangaroo this side of Stroud, and her car needs repairs. Jim Daly will pick it up first thing tomorrow.'

Registering the concern on both their faces, Harriet inwardly cringed as Rose stepped closer and looked into her face. 'Are you hurt Harriet? Perhaps we should get you to the hospital …'

Almost too loudly, Harriet interrupted. 'I'm fine Rose, thank you. A little shaken and cranky with myself for not departing Sydney earlier. I should have known better.'

Harriet met Rose's gaze, then turned to Drummond and smiled. 'It was good of you to drive me here, thank you.'

Rose chimed in. 'Can I offer you a drink Drum? Angus is still out at the Campbell place, drenching their young stock, but he should be home soon.'

2

Drummond returned Rose's smile. About to accept, he glanced at Harriet. He could see exhaustion and something else on her face. Discomfort? Pain? He'd assumed she wasn't injured in the accident, but now wondered if he should have taken her to hospital.

'Harriet, if you're not feeling well, we can drive straight back into town. I should have taken you there as a precaution, in the first instance.' He watched her gather herself, her back straight and her chin up slightly. Small in stature, her thick honey-blond hair fell in waves to her shoulders and her blue eyes seemed too large for her thin, pale face. He recognised she was tired, sore and quite probably drawing on a reserve of inner strength, but her manners were impeccable.

'Thank you, Drummond. I'm fine. Just tired. Thank you again for driving me. I will follow up with the mechanic in the morning.' He wasn't convinced but accepted her assertion.

Drummond turned to Rose, who still seemed concerned. 'Thanks Rose, I will catch Angus in the next day or two. Good-night to you both.'

He smiled briefly at both women, returned to his car and drove slowly along the driveway to the road. Looking in his rear-view mirror he saw Rose pick up Harriet's bags. He noticed the way Harriet favoured her right arm. Damn it! He should have insisted she go to the hospital. He sighed. Not really his problem, but the thought of her potential injuries niggled at him.

3

Ten minutes later Harriet was sitting at Rose's kitchen bench, hands wrapped around a 'hot toddy' – some sort of whiskey, cinnamon and honey concoction, warmed up, that Rose said her grandfather used to brew as a 'cure all.'

Rose had shown Harriet to her room. More than a room, a suite with its own entrance; while explaining this was her parents' quarters when she was young, and her grandparents had lived in the main house. She invited her to come back through the main house for a drink and chat in the kitchen when she was ready.

Harriet went to the bathroom, which was stunning, with an oversize tub she would delight in later, and quickly inspected her sore spots. She could see redness from the seat belt across her chest and her right elbow was swollen; it must have hit the window or door on impact. Her older wound was reddened and a bit tender, but she expected that after the crash. Nodding to herself in the mirror she acknowledged that her injuries may have been far worse had Drummond Murray not alerted her to the mob of kangaroos by the roadside. She just hoped her car would not take long to repair.

Chatting in the kitchen, Harriet warmed to Rose immediately. They had spoken via messenger a few times during the course of booking the accommodation, but Harriet had not expected her to be so young. Probably not even thirty yet, while Harriet herself had turned thirty-one the day before, hence her delayed start that day.

'I'm fine. Some bruising but no real damage.' Harriet took another sip of her medicine. 'Another one of these and I won't feel a thing!'

Rose threw back her head and laughed.

'That's the spirit! Are you telling me you're a cheap drunk?' Rose pushed a small cheese platter a bit closer to Harriet. 'You must be hungry. And tired. Please, try some cheese, it's locally made.'

Looking into her mug as she took another sip, Harriet smiled wanly. How could she tell this lovely young woman just how tired she was? Not tired. Exhausted. Bone weary. Heart sick. Soul sick.

Instead, she reached for a piece of cheese and a stuffed olive, popping it into her mouth while making an 'mmmm' sound. As she did, all hell seemed to break loose. A loud wail from a nearby room had Rose on her feet, while in the same moment the young dog outside began barking madly as headlights swept past the kitchen window.

Rose left the room for a moment, striding back in with a small child on her hip just as the front door banged open and a slightly grubby, but very good looking, and tall, man strode in. He glanced curiously at Harriet for the briefest moment before sweeping Rose into his arms, the child between them, kissing her heartily on the lips.

Watching the scene, as wordlessly Rose leaned into him then handed the child over, something shifted in Harriet. A little flare of envy at the easy warmth between the couple was replaced immediately by a stronger flame of happiness. This was it. This was what she wanted. Aspired to. It really did exist.

She found herself grinning as they all spoke at once, Rose laughingly introducing her partner Angus, 'We're not married yet you know. Living in sin,' and their little boy, Charlie, who was fourteen months old, 'and a wee devil if you want the truth,' Angus added, smiling indulgently at his offspring as he flailed his small arms, sending the dish of olives from the kitchen bench to the floor. The dog outside began barking again.

4

____

Heart pounding, she sensed danger all around, enveloping her like a thick fog. Harriet held her large leather Prada handbag tightly as she hurried toward the train station at Circular Quay. She couldn't shake a deep foreboding of impending danger.

Shaking her head in an attempt to clear the darkness she felt around her, she stepped onto the platform. A group of teenage girls chatted loudly at the other end, and an older lady wearing a floral scarf over her hair sat on a bench to her left. Harriet sidled closer to the older woman, glancing over her shoulder. There was no one else about. It was late. Yet the uncomfortable feeling persisted.

The train approached, its brakes squealing a little as it slowed. The teenage girls stepped into the first carriage, chatting and laughing. One of them was playing a song loudly on her phone.

Distracted for a moment while watching them, she stepped back to allow the older woman to board before her. Without warning the woman backed off the train hurriedly, pushed out of the carriage by a wild-eyed man in rough clothing. She tripped over Harriet's foot and fell heavily. Harriet leaned down to help her up, trying to keep an eye on the vagrant at the same time. He was behind her now. The older woman stood, re-boarding the train quickly. As

Harriet stepped into the carriage, her handbag was ripped from her grasp by the man behind her. Holding it he stepped back on the platform, watching her cautiously.

She hesitated for one moment then stepped out, one hand still on the carriage door, grabbed her bag, tugging it from the man's grasp. He grimaced at her. His breath was foul, what teeth he had were yellow and decaying. His mouth was cavernous, his tongue obscenely red. Then she saw it. The knife. A switch knife, sharp serrated edges. The woman inside the carriage was screaming at her. 'Let it go! Close the doors! Just let it go!'

Jumping back into the carriage with her precious bag, Harriet was not quick enough. He leapt forward, burying the knife low in her abdomen, on the right-hand side. So deep it hit her hip bone. She didn't feel the pain in that first rush of adrenalin. He tore the leather bag from her grasp. Or perhaps she handed it to him. The doors closed, he was standing on the platform, grinning maniacally. He held up his hands. Her bag in the left one, the bloodied knife in the right.

She fell back, the other woman helped her to a seat and pushed the emergency button. Then the pain began to unfurl in her stomach, her hip, up her right-hand side. Looking down, she saw the blood. Red like her attacker's tongue. Obscene. So much blood. Then nothing.

Awakened by the nightmare, Harriet lay in bed, listening to the early morning sounds of a kookaburra on a fencepost only metres from her window. Comforting sounds. Tentatively moving her legs over the edge of the bed she sat up, then gasped. Everything hurt. Her chest, her right elbow, the whole of her torso.

Walking slowly to the bathroom, she took off the tee shirt she'd worn to bed and looked in the mirror. Bruises now bloomed across her chest and right arm and the area around her old wound was red, slightly raised and warm to touch. Damn. Another infection would mean re-opening the wound, probably another drain bag. She still had a couple of antibiotic repeats, she could get them filled at the chemist and see if that killed any infection before it took hold.

Showered and dressed she felt better, but her movements were slow and cautious. Her key mission was to sort out the repairs to her car. Rose had invited her to come through to the main house for breakfast, whenever she was ready. While wanting her privacy, Harriet knew she needed some help with a trip to town, perhaps organise a hire car if hers was going to take more than a few days to repair.

In the kitchen, Rose set a steaming mug in front of her.

'Coffee. Strong. But I can add some rum if you need it,' she raised her eyebrows.

Harriet grinned at her. 'Coffee for now. Maybe rum later.'

'Drum Murray called earlier. Your car is already at the workshop, and he said you just need to let Jim Daly know your insurance details. However, he mentioned that it might take at least a week to source parts for your '*little Italian number*.' His words not mine.'

'Little Italian number? Really? Does no one drive a European car here? Drummond Murray has a Range Rover himself. That's English.' Harriet screwed up her nose.

In a very English accent, Rose added 'English is perfectly acceptable here. European. Not so much.' Harriet snorted into her coffee. Yes, she really likes this woman.

Harriet rolled her eyes and smiled as she picked at the toast Rose plonked down between them. Charlie was in a high-chair, a chewed-up crust in one hand, teaspoon in the other. He looked a lot like his father, but with Rose's colouring. Red-brown hair, although not much of it. He banged his teaspoon a couple of times and Rose cut off a piece of crust from her toast and handed it to him. 'It's not all about you Charlie. Not right now. Eat your crust.'

Rose turned her attention to Harriet. 'I need to know how

you are. I can see you're sore. I'd like to take you in to the hospital, just to be sure.'

'No. No hospital. No need. Nothing that won't heal with a bit of rest.' Harriet shook her head.

Harriet met Rose's eyes for a moment, then inwardly relaxed as Rose conceded. 'Okay. I understand. You call the shots. I'm here if you need help.' Her tone was gentle, but firm.

Harriet shifted in her chair. 'Is there a car hire place in Barrington? Or will the mechanic have a courtesy car …'

'Ha! Small town Harriet. No and Joe Daly doesn't have a courtesy car either. If you don't mind waiting about half an hour, you can ride into town with Charlie and me. You can check with Joe about how long yours will take to repair. If it's just a couple of days, you can borrow mine when you need to. If longer we may be able to get a hire car across from Taree for you. I know you only booked three nights, but do you need to get back to Sydney after that? Work commitments?'

'No. I'm on leave. I planned to head north on Wednesday. Was going to stay by the beach for a couple of weeks, somewhere near Coffs Harbour. But I haven't booked anything up there yet. If I need to change my plans, how long can I stay here? Do you have anyone coming in after me?'

'Nothing booked for the next two months until early January. We only opened the B&B six months ago, and it's been a bit inconsistent. Longer staying guests are a bit easier to manage, just at the moment.' She glanced at Charlie, concentrating on his crust. 'Motherhood has been, um, busier, than I imagined.'

Harriet was curious. 'Do you and Angus run the farm together? I understand from last night's chat he also has a Vet practice with rooms in town. Do you help there too?'

'We do run the farm together, but the B&B and horses are my responsibility, while he oversees the cattle, hay making and so on. I, um, was in publishing before little Charlie came along and you know I grew up here, it's the family property. Actually, I'm also a writer.' She glanced at Charlie. 'When I have time. I've just released my first novel.'

Harriet was impressed. 'Really? Would I know it? I've been reading a lot, recently.' She frowned for a moment, doing a mental inventory of recent releases by Australian authors. 'Wait! I thought I knew your name. I know your book, it's called Controlling something. Controlling Interest. That's it! I've got it on my kindle but haven't read it yet. Wow, I'm so impressed!'

'It's early days yet, but I've had some promising reviews on Goodreads and Amazon. Thanks.' Rose turned to sort Charlie out as she spoke, but not before Harriet saw the flush of pleasure her words had provided. Good. Women need to support each other. Lift each other.

'I'll read it while I'm here and write a review.' Harriet smiled at Rose, who blushed.

'My old publishing house wanted to publish for me, but with my background I've become an Indie Publisher, so I spend a few hours each day on that, if Charlie lets me, plus checking on the horses and attempting to write my second book. And managing Charlie of course, which seems to take up more time and energy every day.' Rose smiled fondly at her son, who had stuffed the crust in one ear and was busy undoing the front of his onesie.

5

_B_iting her lip, Harriet walked along the main street from the workshop. It could take up to three weeks for her car to be repaired, depending on parts availability. Should she go back to Sydney and return when her car was fixed or stay on at Barrington Homestead? Damn. But she was escaping Sydney. There was nothing there for her anymore. She certainly didn't want to run into her dodgy, two-timing ex-husband.

While recovering from the attack on the train, and the subsequent surgeries, she'd decided she wouldn't stay in Sydney one minute longer than her thirty first birthday. She would head north. Start a business of her own. Well, she can still do that. She'd stay at the Homestead, hire a car from Taree, and continue to look around for the right location to start over. A regional town. Not as small as this one perhaps, but somewhere with potential. She'd had plenty of time to think about her business concept while recovering, and knew she was on to something. She just had to find the right place. Another three weeks wasn't going to put her off. She could continue to research and establish plans while she waited for her car.

Houses for sale and rent displayed in the window of a real estate office caught her eye, particularly a rather charming timber colonial cottage. Stopping to read the listing, Harriet drew in a breath. She knew housing was cheaper in rural areas than in Sydney, but could you really buy a little cottage in a lovely setting at this price?

Leaning in, she peered at the description. *Colonial cottage, two bedrooms, functional kitchen, large block.* She looked again at the three photos on the listing card. They were faded; the listing had been in the window for some time.

'No wonder it hasn't sold,' she muttered, 'where's the sizzle? I thought real estate agents always oversold their listings.'

'That's how they do it in the city, Missy, but here in the country we deal with the facts.' Harriet flinched, she hadn't noticed the tall, grey-haired gentleman stop alongside her.

Looking up, she gave him a brief nod. 'The facts are important, but a bit of sizzle wouldn't go astray. Might fire up the imagination of a potential buyer, help them picture themselves in that little cottage.'

'Sizzle you say? Such as …' he looked at her expectantly.

Wanting to make her point, Harriet glanced at the listing again. 'I'd write, *'charming cottage with high ceilings and large bedrooms, cosy living area with combustion fireplace, sun-drenched kitchen and period style bathroom with claw foot tub.'* She peered again at the faded photos. *'Large yard with room for play area and a kitchen garden, close to shops and schools."* She looked smugly at the gentleman beside her. 'And they are the facts as I see them in the photos, which are very poor quality as it is.'

He looked at her again, eyebrows slightly raised. Holding his hand out, he introduced himself. 'Benjamin Evans,' nodding at the sign over the door saying Evans Real Estate, he added 'Principal.'

Flushing, Harriet accepted his handshake. 'Oh. Nice to meet you. Harriet Russell.'

'Just passing through?'

'Yes. No. I planned to visit for a few days but had an altercation with a 'roo last night and it's going to take time to get parts. I must get on, I need to pick up some items before getting a lift back to Barrington Homestead. Nice to meet you Mr Evans.' Harriet smiled tentatively to acknowledge his friendly nod. Was there a glint of amusement in his eyes? Had she offended him? Maybe not.

Walking smartly into the café a few doors further along, she let out an explosive breath as she arrived at the counter, mentally berating herself for opening her big mouth. A small girl, not more than seven, smiled at her from the other side.

'Good morning' she said, her curly blonde hair kept back with an Alice band, 'what can I get you this fine morning?' Her earnest little face dimpled when she smiled, and Harriet smiled back at her.

'Good morning to you. I would like four pieces of caramel slice to take away please.' Harriet watched as the little moppet pulled the milk crate, she had been standing on, further to the left, step up on it and stretch to reach the tray of caramel slice. She expertly used wooden tongs to manipulate four pieces into a brown paper bag. Almost disappearing from view as she jumped off the crate, she dragged it back to its original position where her smiling face popped up again, placing the bag on the counter in front of Harriet.

With a serious expression she said, 'We don't use plastic bags anymore. They're not good for the 'vironment.' Frowning slightly, she added 'the caramel slice is four dollars apiece.' Punching it into the screen of the cash register, she smiled again, saying 'that will be sixteen dollars, thank you.'

Harriet nodded, while internally chuckling, as she reached for her wallet. Cute as a button and smart to boot. Harriet couldn't see evidence of any adult supervision and wondered if the child was in the cafe alone.

'Are you the owner of this cafe, young lady?' Harriet handed across a crisp twenty-dollar note.

'Oh no! I'm just a kid. Aunty Debbie had to run some coffee up to the bank and Cathy is in the kitchen out back, so I'm in charge while she's gone. I should be at school, but I felt a bit wobbly in the tummy this morning, so Mummy let me stay with Aunty Deb at work 'til Nanna picks me up.' She handed the change across the counter.

Just then a young woman wearing a white baker style apron over an obvious pregnancy, rushed in. Taking in the package on the counter and Harriet putting her wallet back in her bag, the young woman said with a smile, 'Oh, hello. Has Tiffany looked after you?'

'Tiffany? I thought she was the owner actually, and yes, I have been well looked after.' Harriet smiled broadly.

The young woman laughed as she ducked behind the counter. 'Good job Tiff. Nan will be in to pick you up shortly, so get your bag from out back please.'

Harriet started to turn away, but the other woman spoke again. 'Are you just passing through or did you stay in town last night?'

Friendly town. Friendly people. Or just nosy? 'Oh. Here for a few days. I'm staying at Barrington Homestead B&B.'

'Good. With Rose.' The young woman nodded. 'You'll be very comfortable there. I might see you in here again. I'm Debbie Tait.' She smiled and held her hand out.

Small town friendly. Comforting. 'Harriet Russell, nice to meet you.' They shook hands. Harriet nodded at Debbie's obvious bump. 'When are you due?'

'Six weeks, just before Christmas. Can't wait. Getting a bit hard to lug this monster around all day.' Hands over her tummy, she laughed.

'You're doing well to keep working.' Harriet smiled warmly. 'Thanks Debbie. I'm sure I'll see you again while I'm here.' Turning away from the counter, the package in her hand, Harriet walked straight into Drummond Murray as he strode through the door.

6

'*O*oof!' Harriet dropped the bag, caramel slice spilling out, while she clutched her side, suddenly light-headed.

'Harriet! Sorry! Thought you saw me there. Are you hurt?' Drummond put a steadying hand under her swollen elbow, leading her to a chair at the closest table. Debbie rushed out from behind the counter.

'Are you okay? What did you do Drum? Bloody men.' Harriet knew Debbie was saying it more for her benefit than Drum's, and now the pain was subsiding she just wanted to get up, walk out and deflect attention from herself.

'Harriet hit a 'roo with her car last night coming into town. She said then she wasn't injured. I should have taken her to hospital anyway.' Drummond was crouching in front of Harriet, one hand on her shoulder, while talking to Debbie, hovering beside him.

'Just sit Harriet. Catch your breath.' Debbie turned back to the counter and called out, 'Cathy, bring me a glass of water please.'

Harriet tried to control her features and straightened in her seat as Debbie spoke to her, feeling embarrassed at all the attention. 'Shall I call the hospital Harriet. Tell them we'll bring you in?'

Shaking her head, feeling ridiculously close to tears at the kindness she heard in Debbie's voice, Harriet took a sip of the water Cathy offered and muttered, 'I'm okay. Just winded for a moment. Yes, I've got a few sore spots, but it's just bruising. Honestly, I'm fine.' Looking up, seeing genuine concern on Debbie's face and a slight frown on Drummond's, she straightened her back and tried to smile.

Placing the water in front of her, Debbie picked up the fallen goods, returning them to the counter just as Rose walked in, Charlie on her hip. Coming straight to Harriet's side she thrust her chin out at Drummond and said, 'What have you done Drum?'

Standing, Drum reached for Charlie, swinging him into the air before tucking him into his side, holding him steady with one gigantic hand. 'Harriet says she's okay. I bumped into her as I came in.'

Rose looked at Harriet and promptly sat down in the chair next to her, taking Charlie from Drum's arms as she did. 'Well Okay. I was going to bring you here for coffee this morning and introduce you to Deb. So, Drum Murray, be a good fellow and order some coffee for us. And something sweet. How do you like your coffee, Harriet?'

While Rose was speaking, Harriet had gathered herself, grateful Rose had noted her embarrassment and given her a moment to do so. 'What a lovely idea. I'll have a chai latte please.'

'Caramel latte and chai latte please Drum. Large. And caramel slice to go with it. Harriet can afford the calories.'

Harriet mouthed 'thank you' to Rose as Drum stepped over to the counter, pulling his wallet out of his back pocket as he did.

'Bloody men. Clumsy oafs. Drum's usually pretty quick on his feet, but he doesn't realise that walking into him is like hitting a brick ...'

'Wall?'

'Shithouse, I was going to say. But wall is more ladylike so let's go with that.'

Harriet laughed out loud at Rose's words. Rose gave her a conspiratorial nod, while bouncing Charlie on her lap, who was now fascinated with Rose's watch, tugging it until she released the clasp and gave it to him.

Drum returned, caramel slice on a plate and a cookie for Charlie. Turning to Harriet he said, 'I've been to Joe Daly's this morning too. Just after you were there. He says three weeks, at best, for parts and repairs.'

'Yes. Apparently getting parts for my 'little Italian number' may take some time.' Harriet was trying not to laugh as Drummond looked at her suspiciously.

'Hmm. Yes. Well. I've got a spare vehicle you can use. It's an older model Land Rover. If you'd care to come home with me today, you can pick it up, drive it back to Rose's.'

Shocked, Harriet looked at him. 'Why? Why would you lend me a car? You don't know me at all.' Shaking her head in disbelief, Harriet waited for his response.

'It's just a car Harriet. I'm not using it. You'll be without one. You may use it until yours is repaired.' He stood as he spoke. 'I've got a meeting to go to, but I'll be back inside an hour.' He ruffled Charlie's hair, touched Rose on the shoulder, nodded at Harriet and walked out.

Still shocked, Harriet looked at Rose, eyebrows raised. Rose shrugged. 'He has a spare car. You need one. You're not about to drive off in his ten-year-old Land Rover leaving your Alfa behind. It solves one of your problems.'

'Yes, it does.' Harriet spoke quietly, slightly ashamed by her own reaction. 'I will thank him. And I will look after his car.'

'Good. Here's our coffee. Let's see if Deb has time to join us.'

7

Driving with Drum to pick up his car, Harriet asked how long his family had been in the area. It was obvious Rose and he had known each other a long time, and she wondered if he was also a generational local.

'Murrays arrived in the early eighteen hundreds. Two brothers, timber getters. While others were rushing to the gold fields to make their fortune, they cut and milled timber, taking advantage of the rapid growth of towns outside the main cities. The next generation diversified, started grazing sheep and cattle on the country they'd cleared. They always left timber in the steep valleys and hillsides, not because it was harder to get, but to prevent erosion, provide cover for the stock and allow re-growth of rosewood, cedar and local hardwoods.'

'So, you're on the Murray family farm, er property, yourself?' He glanced at her sharply before he answered. Was she being too nosy? No. Damn it. She was interested.

'Yes, I'm in the original homestead. There are Murrays, cousins, further up the valley and another lot of second cousins in the next valley over. We have spread out across the country really, six generations now.' Drum turned onto a smaller road, heading south-west from Barrington.

Harriet nodded, sensing Drum had shared as much of his family background as he was comfortable with. She looked to the north, catching sight of an unusual mountain formation. About to ask, Drum anticipated the question.

'The Bucketts Range. Steep, great for bushwalking and rock climbing. Not the Barrington Tops proper though.' He slowed the vehicle, the road dipped down to a cement bridge over a clear, fast running river. Harriet could see the river was lapping the low bridge that was almost just a causeway.

'Rocky Crossing. Impassable after really heavy rain. The water can rise quickly. Every year we have a tourist or two drive through when the water is too high, too fast. They don't note the markers and warnings.'

Harriet wound down her window for a better look at the river as they crossed. Not large, but clear and fast. She wouldn't like to drive through when it was well over the bridge.

A few minutes later they turned into a driveway with old, and impressive, stone pillars on either side. They drove up into a valley, a creek winding along beside them. Tall eucalypts lined the driveway, with green fields beyond peppered with large, healthy-looking cattle. Some black, some white. Angus and Charolais, Harriet thought, but didn't comment. Turning slightly to the left, a cottage came into view. Backing on to the creek, it sat to one side of an enormous, aged oak tree. The timber cottage was old, yet well cared for, painted a rich cream with highlights in deep russet and white trim around windows and doors, veranda rails and front steps and the picket fence all round.

Harriet was entranced. 'Oh, your home is so pretty. How lovely. What a beautiful spot, right by the creek.'

Drum grinned, then drove on. 'Oh, that's just a worker's cottage. You'll see the homestead in a moment.'

Harriet looked back at the cottage as they passed, then turned when Drum cleared his throat.

The homestead. It belonged in a Country Living magazine. Harriet had admired Rose's family home, but this was something else again. It sat proudly on a slight rise, a large, fenced yard with a thriving, well-established English-style garden in front. A sandy path wound through roses and shrubs to the front steps that led up to the veranda. It was a sandstone homestead, single level, with French doors onto the veranda that Harriet felt sure wrapped right around the house. Four large stone chimneys rose above the iron roof and slightly behind Harriet could see the high fence of a tennis court. Outbuildings beyond the house could be seen, and a few hundred metres further away were a series of large modern sheds and silos, cattle yards and farm vehicles.

'Oh gosh. Wow! This is the most amazing home I've ever seen up close. What a privilege to live here.' She turned to Drum, eyes shining. 'Any chance I can take the tour?'

Harriet gazed enraptured at the homestead, then glanced at Drum, to note a slight smile playing around his mouth.

'I'll have to give you 'the tour' of Montrose another day Harriet. I'm sorry, I have to go to Sydney today. The Land Rover is just here.' He stepped out of the car and came around to the passenger side. Harriet had already opened the door, but had turned in her seat, swinging her legs out first, before beginning to step out.

'You're obviously sore from the accident Harriet. Take my hand.' Drum held one strong hand out to Harriet, who ignored it and half jumped the last few inches to the ground, causing her to double over as the small jolt sent a sharp pain to her side.

8

His hand below her elbow, Drum steadied her. It was obvious she was in pain, just getting out of the vehicle had winded her. He could also see she was embarrassed. Why? She had been in an accident the day before. He moved closer, placing his left arm gently around her back, encouraging her to lean into his side. She was small in his arms, thin, her head barely reaching his shoulder. Something stirred in him. He felt protective, wanted to interrogate her about the pain, her injuries, but sensed she would back away.

He felt her stiffen after a moment, then straighten her back. He removed his arm and took a half step away, silently willing her to meet his eyes.

Drum watched as Harriet took a deep breath, then raised her eyes to his. 'Thank you. Bit awkward getting out, should have known better. Only bruises, but a bit tender still.' Her eyes slid away from his, taking in the homestead beside them. She added quietly, 'I really appreciate the loan of your car. I'll take good care of it.'

There had to be more to it, but it wasn't his place to pry. Her fragility moved him and he wasn't looking for that. To feel tenderness for a woman. Didn't need it. Didn't need any complications just now. Stepping away, he walked toward the white Land Rover parked to one side. He opened the door, took the keys from under the mat on the driver's floor and handed them to Harriet.

'Probably about half full of fuel. It was serviced a few weeks ago so you won't have any problems.' He knew he sounded a bit gruff, but the woman beside him was a contradiction. She had strength, he could see that. Strong will and determination. Yet he sensed a vulnerability too, and that touched him.

Taking the keys Harriet stepped up into the car. If it caused her pain she didn't let on, yet her face was pale. Putting the seat belt on she reached her hand to close the door. Looking straight at him, she said quietly, 'Thank you Drummond.' Somehow, he felt she was thanking him for more than just the use of the car.

Nodding he stepped back as she backed out. He was going to give her directions back to town, but there was little chance she would get lost, and she seemed capable enough. He had to get going himself, he was due in Sydney by early afternoon. He watched as the vehicle drove slowly past the homestead, then turned on his heel and strode to the house. Damn. He had enough drama in his life without Harriet bloody Russell getting under his skin. She'd be gone in a couple of weeks, he didn't have to be any more involved than lending her a vehicle.

9

Next day, other than a quick trip to town to get supplies for her little kitchenette as she didn't want to bother Rose for all her meals, Harriet spent time on her emails, polishing her business plan and even napped for a while. Feeling relaxed and refreshed by late afternoon, she had a long soak in the beautiful big bathtub, which seemed to take some of the soreness out of her bruises.

A dreamless sleep saw Harriet up just after dawn. While the bruises were turning ugly on her torso, the swelling in her elbow had receded and the old wound was less tender. She felt energised, as if something had shifted overnight. If she had to stay in the region until her car was fixed, perhaps she could explore and do some research on her business idea.

It was after nine thirty when Harriet drove into town, her laptop in a satchel on the seat beside her. She decided to take the long way, via Rocky Crossing, telling herself she took the route because it was such a pretty drive. The possibility of bumping into Drummond Murray was definitely not behind that decision.

Over the bridge, the water had receded somewhat, and up a

slight incline she saw a sign on the side of the road indicating caution, cattle ahead. Harriet knew many farmers use the side of the road for cattle feed, droving them along the 'long paddock' as it was called. She slowed to first gear, seeing a herd of beef cattle just ahead, moving quietly along the side of the road, a stockman on horseback followed them and a couple of cattle dogs worked quietly behind the animals, running back and forth, tongues lolling. The rider's hat was pulled low as he glanced at the car idling behind him, moving to push the stragglers from the road to the verge to let her pass. On the other side of the road a child sat on a smaller stockhorse, helping guide the cattle across.

As she began to idle past in low gear, the rider came alongside the vehicle. Harriet wound down her window to give him a nod or a wave. He leaned down from the back of his horse, taking his hat off as he did.

'Harriet. How are you feeling? No ill effects from the accident, I hope?' She blinked when she recognised Drummond Murray, not as finely dressed today, in dark jeans and a flannel shirt.

Under the intensity of his scrutiny, Harriet struggled to find her words. 'Er, good morning, Drummond. I'm Okay. Good actually. A few bruises but nothing to worry about. Yes. I'm good, thank you.' Damn, what was it about this man that made her chatter away like an unhinged fool?

'Pleased to hear it.' She was sure he was about to say more, but he sharply wheeled his horse around and cantered directly to the child slightly ahead. There was a car coming the other way, on the other side of the mob, moving quickly. The pony danced sideways, and she could see the child, a girl with a long plait beneath her riding cap, was struggling to keep it in check as the other vehicle came through, too fast. Harriet stopped, thinking to get out and help the young girl, but Drummond was already there, grabbing the horse's bridle as he pulled the child on to his own horse, perched on the front of his saddle with his arm firmly around her as the other car sped by.

Harriet wanted to say something further but could see he had his hands full. There was a gate open on the side of the road and the stock were beginning to move through it. Not droving then, just moving cattle to another paddock. Harriet waited until they were all through. Drummond lifted the little girl back on to her horse inside the paddock and gave Harriet a wave as she moved off. Married then, obviously. The little girl would be his daughter.

10

The café was busy when Harriet walked in. Debbie was serving coffee to a table of young women, most with babies on their laps, some sleeping in strollers. Debbie gave her a brief smile and a nod before bustling back to the counter and returning with another laden tray of morning tea snacks.

Harriet chose a small table at the rear of the café, setting up her laptop before strolling to the counter to order a coffee.

'Hi Harriet. Nice to see you again. What can I get you?'

'Large double shot caramel latte please Debbie. Is it okay if I hook into your Wi-Fi while I'm here?' Harriet nodded to her laptop on the table at the back.

'Sure. Take this card, the password is on the back. We have unlimited data, all good. Six dollars thanks.'

Handing the correct money to Debbie with a smile and thank you, Harriet returned to her table and began reading the local government website, interested in tourism and business development. She barely registered the coffee delivered to her table by Cathy a few minutes later, the lady usually in the kitchen. Glancing up she watched Cathy hurry back to the counter.

The young women seated at the front of the café chatted comfortably; loudly enough to cover the crying of a baby, which stopped when his mother arranged her shirt to discreetly breastfeed.

Debbie had reappeared at the counter, taking orders for four middle-aged women who had just arrived. They stopped for a moment and chatted with the group of young mothers. Small town, Harriet thought. Everyone knows everyone. It bothered her as a teenager in an even smaller town, but she could see the benefits now she was older. The women settled at the next table. The mother who had been breastfeeding stood up, handed her baby to one of the older women, her own mother perhaps, and re-joined the conversation with the young mums, obviously enjoying her coffee and cake, glancing only occasionally at her baby, now sleeping.

Harriet googled real estate agents. How many were there in a town this size? Five at first glance. Most handled residential, commercial and rural. Very traditionally styled websites and offerings. She spent some time on residential listings. Quite a number of gorgeous homes, some even with acreage, many for the cost of an inner-city apartment.

Interesting. Harriet sat back, finishing her coffee. The younger women were preparing to leave, wrangling small children and large tote bags bulging with baby necessities. They departed, chattering happily as they left, calling out goodbyes to each other, the group of older women and Debbie at the counter. Harriet watched as Debbie served another customer, one she recognised. Evans. From her first day in town. Benjamin Evans, the real estate agent. He was quite a well-dressed, dignified sort of person. Tall, thick salt and pepper hair. Mid-fifties perhaps.

The real estate agent sat at a table in the alfresco area, took out a newspaper, folded it carefully and began to read. Watching Debbie bring the order to Benjamin Evans, Harriet thought she wasn't moving freely. In fact, she almost seemed unsteady. Frowning, she watched more closely, her scrutiny unnoticed from her vantage point in the slightly darkened rear of the café. Having considerable experience with pain herself, Harriet recognised it in Debbie's movements. Glancing around the shop, she saw there was only the real estate agent as the four older women had also left. Cathy was now serving at the counter.

Without giving it any serious thought, Harriet stood and waved to Debbie, who was almost shuffling, back to the counter. Debbie turned toward her, and slowly walked across, smiling as she arrived at the table.

'Can I get you something else Harriet? Wi-Fi working okay for you?' Debbie smiled, but Harriet could see tiredness in her eyes.

'Actually, I'd like to get you something.' Speaking quietly, yet firmly, Harriet pulled out the chair beside her. 'Debbie, can you sit please? I'd like to get you a drink. Maybe a snack too. What would you like?' Harriet stood as she spoke, noting with pleasure that Debbie sat down with a sigh and no argument, although she looked surprised.

'Nice of you Harriet. Just for a few minutes. We have a tourist mini-bus booked for lunch at twelve.' Leaning back, Debbie closed her eyes briefly. When she opened them, Harriet could see Debbie was holding back tears. Harriet leaned in to speak again, quietly, but Debbie shook her head. 'I was making myself a chai latte when Ben Evans came in, can you grab it for me please Harriet?'

Harriet walked quickly to the counter. Cathy greeted her with a nod, handing her a large takeaway coffee. 'I don't know what you said, but well done. Get her to rest for a bit, put her feet up, they're swollen. We'll be fine with the minibus. Actually, tell her to go home.'

'I'll try. Cathy, isn't it? I'm Harriet.'

'I know. You're a friend of Rose Gordon. Saw you here with her on Monday. Rose has been trying to get Debbie to slow down, but without much luck.'

'Um, not a friend exactly. I'm staying at Barrington Homestead. Perhaps hearing it from a stranger made the difference.' Walking back to Debbie, who had one leg up on the chair opposite, under the table, Harriet wondered if she needed more than just rest.

Sliding into the chair beside her, Harriet placed the coffee in front of Debbie, who took a sip. 'Thank you. Just what I need. I'll be fine after a short rest.' Looking at Harriet she sighed, before lifting the container to her lips again. 'How did you know Harriet? I thought I was doing a good job of hiding how tired, and uncomfortable, I'm feeling.'

'Your smile and warmth distract most from noticing. But I watched you from back here, and your movements gave you away. Cathy wants you to go home, said she'd manage the customers you have booked in. How about you have your chai and then do just that?' Harriet looked hopefully at Debbie.

'Good try Harriet. And Cathy. Really, I'm fine. I've got six weeks to go, and I want to work right up until the week before my due date. But I don't have to, not really. Cathy's daughter Kristen will be home from Uni in two weeks, and she can cover here for four months before she has to start again in the new year, so I just need to hang on until then.' As she spoke, Debbie removed her foot from the other chair and stood up awkwardly. 'Here's the mini-bus now. Thanks again Harriet. I hope we see more of you while you're here.'

A dozen people arrived, directed to the table set for them in the alfresco area. Debbie took their coffee orders as Cathy brought out beautifully arranged trays of pre-prepared sandwiches and wraps, followed by cheese and fruit platters.

Standing, Harriet stretched, then packed her laptop into her bag, slinging it over her shoulder carefully. She picked up her empty coffee mug and walked toward the counter. Cathy was clearing the real estate agent's table, as he also stood, folding his paper under his arm. Movement caught her eye. Debbie was standing at the coffee machine and Harriet watched, as almost in slow motion, she crumpled to the floor, disappearing behind the counter as she did. Harriet rushed toward her, not wanting to scream out as the other customers were chatting together, oblivious to the drama unfolding. As she sped around the counter, dumping her bag and dropping to her knees beside Debbie, she realised Benjamin Evans was right beside her.

Debbie was sitting on the floor, leaning slightly to one side, but conscious. The real estate agent crouched behind her, putting his hands under Debbie's armpits. Harriet grabbed an upside-down milk crate from against the wall and helped him lift her gently on to it. He was still crouching, rubbing Debbie's back.

'I'm going to call Jamie now love. We'll get you up to the hospital to check you out, he can meet us there.' Benjamin already had his mobile in his hand. Harriet stood, saw Cathy was still serving the table of tourists, but she glanced at Harriet indicating she was aware of Debbie's collapse.

Grabbing a bottle of water from the drinks fridge, Harriet removed the top and held it to Debbie's lips. She was pale, and definitely in pain. She took a sip, then struggled to stand. 'Stop it, Debbie. You need to be checked out.' Looking at Benjamin, Harriet said, 'shouldn't we call an ambulance?'

'It's quicker to take her to the hospital ourselves. You sit with her while I bring my car closer. Jamie will meet us there, he's on his way.' Harriet assumed Jamie was Debbie's husband, so she sat with Debbie, murmuring quietly to her that everything would be fine, Cathy had the café under control and the customers weren't even aware there was an incident.

Benjamin was back in less than two minutes. He helped

Debbie to her feet, one arm around her back, holding her close to his side.

Shaking her head, Debbie looked panicked for a moment. 'I can't. There's another group at one. Cathy can't manage. I'll just sit for a moment …' She hesitated, her legs shaking as Benjamin held her up.

'The café doesn't matter. Cathy will cope. You need to see the doctor Deb. Not just for you. For your baby.' Benjamin spoke kindly, but Debbie continued to shake her head, crying now.

Turning to Harriet, Benjamin said 'Can you stay Harriet? Just for today. Help Cathy through the lunch rush? We'll sort something out for tomorrow, if needed. But it might help her to know there's someone else here.'

Harriet looked around the café. Another four people had arrived, Cathy was looking after them. But there was no one on the coffee machine, and there was no way Cathy could serve out front and prepare meals in the back. Without hesitation she nodded. 'Sure. I've waitressed a bit. And I can make coffee, we had a commercial machine at my old office. Go. Go get checked out. Then rest. We'll be fine here.'

Leaning against Benjamin, Debbie allowed herself to be led out to the car, parked right in front. Harriet watched while Debbie was helped into the passenger seat, then she turned back to the job at hand, taking an apron from beneath the counter, tying it around her waist. Cathy rushed behind the counter with four coffee orders. She raised her eyebrows at Harriet with the apron on but shoved the orders into her hand. 'Can you make coffees? Or prefer plating up sandwiches, lasagne and salad?'

'Coffee. Happy to do coffee, take orders, clear tables if you can manage all the cookery stuff.' Harriet stepped up to the coffee machine, peered at the order, then tamped the coffee grounds, while placing the cups on the tray. Cathy was in the kitchen before Harriet had completed the sentence.

11

Drum met Ben Evans at the café at eight. He liked to have a quick 'meeting before the meeting.' They had their monthly Council meeting at nine, and there were a few matters to discuss beforehand.

Reading through the agenda and accompanying documents, speaking quietly to Ben, Drum didn't hear Harriet arrive at the table with their order.

'Good morning gentlemen,' Harriet smiled brightly as she set their coffee order down. 'Coffee; long black for you Drummond and a cappuccino for you Mr Evans.'

Startled, Drum looked up to see Harriet wearing smart black pants, very expensive looking leather loafers in tan, and the staff tee-shirt, crisp white cotton with the logo embroidered in sky blue above her right breast.

Damn. Don't look at the woman's breast, look at her face you idiot! He met Harriet's eyes, amusement plain to see. Bugger! Caught. Before he could make an appropriate comment, Ben spoke up.

'Harriet. Please call me Ben. Thanks so much for stepping in to help Debbie, she may be off until next week, at least, well done. Lovely to see you again.'

'Again?' Drummond looked at Ben, then back at Harriet.

'Yes, we met three days ago, then bumped into each other again yesterday, when Debbie, er, had an unexpected turn. Small town Drum, as you well know.' Ben arched an eyebrow at Drum.

Just as Harriet seemed about to respond, Cathy bustled over. 'Morning Councillors.'

Drum could see the slight frown of confusion on Harriet's face. 'Local Council, Harriet. It's a part-time role in small towns. We have our monthly meeting today. One Mayor, eight Councillors, mostly local business people.'

'Oh. Of course. I won't keep you. Let me know if you need anything else.'

Drum looked at Ben. 'Really Ben? I understand she was on the spot when Debbie collapsed yesterday. Very good of her to help out. But again today? Isn't there anyone else who needs the work? Harriet doesn't look like she needs work. She's from Sydney. Pretty sure she doesn't do café work there either.'

'Don't be a snob Drum. All I know is that Harriet has left the city, and she's here while her car is repaired. Says she likes this area. Debbie likes her. Rose likes her. So, do I. There may be a story there, but I'm happy to take her on face value and so should you.'

Feeling chastened, Drum nodded to Ben. Debbie had done wonders with the café, it was a great addition to the main street business offering. He didn't think Harriet would stay long, only until her car was repaired. She looked like a city girl to him, but if she could help out for a few days, and stopped Debbie from rushing back before she was ready, well that was okay.

'Sure Ben. She'll be fine.' Drum could see Harriet smiling and chatting with Angus Hamilton, local Vet and Rose Gordon's partner. If the woman had Rose and Angus, Debbie and Jamie on side, not to mention Ben Evans, she'd be Ok.

Breaking into his thoughts, Ben murmured. 'She's smart too. Gave me a bit of city girl advice about my window display the other day. A bit cheeky, but she hit the nail on the head. There's something about her. She's got a bit of class. But I'd bet my bottom dollar there's a story behind her sudden appearance in town.'

Drum answered quietly, glancing again at Harriet, looking confident and relaxed behind the front counter, 'You might be right about that.' He wondered if she was running away from something. Or someone.

Looking at his watch, he added, 'there's two items on the agenda I want to discuss with you quickly Ben. We need to be on the same page when we vote today.'

1 2

The day seemed to fly by. The café was busy from seven right through until two-thirty. Harriet had thrown down a coffee early in the morning, then finally sat down at the back table with a toasted sandwiches and cold drink when Rose came in with little Charlie.

Rose ordered at the counter, then joined Harriet at her table. She wrangled Charlie into a highchair, giving him a rusk from her bag which he promptly threw on the floor, laughing and gurgling. 'So glad you were here yesterday, Harriet, thank you so much.' Rose picked the rusk up, wiped it on a napkin and gave it back to Charlie. 'Cathy is hoping Kristen can get here by the end of next week, and there's a few locals we can call on to help out if you'd rather not do it.'

'Actually, I'm enjoying it. I'm here anyway. I'm doing some research on a business idea and this is helping clarify my thoughts. I don't mind at all. Today was really busy, but it felt good to be working again.'

'Business idea?' Rose was curious, but Harriet wasn't ready to share. 'Cathy said you did really well. What with getting the lunches ready for the Council meeting, the group from Stroud Mine at the same time, then the late lunch for the tennis ladies, she said you were run off your feet.' Reaching for her glass, she looked over it at Harriet, 'How are you holding up? Talk about throw you in the deep end …'

Harriet finished her sandwich, leaned back and let out an exaggerated 'aaah!' 'Honestly? I loved every minute. Cathy did all the hard work out the back. I just manned the register, made coffee and delivered orders, cleared a few tables. And answered many, many questions about Debbie's health.' She raised an eyebrow. 'The tennis ladies even cleared their own table for me. I've had a great day, and it was really nice to be busy and useful again.'

'Again? Hmmm. I know you have a story, Harriet. Would love to hear it. When you're ready of course.' Rose leaned forward slightly.

'I'd love to tell you my story Rose, there's really not much to tell. But I need to go help clean up now.'

Laughing, Rose sipped her coffee, giving Charlie the teaspoon with a little bit of froth on it. 'And personal question nicely dodged by the way.'

'Not dodging, not really. But it's a story for another day.' Standing, Harriet cleared her lunch things on to a tray.

As she walked toward the kitchen, Rose called out. 'So, you'll come again tomorrow?'

'Wild horses wouldn't keep me away.' Harriet loaded their lunch things into the dishwasher, said goodbye to Cathy and walked down the street toward the car park behind the town hall where she'd left Drum's car.

Nearing Evans Real Estate, Harriet noticed a very tall, very broad-shouldered man leaning against the door jamb with his back to her, chatting on his phone. He was dressed in typical stock and station agent gear; moleskins, riding boots, long sleeve blue chambray shirt, and an Akubra hat. A bit of a cliché, she thought, but exactly what you would expect in a country town in the middle of a beef growing region.

Glancing up at him as she went past, he seemed intent on his phone call. Dark hair, large nose, strong face. Good looking, in a rugged way. Two steps past, she heard her name called. 'Harriet? You have to be Harriet.' It was more a statement than a question. She stopped and turned. He was before her in one large stride, hand outstretched. With a questioning look, she placed her hand in his, where he firmly, almost too firmly, shook it, while heartily introducing himself. 'I'm Little Ben. Evans.' He jerked his chin at the real estate agency window. 'Big Ben told me about you. How you stepped in when Deb collapsed and now, you're helping out at the coffee shop.'

Trying not to laugh at this man-mountain referring to himself as Little Ben, she said 'Big Ben?'

'Yep. My Dad is Benjamin Evans Senior. I'm Ben Evans Junior but everyone calls me Little Ben.' His smile was infectious. 'It started when I was a kid playing footy. Once I shot past Dad, somewhere around thirteen I guess, they started calling him Big Ben. It may have faded out if I'd left town, but I chose to stay and work in the business, so I think we're stuck with the nick-names. I really don't mind, although Dad thinks it's a bit disrespectful, he is on local Council after all.' Trying to look serious, but failing, Little Ben threw his head back, laughing loudly.

His laugh was hearty, and Harriet chuckled too, before asking 'Why would Big Ben think to mention me at all? I've only been in town a few days.'

'Hmm. Said you had a few ideas about our window ads, said I should introduce myself.'

'Oh, well. Yes. Thank you. Nice to meet you. Does your dad, ummm Big Ben, want some help with your ad copy?'

'Maybe. Not sure what he had in mind. Just told me to watch out for you and say hello. I was going to come by the café for lunch, but I've had some beef buyers in the car, been out to Cobark and Scone today, only just back. I'll let him know we've met, maybe pop by the café tomorrow. What hours are you working?'

'Seven until two, but we were busy today, so I stayed a bit longer. Just for a few days until Debbie can come back or she organises something more permanent. Yes, good. Drop by the café. See you then.' The phone in Little Ben's pocket started to ring.

'See you then Harriet.' Little Ben nodded as he answered the phone.

HARRIET ARRIVED HOME TIRED AND A LITTLE BIT SORE BUT QUITE euphoric. Maybe this town was a good location for her business concept. She'd only been here a few days and already she was building relationships. Trust even. After a brief nap, she thought about having a soak in the bath. The day had been hot. Rose had mentioned a swimming hole on her property, but Harriet wasn't sure how to get to it. She did know how to get back to Rocky Crossing however, there looked to be a couple of spots not far from the bridge where she could have a dip. She'd seen a couple of people kayaking there this morning.

Having decided, Harriet hurried to her room to change. She fished out the only swimsuit she had with her, a black one piece. Putting it on, she acknowledged that her bikini days were over. Only a one-piece would hide the hideous scars on her lower abdomen. Quickly pulling on shorts and a loose tee over the suit, she slipped her feet into a pair of white canvas tennis shoes and grabbed her towel from the bathroom. She waved to Rose who was driving in as she went out.

Parking off the road in a flat area to one side at Rocky Crossing, Harriet got out and walked upstream beside the river, making her way through scrub and saplings. She followed a small path, possibly made by kangaroos.

Only fifty metres or so along, she saw a potential swimming hole. The water was quite high and flowing swiftly across smooth rocks sticking out in the middle of its path, creating a set of small rapids. Laughing, Harriet slipped off her shoes, shorts and tee and waded through waist-deep water to the rocks. The water was cold, but not icy, as she lay back on the rocks on her back, hands behind her head, letting the water run across her torso and legs. It was like a little spa, and she giggled to herself, feeling happy and relaxed.

In the distance she heard a motorbike but knew there was a dairy farm on the other side of the river, so probably the farmer bringing his herd in for milking. Closing her eyes she listened to the sound of the water, a vehicle slowing down in the distance to cross at Rocky Crossing, the motorbike further away now.

A splash nearby made her sit up quickly. Blinking with the sun in her eyes, now low in the sky she could see a person wading toward her, and another sitting on the bank of the river. Feeling suddenly vulnerable she turned her back, wishing her towel was in reach, rather than several metres away on the riverbank.

The person wading toward her was a child. A little girl with a dark blonde plait, wearing a blue bikini. 'Hello.' The child smiled shyly at Harriet. She looked familiar. Then Harriet remembered. Drum's daughter, she'd been on her horse two days before.

'Hello. Did you ride your horse here today? I saw you moving cattle on the road the other day.'

'No. Daddy drove here.' She looked back at the bank. Now Harriet could see Drummond Murray sitting beside her clothes, looking relaxed in shorts and an unbuttoned shirt. He raised a hand in greeting.

Harriet nodded to him. Damn. How was she meant to get back to her gear? He would watch every step she took. For sure he would see where her swimsuit caught on the scarring on her body. The little girl was speaking again.

'I'm Billy. I'm very pleased to meet you.' She held her little hand out to shake Harriet's. So old fashioned, Harriet thought, but lovely manners.

'Hi Billy, I'm Harriet. I'm very pleased to meet you too.' She gave the child's hand a quick shake.

'My name is spelt B. I. L. L. I. E. Billie. You need to know that, or you will be thinking my name in your head but spelling it like a boy's name.' She gave a serious little frown while she explained.

'Ooh, Billie. Yes, you're right. It sounds different when you know how to spell it properly.' What a serious little thing.

'How old are you, Billie?' Harriet was enjoying the conversation. She looked at Drum out of the corner of her eye. He seemed content to stay where he was, which was just fine with her.

'I'm seven. I'll be eight in April. How old are you, Harriet?'

'Um, I'm thirty-one. Bet that seems old to you?'

'Not at all. You don't look that old.' Harriet grinned. From the mouths of babes. 'My Dad is much older. He's thirty-six.'

'Oh yes. That is quite old, isn't it?' Harriet saw movement

from the corner of her eye. Drum's shoulders were shaking. He was laughing silently.

Enjoying the game, she had stopped thinking about how the swimsuit may look on her. 'Is Billie short for anything, or is that your full name?'

'Oh, my full name is just awful!' Billie shook her head sadly. 'But mother could not be dissuaded.' Harriet snorted, then turned it into a cough. The child was serious.

Billie went on drily. 'You will find out eventually. Everyone does. My real name is Wilhelmina Annabelle Aston Smythe Murray. There. It's horrid, isn't it? I don't know *what* they were thinking.'

Something in the way Billie spoke, her intonation on certain words, gave her a somewhat English accent. Harriet had noticed that Drummond spoke in a manner that Harriet's grandmother would have referred to as 'very well spoken' but did not have the English intonation like Billie.

'It's not horrid at all. But it is long. My full name is Harriet Marion Elizabeth Russell. It's almost as long as yours. And you know what? A few of my very good friends call me Harri. It can be a boys' name too. I like to spell it H.A.R.R.I.'

'Oh, I love that! Can I please call you Harri? I can be your very good friend too.'

Enchanted, Harriet smiled and stuck out her little finger. 'Pinkie promise you can always call me Harri if I can always call you Billie.' Linking her little finger through Harriet's, Billie said solemnly, 'I promise.'

'Can I call you Harri too?' Drum had waded into the river, and lowered himself into the stream beside Billie, letting the water wash over him. He was just in his shorts now and Harriet could see his muscular arms and chest, with a patch of dark ginger hair, trailing down to the top of his shorts.

She looked quickly at his face. He was smiling but it didn't quite meet his eyes. 'Umm, yes, of course. No problem.'

Billie piped up. 'Daddy's name is Drummond Douglas Alistair Murray. But most people call him Drum. You can be Daddy's friend too and call him Drum.'

'Okay. Thank you. I will do just that.' Trying not to laugh she looked at Drum. His smile had reached his eyes. What a change, she thought. He looks quite fierce and unapproachable a lot of the time, but when he really smiles, he's very attractive. And something else. Warm. Yes, he could be warm.

Billie was chattering again, this time about her stockhorse Chippy and Harriet smiled, listened, asked questions and spent twenty minutes just enjoying the company of her new friend. Drum seemed happy to lay back in the water, occasionally correcting Billie or adding a comment, but otherwise watching the interplay between Harriet and Billie with eyes half-closed.

13

The rest of the week flew by, and Harriet found she really enjoyed working at the café. Customers were friendly, if inquisitive, the work was varied. Friday afternoon was a bit of a rush, but finally the customers had left. Cathy and Harriet were just locking up when Debbie arrived, looking pale, but smiling broadly.

Cathy hugged her gently. 'Debbie, we thought you would be in hospital for another day or two.'

'Pre-eclampsia. My blood pressure has come down and feet are less swollen, but unfortunately I can't come back to work until after I deliver.' Debbie spoke positively, but all three women knew the risk for mother and child were high.

Cathy glanced at Harriet before speaking to Debbie, as if seeking reassurance. 'Kristen will be here in a week. We'll be fine. Harriet's been terrific and has already said she can stay on until then.'

Debbie smiled at both women. 'I can't thank you enough. Both of you. Harriet, for stepping in like that.' She pulled a tissue from her bag and wiped a tear away, although she was still smiling.

Harriet touched Debbie gently on the arm. 'It's been good for me too, Debbie. Feeling useful. Getting to know the locals. I like it here. Cathy does the lion's share of the work.' Debbie nodded, smiling through her tears.

'I'm off Debbie, have to catch the bank. Harriet, can you lock up?' Cathy looked at her watch and started for the door. 'Good to see you Deb. Have a coffee with Harriet, then go home.' She waved as she left, turning the sign on the door to closed, before closing it behind her.

'Coffee Deb? Or perhaps a chai latte?' Harriet called over her shoulder as she made her way toward the coffee machine. 'Why don't you sit, I'll bring out a cup for both of us.'

'Chai is perfect, thanks Harriet.' Debbie smiled gratefully, then settled herself at a table near the counter, her feet up on a chair opposite. 'And grab a slice of almond cake, we can have a snack and a chat.'

Harriet smiled and raised one hand in acknowledgement, before returning from the kitchen with two lattes, cake, cream on the side and two forks.

'Oooh, that's the way. Fresh cream too. Well done.' Debbie put her feet down and leaned forward, manipulating a large piece, with cream, on to her fork which she popped into her mouth, eyes closed in delight.

Chuckling, Harriet did the same, then leaned back in her chair and stretched.

'Thanks so much for stepping in Harriet. I'm so lucky you were here that day. Lucky you had the skills to step in for me too. I should have stopped work when my feet started to swell. They're still the size of footballs, and aching too, but slightly better than they were.' To illustrate her point Deb laughingly raised one offending appendage, before resting it back on the chair.

Laughing along with her, Harriet asked, 'so they were just regular-sized feet before?'

Glancing at her feet, turning them slightly from side to side, Debbie added 'I honestly don't know when they stopped looking like proper feet, I can only see them when I have them up, like this.' Debbie grinned. 'Ah, but it will be worth it when peanut monster makes an appearance in about five weeks.'

About to make a comment, they were interrupted by Angus Hamilton, Rose's partner, as he popped his head around the door before stepping in, closing it behind him.

'Ladies.' Angus took his hat off, placing it on the floor and pulled a chair up to the table. 'My good wife tells me that Cathy has baked a lasagne to bring home. Apparently, my offspring has been *a bloody pain in the arse* all day. Rose's words, not mine. I'm to come home with food, wine and be prepared to wrangle the little blighter into submission.' He laughed as he spoke, seemingly delighted with the prospect of wrangling his offspring.

Laughing with him, Debbie added, 'I hope my husband is as keen to help 'wrangle' peanut when he or she arrives. I've hardly seen him this last week, they've been busy cutting the crops in case of rain. I fear he'll be disappointed, the weather reports only indicate a very slim chance of decent rainfall.'

Nodding agreement, Angus turned to Harriet. 'So how have you managed? All I hear is that you're doing a fabulous job and Deb's a lucky girl you came to town when you did.'

Appreciating his interest, Harriet found herself smiling as she confirmed how much she was enjoying the work, the locals, the town and even the visitors. 'I'm almost a local, thanks Angus. On the first day every customer asked me who I was, where I was from and how long am I staying. Today, I don't believe I was asked more than twice. I think I'm almost ready for the keys to the city.'

Putting on a broad Scottish accent, reminding Harriet of Jamie from the Outlander series, he replied, 'Och lassie. Away wid you. You won't be local until ye marry a local. And that local has to be five generations, dinna ken?'

Debbie gave him a nudge. 'So, Angus Hamilton, when are you going to marry Rose Gordon? You've been engaged for two years! If you don't, you'll be an outsider yourself until the end of time. Watch out, or she'll make you take her last name!'

'Now Deb. That hurts. I'm the best Vet in town. I'm a catch. She's lucky she found me.'

Debbie leaned toward Harriet, commenting in a stage whisper, 'Only Vet in town …'

Angus and Debbie chatted some more, while Harriet leaned back in her chair enjoying their good-natured bantering. Harriet had only met Debbie's husband Jamie once, but she could see the strong bonds of friendship between Rose and Deb, and their men. Good people, all of them. Caring people.

Breathing out gently, Harriet smiled to herself. She hadn't had a nightmare since the night she arrived and she hadn't obsessed about her scars and wounds at all during the busy days helping at the cafe. In fact, she felt stronger and fitter than she had since before …. Since before her life changed. For the first time in months, she could imagine a future. It was still fuzzy around the edges, but it was there.

'Earth to Harriet. Where did you just disappear to?' Debbie was laughing, as Angus helped her from her chair.

'Oh sorry.' Harriet mumbled. They were both looking at her. She straightened, smiled brightly and said, 'Actually. You two can be the first to know. I like it here. Helping in the cafe. This town. The people. You. I like it and I think maybe, just maybe, I'll stay.'

'Yes!' Debbie clapped her hands and threw her arms around

Harriet. 'We like you too. You're our kind of people. If you're staying, we're keeping you!' A rush of emotion caught Harriet unawares, Deb's arms still around her. Tears welled up as she extricated herself from the embrace, glancing away from Debbie's keen eyes to clear their plate and forks from the table.

Angus didn't notice, already striding toward the kitchen to retrieve his lasagne. Debbie looked at Harriet, then touched her arm, staying her for a moment. Quietly she said. 'I know you've been through something Harriet. And I know our friendship is very early days. When you're ready, I'm here.'

Harriet nodded mutely, a tear trickling down her cheek which she hastily wiped with the back of her hand. Such genuine kindness. And respect. 'Thank you. I really do love it here. You're amazing Deb.'

Calling out from the front counter, Angus had his foil wrapped dish in one hand, wallet in the other. 'Can one of you please open the till, take my money? Rose has messaged. Now Charlie has been exploring his artistic side, with crayons on the hallway walls. This, she tells me, he gets from me!'

'Oh, poor Charlie. Rose does like everything 'just so.' This will be doing her head in.' Debbie shook her head, grimacing slightly, but smiling at the same time. She called out, 'Don't worry about paying. Just go Angus. Save Charlie. We'll sort it out next week.'

'Save Charlie,' Angus muttered as he waved goodbye, 'and who will save Angus?'

Watching the tall man flee, Harriet and Debbie clutched each other, laughing so much they both had tears falling. 'Oh, cripes Harriet. Now I need to pee. Don't make me laugh like that. Just wait, I'll be back, we can lock up together. I've got something for you before you go.'

Still giggling to herself, Harriet gave the front counter a good clean and took the drawer out of the till, locking it into the safe in Debbie's small office. Most of the banking had been taken care of by Cathy, but it was still good practice to lock it away.

Debbie returned moments later, an envelope in one hand and a small takeaway container in the other.

'Okay Harriet. Take the last piece of apple strudel home to have later tonight. Cathy has a fresh one ready to go in the oven first thing tomorrow.'

Handing over the envelope, Debbie said, 'We've never spoken about pay, and I still need to get your bank account details and fill in some forms to say you're officially on the payroll, if only temporarily, but I've put cash in here to cover you for the last few days. I hope it's enough.' Harriet took the envelope, putting it into her bag without opening it.

'It will be fine. Plenty. I was happy to just work here for free, you know, to help out until Cathy's daughter arrives. I wasn't doing anything else, just waiting for the repairs to be finished on my car.'

'You're worth three times what's in that envelope. Cathy came to see me yesterday afternoon. Told me not to worry and not to come in until after I deliver Peanut. I just wanted to check for myself that you're okay, that you don't mind being here until Kristin arrives.' Hesitating for a moment, Debbie added, 'and you don't have to leave then either, we're busy over summer, if it rains the river will be up, and the tourists will come. Stay on if you want to. I just need to get you into the system.'

Smiling, but shaking her head, Harriet hugged Debbie gently. 'Thank you. For offering to keep me. I'm pleased to help out for now, as long as I'm needed. I'm planning to stay around here, maybe start a business of my own.' Seeing the surprise on Debbie's face, she added quickly, 'not a café of course, but something I think will work well here. But while I'm getting my ducks lined up, so to speak, happy to step in and work a few hours whenever I'm needed.'

Relieved, Debbie hugged Harriet. 'You've just walked into my life when I needed someone with your skills Harriet. I'm really pleased you're sticking around. I'd love to hear more about your business idea. When you're ready of course. Maybe we can have a dinner together before I deliver this baby. You, me, Rose and Mel. Girls' night.'

Nodding and smiling in agreement, Harriet was stunned. Girls' night? She had only known these women a week, and they were including her in a girls' night. It felt right. She had few friends in the city with this rapport. Only one close friend, Larissa, but Harriet had pushed her away during her recuperation from the injury. Once she was settled in, she'd invite her out, she had a feeling Larissa would hit it off with Rose and Debbie too. And Mel, she worked for Angus at the Vet Clinic and had been in every day to pick up coffee and lunch. Mum to Tiffany, the gorgeous child who'd served Harriet on her very first morning in town.

Locking up together, Harriet waited until Debbie had wriggled her tummy behind the steering wheel of her SUV parked in the side lane, before heading up to the bottle shop.

Carrying her large tote by its handle, now crammed with snack food, a bottle of red and the takeaway container, Harriet slowed when she saw Big Ben standing at the door to his shop.

'Afternoon Ben.' Harriet paused. Little Ben had been to the café twice to speak to her, but she had been too busy with customers. They had a tentative time arranged tomorrow afternoon, to have coffee and a chat.

'Harriet. Hello. Finished for the day I see.' Ben raised an eyebrow at the wine poking out of the top of her bag.

'Yep. Going to have a celebratory drink tonight. Debbie's doing okay and the café is still standing.'

'Well done. That's the ticket. Indeed.' Harriet started to move on when he added, 'So two pm tomorrow? Little Ben will pick up coffee and we can have a quick chat here at the office. I'm keen to get your thoughts on our advertising, generally. Not just the window displays.'

'Thank you, Ben. I look forward to it.' Harriet almost did a little jig as she walked on. She wanted to know more about Evans Real Estate and the local market in general. It would fit with her plans.

1 4

———————

*D*rum put the phone down. Hard. He'd had to pick Billie up unexpectedly this week, in the middle of her school term. Annabelle was unwell, needed a break, she'd said.

He'd wanted to keep Billie in Barrington two years ago when Annabelle first left, moving to their Sydney apartment in Edgecliff. But his wife insisted the child belonged with her. Secretly, Drum hoped Billie would be the link, the line of communication they so badly needed to make their marriage work, so he let her go.

Now, he realised Annabelle used Billie as leverage to grasp increased funds for their support, saying his daughter needed this thing or that. After two years it was clear his wife wasn't coming back. And Billie came to him with practically nothing. Annabelle spent the funds he sent on herself.

Frustrated, he now had to tell Billie she wasn't returning to her mother tomorrow as planned. He hoped her heart wouldn't be broken. Annabelle hadn't given a reason, but Drum thought he knew. Billie had mentioned a man in a fancy car taking her mother to dinner. A lot. Annabelle obviously wanted Billie out of the way to develop a relationship. He wondered who the poor sucker was. While part of him was angry, and if he admitted to himself, even a little jealous, logic told him this could be his escape ticket. Keep Billie. Let Annabelle go. For good this time.

Walking quietly down the hall, not sure if Billie was awake, he pushed her bedroom door open. There she was, sitting on the cushions of her window seat, reading. Looking up, she gave him a broad smile. 'Is it breakfast time Daddy? I was just going to finish this chapter …' She lay the book down and ran to him, arms up for a hug.

He reached down and hoisted her into his arms, squeezing her gently as he walked toward the kitchen. Billie. So easy to love.

'Breakfast time indeed. Scrambled eggs? Toast? Coffee?' She laughed and wriggled out of his arms, leaving him momentarily bereft.

'Silly Daddy. Not coffee. I'm not a grown-up. Orange juice please. Can I use the juicer and make it?'

Moving quickly, she knelt on a stool at the breakfast bench, plucking three oranges from the basket of fruit.

'How about two oranges and an apple today? You can juice them up in the bullet blender.' He placed everything in front of her, watching as she struggled to peel the oranges. 'Want me to cut them up for you?'

'No thank you Daddy. I do this by myself at home. Mummy doesn't like mornings, that's why I read quietly until she's awake.'

He winced. Yes, the Sydney apartment is home to her. And she knows her mother well.

Later, two eggs scrambled, and a piece of toast eaten, except for the crust, he sighed inwardly. He'd have to tell her now.

'Billie. I know we planned for you to go home to Mummy tomorrow, but I wonder if you would like to stay on here a bit longer?'

Her wide hazel eyes blinked a couple of times, while she

studied him. He braced himself to expect tears. Or worse, a tantrum. Not that she ever really had tantrums when she was with him, but Annabelle complained about Billie's behaviour constantly, so he was prepared.

'Really Daddy? Stay here with you? How long?' The last was almost a demand. Still not sure of her emotions, he responded. 'I'm not sure Billie. If it was up to me, it would be forever. But I understand you need to be with your mum, it's just that she … um, she's a bit under the weather at the moment.' He didn't want to lie but didn't want to hurt her.

Billie sat back, then looked out the window toward the paddock closest to the house. Her little stock horse, Chippy, was standing at the fence waiting for his morning apple core.

Drum's heart broke when she turned her eyes on him again. They were filled with tears.

'I'd like to stay here forever too.'

Drum was stunned. 'Really? You would?'

'Yes. I want to stay here with you and Chippy. Always.' She nodded firmly. 'I love Mummy, of course I do. But she doesn't really need me. You need me here Daddy.'

Completely flummoxed, he didn't know if he should laugh or cheer. Keep her. Always. Raise her. Watch her grow. Guide her. Love her. It was his dream. One he thought he had given up when Annabelle asked for a divorce. He'd never expected more than a weekend here and there and some time in school holidays. He assumed she would rather be with her mother.

'I do need you, Billie. I want you here always. You can see your mum whenever you like, we'll work something out, but I'd like this to be your forever home.' He leant over, scooped his daughter off her breakfast chair and onto his lap, hugging her tightly.

Billie breathed out. 'That's settled then.' With lightning

speed, she transitioned to a completely different topic. 'We should go for a ride, check the heifers.'

Feeling lighter, happier than he had in the last two years, he nodded. 'Get your jeans and boots on then and we'll check the heifers. And Billie, we need to get you started at school. Barrington School, where I went when I was your age.'

'Okay.' She sang out as she skipped down the wide hallway to her bedroom.

Harriet walked slowly from the car park to Evans Real Estate. She was early, so she strolled past two other real estate agencies, noting their window displays weren't any better, although Bucketts Realty had a window video depicting rural properties mixed with tourist attractions in the area.

'Harriet! Hello. Good timing.' Little Ben approached carrying three takeaway coffees in a cardboard holder; a paper bag in his other hand; grinning from ear to ear as if he was the bearer of impossibly good news.

Grinning back in response, Harriet reached for the paper bag. 'Let me help you with that.'

Handing the bag to her, he opened the door, holding it so she could duck under his arm (he was very tall) to enter the shop.

Big Ben walked toward her, hand outstretched. 'Harriet. Thank you for coming. I can see you two are already working as a team.' Chuckling, Harriet took his hand, but seeing the serious look on his face, turned it into a small cough, as she sat where he indicated, a comfortable chair in front of a large, highly polished, rosewood desk.

Little Ben took the bag from her, placed the coffees on the desk, and disappeared through a door at the rear of the shop to what Harriet assumed was a kitchen of sorts, as he returned moments later with a variety of slices arranged on an old-fashioned bone china serving plate.

Harriet pulled a notebook and pen from her bag. She'd been tempted to just use her laptop but thought it may look a little presumptive.

Big Ben leaned back in his chair. 'We have been aware that our advertising and marketing needs an overhaul, and if sales have been slow, we've attributed that to the ongoing drought. Your comments last week were insightful and made me look at our window display with fresh eyes. Yes, the photos are old and faded. The descriptions bland, factual. No sizzle. You are absolutely right there. We upload listings to the real estate websites but use the same images and text that we generate for the window listings.

'I looked you up on LinkedIn. You worked in real estate in Sydney, for developers, attracting international residential and commercial buyers. You have qualifications in marketing and branding. You are well and truly overqualified to provide some consulting advice.' Harriet raised an eyebrow. LinkedIn. On-line listings. Better than she'd expected. Big Ben leaned forward, taking a sip of coffee.

Little Ben chimed in. 'We need some advice, some guidance Harriet. New window listing templates. Some ideas for better photos. And the words. We need help with the words.'

Jotting down notes as they spoke, an idea was already forming in Harriet's mind. She reached over and picked up a business card from a display on the desk. The logo was uninspiring, at best.

'Templates for the window, help with photos and words is one thing. Depending on your appetite, you could go further. Re-brand. A new logo. Freshen it up a bit. Roll out the re-brand with some press releases in the local paper, but maybe go further with editorial in The Land and the Weekly Times perhaps. Tell the story of the business, then wrap some prime listings around that story. You obviously have LinkedIn. Any other socials? Instagram? A Facebook page? How far do you want to go? What do you want to achieve? But even more than that, who is your market? Locals? Near locals? Have you thought more broadly than that?'

Sitting back, Harriet saw that Big Ben was frowning and a look passed between the two men. She'd gone too far. Possibly scared them off. Perhaps their budget was tiny, and they just want some advice on the window listings.

Little Ben took over. Some sort of silent tag had passed between the men. 'All of that Harriet. We realise you're helping out at Debbie's in the short term, but can you consider this,' he looked at his father, who nodded encouragingly, 'let's look at a logo re-design and re-brand. Then templates for the window listings and a formula for photos and descriptions. And a strategy for social media presence. We don't want to half do this. It will mean new signage, not just here at the shop, but on our vehicles and property signs. How much can you do yourself Harriet? We need you to provide an idea of budget and timing. What can you do and what do you need to outsource? We have a local sign maker, so it's the logo that's important; the look, the image, to begin with. The market. Well. We know there is a market in the city. Newcastle and Sydney for example, but the jobs just aren't here to attract the young ones. It's mostly retirees seeking a tree-change at the moment.'

Impressed, Harriet responded slowly, taking a moment to complete her notes, giving her time to consider all they had said.

'I'm so pleased you're taking this seriously and seeing it as an opportunity to position yourselves as leaders in the market in this region. I'd like to think about this for a couple of days. I'm not a graphic artist but I have one I can call on for the re-brand that would offer reasonable rates. Let me put something together and come back to you – a strategy with proposed budget and timing and an outline of resources.'

Looking around the office, she noticed there were two other desks, plus a small meeting area behind a half wall. 'Do you have other staff? Who uploads the listings to the internet and does the window cards at the moment?'

A shuttered look came over Big Ben's face. His son answered for him. 'Mum used to do the property management and the listings and so on. She passed away last year. We sold the rent roll; we were struggling with it a bit and decided to concentrate on sales. I've been doing the listings at night, but honestly Harriet, there haven't been many new ones lately, the market is poor, so we haven't needed extra help.'

Watching him speak, his sincerity touched her. She wondered, for just a moment, what it would be like to be the focus of this man's attention. His voice brought her mind back to the subject at hand, but not before she saw something like amusement cross Big Ben's face.

Big Ben looked at Harriet as he joined the conversation. 'Rain is predicted and that's increasing buyer confidence, so the market is firming. We're hoping, no expecting, there be a turn-around, and we want to be ready for it.' Harriet nodded, taking in his words. 'We would consider someone part time to manage the office, phones, paperwork and internet stuff. We know you're not available just yet and expect you may move on when your car is repaired and Debbie has her baby, but once you have every-thing set-up, we can look at hiring someone part-time.'

'Sorry to hear about your mum, your wife.' She looked kindly at both men. 'And you have obviously thought this through and had more conversations than just this last week, so that's good. I'm pleased I was the catalyst for action, though.' Harriet smiled, finished her coffee, and began packing her notebook away, an idea already forming in her mind.

'I appreciate the opportunity to look at this for you. I'll get back to you on Monday. Say, three pm?'

A look passed between the men again. Little Ben cleared his throat. 'Um, Monday, yes. We're busy at the saleyards on Monday. Perhaps, er, Monday evening would suit you? We could have dinner at the pub, say six thirty?'

Laughing on the inside, Harriet could see this was a set-up. Little Ben wanted to take her out and Big Ben obviously approved. But playing dumb she responded.

'Of course. Yes, dinner at the pub will be very nice, thank you. I look forward to seeing you both there.' She hid her smile while leaning down to pick up her tote bag, before standing and holding out her hand to each man in turn. Little Ben looked slightly flushed when he shook her hand, and she was sure Big Ben was hiding amusement behind his impressive grey moustache.

The homestead was quiet when Harriet got back, she suspected Charlie was having his nap and Rose was most likely trying to get some writing done while he slept. She set her laptop up on the little table in her suite and wrote a marketing strategy for Evans Real Estate. It was an outline really, just three pages. She pulled up a larger document on her screen, her business plan outline, and read through it again, tweaking it here and there as she went.

Her business would require an office of sorts. Street frontage preferably. She had thought she could rent inexpensive premises in a small town, once she had settled on an area, but now she was wondering if she could share a space. With a real estate agent. The businesses were compatible, rather than competitive. While she had thought to work with more than one agency, it wouldn't hurt to choose one and create a strong relationship. She was chasing a particular market, they would have the stock, the listings. It could work.

Could she trust them though? They could run with her idea on their own. Or could they? Harriet had the connections in the city, the marketing savvy. And she had a feeling the Bens were straight shooters. She would feel them out on Monday, and if it seemed appropriate, she would share her plans, it may be worth the risk. So far, this town had not disappointed.

Creating a timeline and proposed budget for Evans Real Estate didn't take long. Harriet had strong ideas about branding; re-design of the logo. She could already see it in her mind's eye. Could even draw up a rough design, but it would be better to brief a graphic artist. She wondered if there was anyone local she could chat to, rather than giving the work to a city contractor.

Hearing movement in the main house, little feet running on the timber floors, Harriet decided to check if Rose had time for a quick chat. Taking her bottle of red wine and some cheese and crackers, she was about to knock on the door, when Rose flung it open from the inside. Quickly taking in Harriet, the wine and the cheese and crackers, still in their packets, she laughed and stepped aside, gesturing for Harriet to come in.

'Great minds. I was just coming to see if you'd like a sundowner with me. Angus is home and planning to wrangle Charlie into a bath. He suggested I see if you're interested in some girl chat out on the back veranda.'

'And here I was, wondering if it was okay to interrupt you, while thinking a chat is exactly what I'd like right now. With a glass of red and some nibbles, of course.'

'Of course. Nothing nicer. Come through, the door to the back veranda is on your left, I'll just get some glasses and a plat-ter.' Rose was already heading to the kitchen, calling over her shoulder, 'and olives? They're local.'

'Olives. Yes please.' Harriet smiled to herself as she settled into a comfortable wicker chair, one of a pair with a low table between. She set the wine and the food on the little table and gazed out into the larger garden. She could see a fruit orchard beyond and an ornamental pear tree provided shade over a lovely outdoor setting and a little covered sandpit. Harriet could picture Rose relaxing out here while Charlie played.

Rose returned with glasses, a platter, pesto style dip and a dish of olives. Harriet popped an olive into her mouth as Rose spoke. 'This lot will go down nicely with your wine. It looks a good one. Tyrrells?'

'Yup. Love Australian reds.'

'Me too.' Rose laid out the snacks while Harriet poured the wine. 'Here's to you Harriet. I hear you may be staying here. In this district.'

'Yes. I wasn't expecting to find what I was looking for here, thought the town may be too small. But you know what, it's bewitched me. You, Debbie, Cathy, little Charlie. Drummond lending me his car. The Bens…'

'The Bens? Evans? Good men, both of them. Been a bit lost since Rosemary passed.' Rose let her comment hang, a questioning look on her face.

'I made some comments on my first day in town about their window display. Didn't realise Big Ben was the owner. He was standing right behind me. But we've spoken a few times this week, and, well, he looked me up on LinkedIn.' Harriet nodded when Rose raised her eyebrows at this. 'Then asked if I would consult on some re-branding; logo, window card templates, online listings.'

'Excellent. Most of the main street shopfronts could do with a makeover, not just the real estate agents, but it's a great start. Actually, it's something Drum is really passionate about, being on Council. Making the main street more attractive to tourists. Not just tourists but make it tempting for visitors seeking a tree change. Bring more families here as well as retirees. And back-packers doing farm work to meet visa requirements.'

Harriet was impressed Rose was all over it. And Drum. And why shouldn't they be? That was her point exactly. Small towns don't have to be small-minded, or parochial. She grew up in one much smaller, and it had a lot going for it too.

'I've put together a brief marketing strategy, timeline and budget. Most I can do myself, but I need a graphic artist for the finished art for the logo. Wondering if you know anyone local, would rather spend the money here, if you know what I mean.'

'Oh. Yes! I do actually. Got just the person. Laura Harrison. She's brilliant, did the cover of my first book and some of my promo pieces. Has a small farm here, but ex-Sydney. I'll give you her number.' Rose was excited, and Harriet was thrilled to see how keen she was to help. Liking this town and its peeps more and more.

Picking her phone up from the small table, Rose searched for a moment, then, looking up, she gave Harriet a happy nod. Harriet's phone pinged in her back pocket. Taking it out, she saw the message from Rose with Laura's number.

'Thank you. I'll call Laura on Monday, see if she has time to see me.' Harriet took another sip of wine.

Glancing at her watch, Rose said, 'Why don't I call her now, introduce you, and set up a time for tomorrow. She's a farmer, Sunday is just like any other day for her.'

Chuckling at Rose's enthusiasm, Harriet nodded. 'Sure. See if she can see me tomorrow. I'd really like that.' Warming to the idea, she added 'she might be able to knock some concepts together for my meeting with the Bens on Monday night.'

Raising both eyebrows, Rose paused with her finger on the call button. 'Monday night, huh! What's that about?'

Laughing, Harriet said, 'I'm not sure if it's a fix-up actually. I suggested three pm Monday, but they said they had to be at the saleyards. We're having dinner on Monday night at the pub. I'm expecting both Bens …'

'Ha! Interesting. He's a lovely bloke. Not sure why he hasn't settled down. He spent some time in Newcastle at university then travelled for a year or so. Worked in Queensland as a stock and station agent for a while before coming back and joining the business. Since I've been back, I haven't seen him date anyone seriously, although he has friends from Uni and his travels, that visit. Not sure what he's looking for.' Tossing back a large gulp of wine, Rose added, 'Maybe you, Harriet.'

'Funny. I've been here five minutes. I know I'm a new face in town, but really, they know nothing about me.' Suddenly realising the implications of her association with Evans Real Estate, she added, 'I'm not looking. For a relationship. Not a romantic relationship. Not at the moment. Maybe not ever.'

'Really? Bad experience?' Rose topped Harriet's glass, up, looking into her eyes for a moment. 'Are you running from something Harriet? Is that why you're here?'

Taking another sip of wine, Harriet sighed, closing her eyes briefly. If she was planning to make a life here, she needed to be honest. To a point. Some things were best kept to herself.

'I was married. It didn't end well.' Taking a deep breath, she added, 'I was unwell for a while. Couldn't move forward. But a couple of weeks ago I realised that I'm ready to get on with my life. I have a small business idea that I was heading north to find the right sort of town to set up in. Frankly, I was looking for something bigger than this one. But I ended up here. And I'm getting to know a few people.'

Turning in her seat toward Rose, she raised her wine glass. 'Rose, I think it could work here. I could work here. My meeting with the Bens on Monday might provide the next step. I don't know for sure. But I have a good feeling about it.'

Rose raised her own glass, leaning across to clink gently with Harriet's. 'Here's to you, Harriet. Stick around, I'd like that. And I'd love to hear more about your business idea. I'm sure Angus would too. Maybe you'd like to join us for dinner on Tuesday night, tell us how your meeting went. Perhaps we can help.'

'Did I hear my name?' Angus appeared in the doorway, a wriggling Charlie in his arms, wrapped in a very damp towel. In fact, Angus looked like he'd been in the bath too, fully clothed.

Holding her arms out to take Charlie, Rose grinned at Angus. 'How is it that you seem wetter than your progeny? Did you get in the bath with him?'

'Not exactly. It was all going to plan until he couldn't find Ducky among the *many* floaty toys in the bath.'

'Ducky, ducky, ducky.' Charlie was trying to wriggle off Rose's lap.

'So, I turned around to look for Ducky and when I turned back Charlie was standing in the bath, unsteadily I might add. So, I leant over to hold him, and, well, he half pulled me in to the bath. There was a lot of splashing.'

Harriet found the exchange amusing, and sweet. Nice couple. Cute kid, if a bit of a handful.

'So, Harriet. Here we have Vet Hamilton. Capable of wrangling a two-tonne bull into submission without breaking a sweat. But bathing a baby … well, that's a much more dangerous activity.' Rose laughed as she spoke, causing Harriet to giggle too. Glancing at Angus, wondering if he was offended, she saw him looking at Rose and Charlie with affection, laughing with her.

He turned to Harriet, grinning broadly. 'Rose knows full well that bathing Charlie is like trying to pin jelly to a wall. Which is why she leaves it until I get home. Oh yes, she says it's to give me meaningful time with my son, but frankly, she doesn't have the fortitude to tackle the little blighter in the bath herself.' He was laughing loudly now, Rose and Harriet with him. Charlie was giggling and looking from his mother to his father in delight.

'Yes, we are talking about you, young man. It's time you were in your pyjamas.' Rose stood, with Charlie still wrapped in the towel on her hip. 'Stay Harriet. Have a drink with Angus, I'll be back in a moment.'

Harriet felt she should leave them to organise their dinner, feed their child and get on with their evening routine.

'Just a moment Harriet, I'm going to grab a beer.' Angus disappeared into the house. Leaning back in her chair Harriet sipped her wine and popped another olive into her mouth. Looking out into the garden, the sun now almost set, she realised she felt comfortable here. The house was magnificent, the gardens were stunning. Beyond the garden and orchard, was a field dotted with black angus cattle.

Angus reappeared, taking the seat Rose had vacated. 'It's a special place, Harriet. I can see you feel it too. It was owned by Rose's grandfather, he passed away a couple of years ago. That's how we met. Now we'll raise Charlie here, and maybe some more little Gordon-Hamiltons.'

Sensing his pride, in the homestead and his family, Harriet smiled briefly at Angus. 'Your love of this place is obvious Angus. It's been really lovely to share it with you and Rose and little Charlie, even just for a moment in time.

'Did I hear you may stay in the area longer than a moment Harriet? Or was that girl-talk and not for my man-ears?'

'Your man-ears heard right. I'm thinking about it. I thought I was looking for something else. A bigger town. But there is something about Barrington that feels right. Perhaps it's the people. Rose, Debbie, Drummond, the Bens, you. You've all been very accepting of a stranger in your midst.'

'Not everyone will be, Harriet. Small towns can be harsh toward new people sometimes. We've all lived in other places, and that broadens our view. There will be some that won't care for change. But that's not unique to small towns. Participating, *giving*, goes a long way in places like this. And you've already demonstrated that by stepping in for Debbie at the café. You didn't have to at all. You could have walked away that first day. You could have walked away the next day. But you didn't. You haven't. Well done, by the way.'

Flushed from his praise, and perhaps the red wine, Harriet glanced into her glass for a moment. Looking up, she spoke quietly.

'Thank you, Angus. None of this has been by design. But somehow, I was where I was needed, at just the right time. I don't really know why, but I will say, I think I needed this too.'

Angus reached out and touched her arm gently. Just as quietly, he said, 'You may be right Harriet.'

Just then Rose cried out. 'Grab him Angus!' Little Charlie shot through the door onto the veranda, dressed in a singlet, a sock and nothing else. In one swift movement Angus reached his long arm out, scooping his laughing son onto his lap. Rose appeared, carrying a nappy and pyjamas, her neat ponytail now askew over one shoulder.

She knelt in front of Angus, who held the toddler firmly, while she got the nappy and pyjama pants on. Harriet chuckled as she stood.

'It's been lovely to share a drink and chat.' Smiling at Charlie she added, 'I might leave you now, you have your hands full.'

'Lovely to have you here too, Harriet. Don't forget to call Laura. We didn't quite get to it earlier.'

Letting herself back into her accommodation, Harriet went to the bathroom. Staring into the mirror, she smiled wanly. The gaunt look seemed to have gone from her face. She looked better than she had in months. Her skin was healthy, and her eyes were bright. She studied herself more closely. She did look different today. What was it? Realisation struck her. She looked happy. Relaxed. When did she last look like that? Feel like that? Sitting down on the side of the bathtub, Harriet drew a deep breath and let the tears flow. Not because she was upset. Because she was happy. Her life had meaning after all.

Wiping her eyes, she glanced at herself again. She was smiling. Really smiling. Harriet picked up the phone and found the message from Rose. Entering the number, she called Laura.

LAURA WAS HAPPY TO MEET WITH HARRIET THE NEXT AFTERNOON, inviting her out to her farm, nestled between Barrington Homestead and Drum Murray's place.

Harriet knew Laura was English from her accent on the phone. A tall, spare woman aged somewhere in her forties, she exuded a no-nonsense persona and quiet confidence. She told Harriet she'd moved to the area three years earlier with her husband, who had sadly passed away eighteen months after the move. Both professionals from Sydney, her husband a former economic analyst and journalist and Laura a graphic designer, they had chosen the area for a semi-retired tree-change. Losing Gareth made it harder for Laura, who seemed very eager to pick up some design work.

While chatting out on the patio, Harriet noted that although there had been some rain the month before, the area was still very dry. She could see a lot of long grass down by the roadside. Laura's paddocks had little feed and were slashed along the boundary fence. Fire breaks most likely. There hadn't been enough rain in the season to protect from bushfires just yet. There were a dozen or so young bulls eating hay in the paddock nearest the house.

After discussing the project and being delighted that Laura understood the brief straightaway, including a reasonable price for the artwork, they chatted about general things.

'Are you a member of the local firies Laura? I notice you've slashed your boundary line.'

'I haven't joined. Gareth was a member and many of them

sent condolences when he passed. But they didn't approach me to take his place. I'm not sure if the likes of Drum Murray even approve of women in the volunteer firies.'

Harriet raised her eyebrows at this but did not comment. Instead, she asked about the cattle. 'What are you breeding here? Your young bulls there are in great condition, but I don't recognise the breed.'

Laura glanced at the cattle, then turned back to Harriet. 'Wagyu. They're my first crop of bulls. I only have eighty hectares, so my herd is small. The locals would barely refer to my place as a farm. It's just a small paddock in their eyes.' A small frown of worry crossed her face. She sighed. 'I'm having trouble finding a market. No, that's not right. I have a market. But I can't fill a truck to get them there and the freight cost is huge. I made enquiries with Little Ben Evans, to see if I could partner up with another breeder to share freight, but he hasn't responded. When Drum Murray's Dad was alive, he spoke briefly to Gareth about having our stock at their bi-annual bull sale. It's local, no freight to pay. Specialised buyers looking for stud stock.' She glanced again at the young cattle feeding beyond the fence. 'But I don't think Drum will be interested.'

'No? Have you asked him?'

'Not exactly. But I hear he runs things differently to his dad. He's on local Council and I may have rubbed him up the wrong way at one time.' She coughed, looking a little sheepish. 'I blew that opportunity. But it's a story for another day.'

Picking up the brief from the table she smiled at Harriet. 'Let's just go through this once more before you head off, I'm keen to get started straight away.'

An hour later, with agreement reached for Harriet to pick up the concept designs from Laura the next afternoon, she said her goodbyes and decided to head down to the river for a swim before returning to the homestead.

17

$\mathcal{D}$rum squinted up at Laura's place from the riverbank. She'd slashed her boundary. Good woman. The grass was getting long and dry there, it wouldn't take much for a fire to charge up the hill if it crossed the river. He'd slashed his own boundaries and made firebreaks around the main house, the sheds and the cottages some weeks ago. Would do it again in a couple of weeks.

Billie splashing and chattering away distracted him from his thoughts. She'd been brilliant all day, getting more confident riding Chippy and asking lots of questions about the heifers. He'd wanted to laugh at times but could see that she was serious and really trying to learn. Bless her. He hoped she wasn't doing it just to please him, although it certainly did. He had no idea what her mother had told her about him.

He wished his own parents had lived to see her back here on the farm. They'd been heartbroken when Anabelle left with their granddaughter.

His parents were taken too soon. Hit an icy patch of road in the early morning, rolled the car. The police told him his mother had died on impact, his father was holding her lifeless hand when they got there. He passed away before he reached the hospital, although his injuries were not as severe as his wife's. Drum suspected he had just given up. Almost forty years of marriage, they had rarely spent a night apart. He shook his head when he recalled his father asking him gently, on the eve of his wedding to Annabelle, 'Are you sure she's the one for you son? It's not too late to change your mind.'

His father had known. Long before Drum did. He'd been young; entranced by her English accent and family history. Her professed love of country life, how much she wanted children, how much she wanted him.

She had never really settled at Barrington. Hated the summer heat, the house, the farm. The locals were *provincial and boring*, his work in the community, such as local council, *so pedestrian*. The only thing she had adored was staying at the Sydney apartment, shopping and theatre trips, spending his money. The farm's money. She hadn't even supported him when he lost his parents. He shook his head in an attempt to dislodge the deep-rooted anger he felt when he thought about the last ten years of his life. The one shining point was Billie. He adored her, his only child.

'Hi Harri.' He focussed on Billie, on a rock in the middle of the river, waving in his direction. He glanced behind him. Harriet was standing there with a towel over her shoulder, smiling and waving back at Billie.

'Hi yourself. Is it cold in?' Harriet looked down at Drum, nodded, then sat beside him to take off her walking shoes.

'Harriet. Nice to see you.' He sat up a bit straighter.

'Nice to see you too. Drum.' She said his name as an afterthought. As if it was hard to get his name out. He wondered why. She looked healthier than last week. Stronger somehow. Not as pale. Probably just the country air.

'You look well, Harriet. Recovered from the accident?'

She looked at him sharply. 'Recovered? Oh, the car accident. Yes, thank you. All good. They've ordered the parts, Alfie should be fixed in another week.'

Billie had edged closer, although still chest deep in the water. 'Alfie. Who is Alfie?'

'My car Billie. It's an Alfa Romeo, so I call him Alfie.'

'Oh, I like that!' She splashed her way closer. 'Daddy, what do we call our car?'

'It's a Range Rover, Billie. We don't give our cars names.' He shook his head slightly, with a hint of a smile at Harriet as he said it.

'But we should. We should give the Range Rover a name.'

Harriet nodded enthusiastically. 'Yes, you should. Definitely. My car has a boys' name, maybe your car should have a girls' name.'

'Yes. What about 'Princess' Daddy. We could call the Range Rover Princess?' Billie was bouncing a bit in the water.

Drum looked balefully at Harriet. 'Thank you,' he mouthed.

'No. I'm not driving a car called Princess. Under any circumstances. It needs to be a bit more masculine than that.' He sighed and stepped into the water, splashing his daughter to distract her. She squealed and splashed him back, flicking water over Harriet too. He noted that Harriet had slipped into the water while he had his back to her, before wading across to the special rocks that locals called The Spa.

Billie kept chatting about the car and names, while she played around in the water. Stopping only to show the adults the swimming technique she called 'big arms.'

Drum swam a few strokes to the other side of the river where the water was deeper. He watched Harriet respond to Billie's chatter. There was something about her. He shook his head. He was off women. Gold-diggers, the lot of them.

He didn't notice Harriet watch his muscular arms cleave

through the water, mesmerised by the way he seemed to move with an economy of effort and fuss. He stroked languidly back to them. He caught Harriet staring at him and gave her a half-smile. He liked the way she blushed before turning back to Billie.

'Harri. Harri! Are you listening to me?' Billie stood before her, water up to her chest, little hands-on-hips and a trying-to-frown-and-be-cross face, but not really succeeding.

Laughing, Harri mimicked her, hands on hips, frowning and laughing at the same time. 'I do beg your pardon, Miss Billie. What can I do for you?'

'I was telling you about starting school. On Monday. I'm going to Barrington School. It's where Daddy went a long, long time ago.'

He watched Harriet control her features as she dipped her hair back in the water. Looking back at Billie, she said in a loud whisper, 'Did they even have school way back then, when your dad was a boy?'

'Don't be silly! Course they did.' Billie looked from Harriet to him. He got out of the water, shaking droplets from his hair, not sure if he should laugh or be peeved.

'I would have thought you were old enough to already be attending school Billie.'

'Oh, I've been going to school, I'm in grade two. But that was in the city. Now I'm living here with Daddy I'm going to Barrington School.'

Drum saw Harriet steal a glance at him. She started toward the riverbank, saying to Billie, 'Come on, let's get out and dry off, I'm starting to get goosebumps.'

No more was said, although Drum felt her gaze on him more than once. In a different time, he may have liked this woman. May have tried to get to know her. But he had Billie now. That was enough. He wouldn't do anything that could instigate further hostilities with Annabelle. She could demand Billie back at any time. He needed to make an appointment with his Solicitor Barlow, understand his rights. Maybe he could buy Annabelle off for good.

Taking a deep breath, he chastised himself. He had to do what was best for Billie, not for him. She still needed contact with her mother. He sighed, watching Billie wave goodbye to Harriet who looked at him again, quizzically, over his daughter's head, but he gave nothing away.

18

Monday morning was busier than ever at the café. Harriet was thrilled when Debbie walked in just after lunch, although she seemed tired and somewhat uncomfortable. She spent some time in the office, going through stock orders with Cathy while Harriet manned the counter.

Cathy suggested Debbie should head home, but she laughingly told her she was having lunch first. As she spoke, Debbie took two slices of quiche and a salad from the fridge and beckoned Harriet to follow. 'Grab something cold from the fridge Harriet, join me for a bite.'

Harriet looked at her watch. She was meeting the Bens at the pub at six-thirty, but her stomach was rumbling. She'd had a coffee and croissant around nine and nothing since. She took two bottles of spring water from the fridge and followed Debbie to their usual table at the back.

'How's the re-branding for the Bens' coming along Harriet?' Debbie took a bite of quiche, closing her eyes momentarily as she chewed.

Harriet had told Debbie about her 'side hustle' earlier that day. Knowing how small towns operate, she'd wanted to be up front and assure Debbie that the café was her first priority for the moment. Debbie had been enthusiastic. 'Setting up to do freelance work, plus your hours here means you won't have any need to leave and go back to the city.'

'Please, call me Harri.' She smiled. 'The re-branding is going well, I'm really excited about it, thank you, Deb. Yes, I think I can make a living here, maybe even make a life.' Harriet felt herself flush slightly at the words. In the city they'd have seemed trite, but here her growing friendship with Debbie and Rose felt real and solid. Harriet realised she hadn't had any bad dreams since the first night and she felt stronger and healthier than she had in a long time. She'd stopped obsessing over her wound and the scars that would be with her forever, both physical and emotional. She felt ready to look forward, instead of back.

'I've got a meeting with the Bens' at the pub tonight, to show them some concepts and the overall strategy and budget. Once they sign off, it will be all systems go. But this is something I can do after my work here.'

'Good. Well done. I look forward to seeing what you do for them. Their branding is seriously stuck in the nineteen-eighties.' Debbie chuckled, then drew her breath in sharply.

'Are you OK? Pain?' Harriet pushed her chair back and stood.

'No, no, sit down. I'm fine. Jamie Tait's bloody offspring is pushing on my back, I get this ghastly lower back pressure!'

'Well. I think that's also your body's way of telling you that you need some rest. Cathy is okay here. I'm heading off now, how about I walk you to your car and you go home and lay down for a bit?'

'I give in. Yes. I'll go and put my feet up at home. Good idea.' Debbie pushed her plate away and levered herself out of the chair. Harriet quickly picked up their plates and dropped them in the kitchen, telling Cathy she was going to walk Deb to her car. Cathy nodded her approval and by the time Debbie had walked to the front of the café, Harriet had both their tote bags over her shoulder.

'Do you want anything from the fridge to take home for dinner Deb?' Cathy asked as she closed the kitchen door.

'No, thanks. Jamie's cooking a barbeque tonight, so I'm off duty. Bless him, he's been working crazy hours getting the crops in.' Reaching for her bag, Debbie waved to Cathy and followed Harriet outside. Harriet waited until Debbie pulled away from the curb, before hurrying to her own vehicle.

PUSHING OPEN THE DOOR OF THE AVON VALLEY INN JUST BEFORE six-thirty, Harriet was unsurprised to find both Bens sitting at the bar with welcoming smiles.

'Hello Harriet. You're very punctual, thank you.' Big Ben stood up, shook Harriet's hand, 'What would you like to drink?'

'A glass of house red will be fine, thank you.' Harriet didn't want to have more than one glass, while chatting about business.

Little Ben ordered the drinks as Big Ben led her to a table. 'Business first, then we'll order some dinner.'

'Thank you, that's perfect.' Harriet settled herself on one side of the table, Big Ben on the other side. Little Ben took a seat at the end when he arrived with their drinks.

'I have an outline for a strategy, some re-branding concepts and a budget to show you.' Harriet retrieved the folder with her notes from her bag, placing them on the table along with her notepad and pen.

Turning the document so the men could read it, Harriet walked them through her strategy and budget. She had provided a range of costs, depending on how many hours of her time (and

Laura's) they needed, and on how much they might do themselves.

They asked a few questions, negotiated some of the items slightly, but largely agreed with her proposal. Harriet was outwardly calm and professional, but ecstatic on the inside. It wasn't just that they liked her proposal, it was their level of trust and belief in her abilities.

Finally, Harriet brought out the logo concepts she had picked up from Laura that afternoon. They were professionally rendered and, Harriet thought, quite stunning and a very good fit for the business.

She worried for a moment as the Bens' looked at the logo, drawn in a couple of different sizes and on a sample window card template, then looked at each other. Her heart sank when they both leaned back in their chairs.

'It's only a first concept ...' she began, but Big Ben put his hand over hers for a moment, effectively silencing her. 'It's perfect Harriet. If I could have imagined a new look for us, this would be it. But I would never have come up with it myself or even briefed someone to develop this. How on earth did you do it?'

Flushed with happiness at the warmth of his praise, Harriet responded, 'I pictured myself in your business. The customers you would have, and the ones you'd like to have. My colleague, who developed the graphic art, perfectly understood the look I wanted and created something really simple, and I think, quite timeless. I'm so pleased you like it as much as I do.'

Harriet looked at Little Ben. He hadn't said much but was watching her in a way that made her blush again. 'Yes. Well done Harriet. We knew you would produce something wonderful. Thank you. What's the next step?'

They chatted for another twenty minutes about the steps to complete the logo, organise new signage and business cards and complete the window card template. 'I'm not a journalist, but I can knock together some press releases too, if you like, and create a launch for the new branding. Do you have anything major coming up? A spectacular homestead or rural property perhaps, that we could use as leverage for stories in the press?'

'We have a few smaller properties listed, some have been on the market for some time. The Barrington Bull Sale at Drummond Murray's could be a good launch although it's not until early March next year. But it does attract interstate buyers. It's held at Murray Homestead; Drum has all the facilities there for a sale and good access to load stock, but he invites the cattle studs from Cobark, Moppy and Rawden Vale to join with him on the day. Rose and Angus from Barrington Homestead put a small number in the August sale this year, for the first time. It's one of the most prestigious sales in the State, held twice a year.'

Harriet's brain was ticking over. Could Laura get a few of her bulls into this sale too? She could work on it. Aloud she said, 'That's perfect, let's work on March then, although we may do a soft launch prior to that. That gives us a little over three months with Christmas and New Year in between, of course.'

Little Ben thrust a menu into Harriet's hands. 'Great. Sorted. Let's order, I'm starving.'

Chuckling, Harriet looked at the menu. She chose an Angus eye fillet, medium rare, with salad. Little Ben ordered a T-bone, Harriet wasn't surprised, and Big Ben settled for the rib fillet. Another round of drinks arrived, and Harriet told herself to go steady, she had to drive back to the homestead after this.

Their meals were delivered, and they ate in silence for a few moments. Harriet laid her knife and fork down, picked up her wine glass and took a large sip. She cleared her throat, looking across the table at Big Ben. Also laying down his cutlery, he looked enquiringly at Harriet.

'There is something else I wanted to talk to you about. A

couple of things actually.' She set her glass down and glanced from one man to the other. Little Ben, somewhat reluctantly, laid his cutlery down too.

'Go on Harriet, we're all ears.' Big Ben smiled kindly, and Harriet drew a deep breath before commencing.

'Firstly, please call me Harri.' She beamed at them. 'While I can stay at Barrington Homestead until just after Christmas, I'm thinking of finding something, um, more permanent.' She paused again, noticing Little Ben's hand reaching for his fork. 'Oh, please eat.' Little Ben happily resumed his steak but nodded to indicate he was listening. His father leaned back, sipping his beer, watching Harriet with a slight smile.

'There's a cottage in your window. For sale. The one I noticed the first day I met you.' Picking up her own knife and fork she smiled at Big Ben, who also resumed eating. 'It's been on the market for a while. Is it a deceased estate? The furniture in the photos, is that still there? For sale too?'

'Bellbird Cottage? It's been on the market for a couple of years. It was once attached to Drum Murray's property. Miss Boxshall lived there until she passed away three years ago. She was in her nineties and was gifted the cottage and a half acre by Drum's father many years ago. She came as a young girl to nanny Drum's father, then stayed on as a part-time teacher at Barrington School until Drum and his brother Fergus were born. She was their nanny too and retired when they went to boarding school. She never married and her only family are two great nephews and a niece, the boys in Sydney and the girl in London. They just want it sold. I doubt they want any of the furniture. I remember them coming for her funeral and taking what they wanted from the house at the time. Some of the furniture would likely have originated from the Murray Homestead.'

'Drum would like to buy it back and return it to the Murray property, but his parents' death, the drought, and now his, er situation with his, er wife, leaves him reluctant to spend his capital on it. I think he's hoping no one will buy it in the meantime until he can buy it back himself.' Little Ben glanced at Harriet before taking a mouthful of beer.

Nodding, Harriet returned to her meal, thinking over Big Ben's explanation. There was an opportunity if the family of Miss Boxshall agree.

'Bellbird Cottage. Nice name. I'm interested in it. It's on half an acre and has the creek at its back. Established gardens, although a bit overgrown despite the drought, and a small orchard. I'd like to have a look at it, of course, then make an offer to buy. A low offer, but I want a quick settlement. Within thirty days if possible. What do you think?'

Little Ben laid his cutlery down, his meal finished, beaming at Harriet. 'So, you're staying then Harri? Putting down roots here?'

'Yes. Yes, I am Ben. I have a business I'd like to start. I was looking for a slightly bigger town, closer to the coast, but since I've been here this last couple of weeks, I can see this is the place for me. For my business. To start over.' Fearing she'd said too much she picked up her fork, fiddled with her salad a little, not looking at the men, although she could feel them both studying her.

'That's good. You're young and smart. I think you'll be good for this town, this region. Good for you. The cottage needs a bit of work; mainly a good clean and the gardens cut back a bit. I'll take your offer to the sellers and enquire about the furniture. There's even a fridge and washing machine there, but we'll have to check they still work. I'll get back to you, we can have a contract ready later this week if price and terms are agreed.'

A fluttering of nerves hit Harriet for a moment while she digested his words. So that's it. I'm committing. I'm doing this. Taking a deep breath, she realised it felt right. Okay, it was quick and maybe a bit spontaneous. What's the worst that can happen?

The business doesn't take off and she moves on in a couple of years and has to sell. Property prices won't go down here, in fact she could make a nice little capital gain. She frowned. Drum Murray. He wants it back.

Looking directly at Big Ben, Harriet spoke firmly. 'This is business Ben. I don't expect you to let Drum Murray know I've made an offer. I don't want this to turn into a bidding war. I'll make one low offer and that's it. The sellers can take it or leave it. There are other properties.'

Big Ben leaned forward while his son gave him a quick, slightly worried look. 'Harriet, it would be unethical of me to advise Drum of your offer. He's not the seller, merely a neighbour in this case. He hasn't made an offer himself and has had plenty of opportunity to do so.' He included his son in his gaze as he added, 'I will present your offer and get back to you when I've spoken to the sellers. I sincerely hope they accept.'

Relieved, Harriet smiled, a warm glow of excitement in her core. 'Thank you, Ben. I felt that would be your response but needed to be sure.'

They spent the next twenty minutes talking price, deposit and terms. Big Ben made notes in a small notebook he pulled from his top pocket, while Little Ben spent a few minutes chatting to locals at the bar as he ordered another beer.

Around eight Big Ben took his leave. Harriet was sipping a soda water, hoping it would dilute the two glasses of red she'd consumed. 'Thank you again for the opportunity to work on this with you. I'll get draft designs for all elements to you within a week. I expect we'll speak on the cottage before then. Thank you for dinner too, great food, lovely company.'

Big Ben smiled. 'See Harriet back to her car, son.' To Harriet, 'I'll find you at the café Harriet, or will send you a message to drop by the agency. On our re-branding, just let me know when you want to have another catch up. No pressure, you know our timeframes, we'll let you manage this now.' He laid a hand gently on Harriet's shoulder as he spoke. She could feel a slight warmth there after he strolled away.

'Do you mind if I finish my beer, Harri?' Little Ben still had half a glass in front of him.

'Of course not. I'm fine to walk to the car by myself, you enjoy your drink.' Harriet stood up, smiling, and slung her bag over her shoulder. 'Goodnight, I'll see you during the week, no doubt.'

Little Ben stood at the same time, draining his beer in one gulp. 'I'll walk you to your car.'

With a cheeky grin Harriet said, 'I'm sorry, you didn't have to chug your beer. I'm perfectly fine to get to my car, it's less than two hundred metres away.'

'And deny me the pleasure of walking you there?' The look he gave her sent a shiver up her spine. He was very good looking, and quite charming, if a little old-fashioned. She decided she didn't mind old-fashioned. Harriet led the way to the door, hearing various people calling their goodbyes to Little Ben as they left, and even a couple of regulars from the café calling out ''Night Harriet,' to her. This gave her a small sense of belonging and a warm glow of pleasure.

Once at the car, Little Ben opened the door for her. He leaned toward her a little and Harriet leaned back, unsure if he was going to try to kiss her. But he just smiled, said goodnight and drive safely, and closed the car door once she was settled with the seatbelt on. She waved as she drove away and wondered if she had imagined that brief moment when she sensed his interest. Possibly not, she was being oversensitive. On the way home she hoped Laura was still up, she would call and share their good news.

19

Harriet found it hard to sleep after her quick call to Laura, also excited the Bens were moving forward with the re-branding. She fell asleep with a vision of Bellbird Cottage in her mind. How it must have looked when it was lived in and loved. How it could look again. Although she hadn't inspected it in person, she had scanned through the photos on the online listing a dozen times. It felt right. She could make it work.

Images of Little Ben Evans ran through her mind when she woke briefly in the wee hours, leaning toward her at the car, his eyes looking into hers. She hadn't imagined it. He was interested. Just a gentleman with old fashioned manners. Smiling, she fell asleep thinking about Ben, but he morphed into Drum Murray. Drum Murray standing at the door of Bellbird Cottage, hands on hips, legs apart, glowering at her. Warning her to keep away. She woke feeling confused and somewhat irritated. Men. She wasn't looking for one. Why was she even thinking about them?

Big Ben dropped by the café just after Harriet and Cathy opened on Thursday. Kristen was arriving in the afternoon, which would take the pressure off both of them. Harriet made his coffee and delivered it to his usual table. He laid the paper down and smiled at her. 'Harriet. Good morning.' He indicated she should sit for a moment. Harriet glanced at the counter, Cathy was busy loading cakes and slices into the front cabinet, there were no other customers. She pulled out a chair, not sure what news he had.

Ben spoke quietly. 'I've spoken to the oldest great nephew. He's Executor of the estate. He will have spoken to his siblings over the last couple of days. He seemed receptive. To your offer and quick settlement. It's the only offer they've received, the market has been slow due to the drought since the old lady passed. They've been paying the rates for the last couple of years with no return. No one has been interested in renting such a small place out of town either. While the light rain we got last month has helped the market and the drought is due to break, it may be another six months before it truly rebounds. He knows that.'

Harriet gave him a quick grin. While her offer was low, it was not unreasonable. Ben Evans was ethical, he would always try to get the best deal he could for the buyer. But a bird in the hand … they both knew her timing was good. Regular customers started to come in and Harriet stood, she needed to get to work.

Ben touched her hand, staying her for a moment. 'I'll pick you up here at two-thirty Harriet. We'll run out and open the place up, you can have a good look through it before you commit. I want you to be sure.'

Sudden tears pricked her eyes. She blinked quickly, willing them away. Of course, he was being professional, but the kindness in his voice almost undid her. If he noticed, he didn't comment. She nodded without speaking, hurrying to the counter to serve Angus Hamilton, in for his morning takeaway coffee before he started his Vet clinic.

Busier than usual, with a visit by Deb for half an hour just after lunch rush, Harriet made herself a quick snack after two, finishing just as Big Ben looked in. She grabbed her bag, waved to Cathy and walked out to meet him. He led her to a recent model Land Cruiser, holding the door open while she climbed into the passenger seat. They chatted amiably in the large and luxurious car as he drove them out past Laura's little farm to a small dirt road just before the gates to the Murray property. About a kilometre up the road Bellbird Cottage came into view.

Harriet gasped. It was picturesque. It was already late spring and the garden, while overgrown, had a myriad of colourful plants. Traditional roses, camellias, geraniums and lavender as well as a large number of flowering plants native to the region such as wattle, and bottlebrush. The garden was a-buzz with bees as they pushed open the wrought iron gate, sadly rusted, and the picket fence was leaning over. Nothing a good paint and few new pickets wouldn't fix, Harriet decided as they walked up the path paved in old red bricks, faded now with grass growing between some of them.

The exterior of the cottage needed a paint too and Harriet could see the iron roof may need replacing at some stage, but that was an expense she could deal with later on. The weatherboards were in good condition but when they stepped on to the veranda, up just three steps. She felt a bit of sponginess in a couple of floorboards. But most of them looked solid enough.

Standing back, she waited while Ben inserted a large old-fashioned key into the front door, made from solid wood with dusty stained glass set into the top section. A good clean would bring that up beautifully, she thought. Dust motes swirled around once the door opened, but the dull golden sheen of the wide floorboards welcomed them in. The hallway was high ceilinged, making it seem larger. Flushed with excitement, Harriet moved ahead of Ben, walking from room to room.

Two spacious bedrooms, one with a small air conditioner and ceiling-high built-ins, a living and dining area with a wood-burning heater and a larger reverse cycle air conditioner. A spacious bathroom with original checkerboard tiles and a deep claw foot bath and pedestal hand-basin had her clapping her hands with pleasure. There was no toilet in the bathroom. At the time the house was built in the early nineteen hundreds, the toilet would have been outside. Biting her bottom lip, Harriet looked at Ben.

'This way Harri.' They walked through a small, yet sympathetically renovated kitchen, with tiles matching the original ones in the bathroom. She noted a gas stove, dishwasher, fridge and microwave, all less than ten years old, and white matte cupboards in keeping with the original style of the cottage. Harriet followed Ben through the kitchen to another room, an addition to the home and probably part of a back veranda at one point. The room contained a laundry in a built-in cupboard on one side and a large shower and basin with a toilet cleverly placed behind a half wall on the other.

Clapping her hands, Harriet turned in a circle. 'I did not expect this. So modern but fits beautifully with the original part of the cottage. How fabulous.' Turning back to Ben she waggled a finger at him. 'Better photos and description would have sold this place Ben, it's gorgeous. Small, yes, but very sweet.'

'Jock Murray had the bathroom put on when Miss Boxshall became a bit frail. She had a fall, broke her hip, getting to the toilet out here one afternoon. It used to be where the laundry stands now, and no one found her for several hours. She couldn't afford to renovate it herself, so Jock organised it while she was recovering in hospital. They brought her home to the new kitchen and laundry, with the shower made wide enough for a wheelchair if she ever needed it. But her hip healed, and she lived here for another six or seven years until she died in her sleep, only a few weeks after Jock and Lorraine were killed in a car crash.'

Harriet was delighted by the original floorboards, high ceilings and veejay timber walls, some needing a coat of paint. It combined charmingly with the gardens at the front and the lawn at the back, leading past an abandoned kitchen garden to a little gate in the back fence, with the creek only metres away down a slight slope. Standing at the back fence looking toward the house, Harriet could see two large rainwater tanks against the wall on one side and a small pump sitting under a cover beside them.

'Permission to pump from the creek if the tanks run low?' She pointed toward the pump.

'Good pick up. Yes, and it would have been needed during the drought had anyone been living here. But once the tanks are full, with just one or two people living in the house it's unlikely you'd need to pump very often, if at all. Those tanks hold five thousand litres each. Plenty of water once we get the summer rains they've predicted.' Strolling back to the house, Ben added, 'Would you like to walk through again Harri? I'll walk around the outside and meet you in front.'

With a clap of her hands and a small skip, Harriet entered the house from the back veranda, stopping for a moment to look beyond the creek, to the line of trees in the distance that marked the driveway to Drum Murray's homestead. She could see the smaller home in the distance, and just the chimneys of the heritage homestead beyond.

Walking slowly through each room, some still furnished, the main bedroom had a dresser but no bed. The other bedroom had an old-fashioned double bed, made from timber. She could use that until she bought a queen size for the master bedroom. Under a dust-sheet there was a quality oak dining table with eight chairs and a matching sideboard. Harriet opened a drawer, finding tarnished cutlery in one. She picked up a fork. Silver. Just needs polishing. She was surprised the family hadn't taken it. There were dark patches on some of the walls where paintings had hung. That's OK, she had a few paintings stored in Sydney that may work in the cottage. A pair of grandfather chairs sat on each side of the fireplace, their upholstery dark and threadbare, but they could be re-covered and there was room for a sofa. Lighter paint on the walls, soft furnishings and a bit of colour here and there, it could be a little colonial showpiece. Harriet felt momentarily guilty. This would fetch a high price in the city, but out here, she could buy it for less than half the cost of an inner-city apartment.

Stepping back into the kitchen, the fridge suddenly hummed. Ben must have turned the power on at the mains. Harriet opened the fridge door. It had been cleaned. It worked. Perfect.

Back at the front door she looked from the hallway through to the main living area. The cottage felt welcoming. A good clean, some fresh paint, her own pictures on the walls and a few extra pieces of furniture, the place was perfect for her.

Grinning broadly, she stepped out on to the front veranda and waited while Ben locked the front door.

'The look on your face tells me everything.' Ben gestured for her to walk up the path to the front gate before him. Going through the gate she turned and smiled at him.

'I love it. It's better than I expected, doesn't need much spent on it, which is good as I have to keep some of my funds for my new business venture.' Harriet looked at the cottage again before turning back to Ben.

'I'm pleased to hear that, Harri.' He held his hand out. Harriet put hers in his, puzzled, as he shook it firmly. 'Congratulations my dear, you've bought yourself a house. I got a call from the seller when you went through the second time. They've agreed on price and terms.'

Harriet pulled her hand from his, stepped forward and spontaneously threw her arms around his neck and standing on tip toes kissed him on the cheek. He hugged her for a brief moment, before taking a step back. His smile was broad, the corners of his eyes crinkled with pleasure.

'Bless you, Harri. Your joy in this little place is a gift in itself.' Opening the passenger door for her, he waited until she was safely inside before closing the door. She admired his stately stride as he returned to the driver's side. As he got in, he said, 'it's been a tough few years in this region Harriet. The drought has hit the farmers hardest, but the town has been affected too. Good people have sold up and moved on. Some with farms, others with businesses in town. Precious people have passed on. My Rosemary, Jock and Lorraine Murray, Charlie Gordon.

'But with death comes new life. Debbie Webb, now Tait, and her cafe. It has become a hub and visitors stop here now, instead of driving through. Angus Hamilton has taken over the Vet practice and Rose Gordon has come home, writing her first book and starting her B&B business. She's encouraging others to do the same. This cottage, yours now, would have been perfect for tourists too but the owners live too far away, couldn't be bothered. Now you, Harriet. Your help with our business re-branding may encourage others in the main street to reconsider their presentation. I'm not sure what your new business idea is, but I feel confident you'll tell me when you're ready and my gut tells me it will be good for us. For this town.' Changing gears, he turned from the dirt road on to Barrington West Road to head into town.

'I will tell you Ben. And soon. It's something I think you may be more than interested in. Let's get the contracts done, I need to organise the deposit into your trust account and sort out the settlement details. I want to keep your project moving too. But I will need to move out here in four weeks, and that includes some cleaning and reorganisation. Once I'm in, I'll make time to talk to you further about my long-term plans.'

Nodding, Ben slowed slightly as a vehicle approached. It slowed too and Harriet clearly saw the look of confusion on Drum Murray's face as the vehicles passed. He raised his hand from the steering wheel as he passed, as did Ben. The country person's wave of acknowledgement.

'You might want to tell Drum sooner, rather than later, that you've bought Bellbird Cottage.'

'Yes, I should. I will.' Harriet sat quietly as Ben turned on to the main road to town. Damn, she was using Drum's car. The least she could do was tell him. Why did the thought make her nervous?

2O

The next week flew by. Kristen had jumped straight in, she'd worked in the café during previous holidays and knew the ropes. Harriet started each day at the café and spent two afternoons sorting out her finances for deposit and settlement and organising some of her belongings to be transported from Sydney within a month.

The contract became unconditional once Harriet paid the deposit, so she forged ahead with her plans to move in. Rose had recommended the cleaner she used for the B&B, so Harriet sent them to Ben to get the key and give the cottage a thorough clean. And Joe Daly had called to advise her car would be ready to pick up on Monday, as the parts were in.

Finally, on Thursday afternoon, she spent time with Laura at her place, working on the finer points of the marketing plan for Evans Real Estate, going through the final logo design together.

Harriet floated the idea of getting a small number of Laura's bulls into the Barrington Bull Sale at Drum's in March, but Laura just shook her head. 'You could try Harri, but I'm worried that you might lose this work if you go in to bat for me. They just don't like me. My farming style is different. Modern, conservation-based. They see me as outspoken, I'm a woman running a farm on her own …'

'I understand. I'm not planning to rush in, but if I see a suitable opportunity I will try. I appreciate your work on this and I want to help you in return, if I can.'

'You are helping Harri. Your company this last week has been a blessing and such a welcome change, not to mention the opportunity to pick up a bit of off-farm income. But it has made me see how lonely I've been. If I can't find a market for my stock, make the farm pay for itself, I may have to consider selling up and returning to the city where I can still get some work. Chris and Caro and their two little ones are living on the coast north of Sydney and they've made it clear they'd love me to move closer. I don't want to give up – this was our dream. Mine and Gareth's.'

'I get it Laura, really I do. Step one; you need to get some of your stock sold and an ongoing market. Step two; you need some friends here, locally Laura. Have you considered service clubs? Rotary? Country Women's Association?'

Laura threw back her head and laughed. She reached into a drawer in the cabinet in the dining area and pulled out an old-fashioned-English-gentleman-sort-of-pipe and a pack of tobacco. Harriet's jaw dropped as she watched Laura pack tobacco into the bowl, stick the stem between her lips and suck on it as she held a match to the tobacco. In seconds the pipe was lit, and Laura leaned back, her teeth clamped around the stem and a slightly belligerent look on her face.

'Wow. I'm stunned. I've never seen a woman smoke a pipe before. Actually, my grandfather had one like this.' Harriet collected herself mentally. Laura was a bit eccentric, but it was becoming one of the things she loved about her. Eccentric and didn't give a fig for anyone's opinion.

Then it dawned on her. This must be Gareth's pipe. More quietly she said, 'does Gareth feel closer when you light this up Laura?'

Laura nodded, taking the pipe from between her teeth, holding it in her hand.

'Yep. Yes, he does. About two weeks after he died, I realised I could no longer smell his tobacco around the house, or outside under the eaves where he used to smoke. So, I found the damn thing, filled it and tried to light it, just to, you know, have the scent around. I couldn't light it without sucking on the stem and I dunno, it just seemed ok to do it. Now I light up most evenings; it soothes me. I'll put it out if it bothers you.'

'Leave it. It's a nice aroma. Masculine. Very different to ordinary cigarettes, don't you think.' Harriet watched as Laura drew back again; little red embers lighting up the bowl of the pipe. It looked very good quality. 'But I'm guessing there is a story regarding the women of Barrington? Hence you resorting to your pipe in an effort to shock me.'

'There is. Ben's wife, Rosemary, dropped out here unannounced one day. I realise now that she meant well, but I was grieving Gareth. The kids had returned to the coast, and I was feeling lonely and doubting my ability to make the farm work by myself. Rosemary caught me unawares. I was wearing a pair of Gareth's overalls, hadn't been out of them for days and they were so filthy they could have walked to the laundry on their own.' She coughed and tapped the bowl of the pipe against the ashtray.

'I wasn't very gracious, knew who she was but had no idea at the time that she had been diagnosed with cancer. She invited me to a CWA meeting. I refused, said I'd prefer Rotary and the company of men. Pulled the pipe out of my pocket and lit it, to make my point. She scurried away, never came near me again. I heard she died last year from aggressive breast cancer, and I berate myself for treating her that way when her only intention was to include me in something. Legend has it the woman was a saint. I'm sure she told her husband about that day, and probably the CWA ladies, and they laugh at me behind my back. Now I'm nervous about reaching out to anybody. So, I don't.'

'Oh Laura. What an awful time you've had of it.' Harriet stood up and draped her arm across her new friend's shoulder. 'But you know, she may not have told anyone. If she was such a good woman, why would she tell this story when she knew you'd just lost your husband? You may be over-reacting to something that was never true in the first place.'

'We-ell. I made it true. I was still on my high horse when I approached Big Ben about the farmer's market idea. I did it at a public council meeting. Everyone was there. The look on their faces when I turned up in Gareth's overalls, a clean pair I will add, and lit up my pipe right there on the lawn in front of the Council building, loudly requesting consideration for this farmer's market idea I'd mentioned to a few people around town. A couple of people looked interested, but Ben Evans shut them down. Drum Murray gave me such a look, then started to walk across to me. I lost my nerve and bolted. Hardly go to town these days.'

'Oh Laura, gosh, I don't know what to say.' Harriet started giggling, 'but I'm picturing their faces. A woman in men's overalls, with a lit pipe, daring to speak out at a public meeting.' Laughing loudly now, she held on to Laura's arm for a moment. Putting her pipe down, Laura laughed with her.

'Damn Harri, you are just the ticket. I've laughed more since you've been here than I have in two years!'

In that moment, laughing with Laura, recognising the grief and loneliness she'd experienced, Harriet felt something shift inside herself. She stopped laughing, looked out the window for a moment, before looking back at Laura, tears welling in her eyes.

'Laura, can I tell you my story? I haven't wanted to talk about it. But just now. I don't know. Suddenly I want to tell *you* …'

Laura leaned forward. 'I feel it too Harri. We share something. Is it grief? I feel privileged that you want to share it with me.'

21

Drum marvelled at how well Billie settled into Barrington School. Only seven, she was in Grade Two and he was relieved to learn that after just one week, her teacher Miss Grayson confirmed she would move up to Grade Three at the start of the next school year.

From snippets of conversation with Billie at home, he had gleaned that she had not been attending school every day, as some days her mother wasn't 'well enough' to drive her. Drum berated himself for not knowing the true situation at the Sydney apartment. It seemed that Billie took better care of her mother than her mother did of her. He also learned that Annabelle often went out in the evenings after Billie was in bed, leaving her alone in the apartment.

Due to this, or perhaps in spite of it, Billie had become quite resourceful and independent and had told Miss Grayson that on the days she didn't attend school, she read quite a lot and practised her times tables. Drum had been somewhat embarrassed to hear this from the teacher, and when he questioned Billie she clammed up and said she 'didn't want to get Mummy into trouble, but it was much better to be attending Barrington School and be looking after Daddy.'

At five to nine, after his catch up with Miss Grayson, he parked near the café and entered the old bank building, taking the polished rosewood stairs up to the offices of Barlow and Maxwell two at a time.

Frances Barlow smiled warmly, walking around the reception desk to greet Drum. 'Right on time, as always Drum, just like your dear father. How are you? And how is Billie settling in at Barrington School?'

'Good morning Frances. I'm well, thank you. Blessed to have my child with me, permanently, I hope. I've just come from school, and she's settled quickly and will graduate to Grade Three in the new year.' Laughing, he added, 'I don't know why I was concerned, she is very grown up for seven. At home I wonder sometimes if she is channelling my mother, with her funny little ways.'

'That would be no bad thing Drum. Your mother was an amazing woman. She knew everything your father knew about farming and animal husbandry, and perhaps even a little more about horses. And she kept a beautiful home and was active in the community.'

Frances stood at only five foot two and leaned back to look up into Drum's face. Quietly she said, 'You're a fine farmer, Councillor and father Drum Murray. Your parents would be proud.' Stepping away, she added, 'I'll let Douglas know you're here.'

Drum watched Frances open the door to her husband's office. She'd been a close friend of his mother's and he admired her enormously. Small in stature, she was always immaculately dressed, highly professional and absolutely discreet. He knew the discussion he had with Douglas today would remain confidential. Not always the case in small towns.

~

Leaning back in his chair forty-five minutes later, a cup of tea half-finished in front of him, Drum frowned slightly and looked directly at his Solicitor.

'Make Annabelle an offer, you think? Iron-clad. Let her have the Sydney apartment to live in for life, or until she remarries, along with a monthly allowance. The allowance to be discontinued if she remarries. Request sole custody of Billie. It seems she isn't that keen to have her full time anyway. Additional allowance if and when Billie stays with her in Sydney. Have I summed it up correctly?'

'Yes, Drum. Our key concern is to protect your rural holdings from a claim during the divorce. The properties, including your parents' home and the lovely cottage you shared with Annabelle when your parents were alive are entirely in your name now. Fergus holds title to the Armidale and Glen Innes properties, has done since your parents passed. As the Family Trust owns the Sydney place, it's not yours to give as a settlement without your brother's permission. As it is, you will need his approval for Annabelle to live there for life, or until she remarries, as Fergus and his family are effectively excluded from using it themselves now.' Douglas made some notes as he spoke.

'I spoke to Fergus last night. He never really liked Annabelle. Moira and she didn't get on particularly well. He believes Annabelle will remarry. It's likely she's seeing someone at the moment. If she doesn't and it becomes a problem, I may have to buy her a place in Sydney of her own. But for now, Fergus is happy I'm taking some action to remove myself from the relationship, especially if I can keep Billie.' Drum stood, reaching across the desk he shook Douglas by the hand.

'So, you will write a proposal Douglas? I will speak to Annabelle, see if she has legal representation.' Sighing, he added,

'I'm sure it will be the best and I'm also sure I'll be paying the account. But it's worth it to have legal custody of my daughter. I'll let you know who to speak to.'

Leaving Douglas in his office, Drum spoke to Frances before going downstairs. 'Have you met Laura Harrison, Frances? She's my neighbour and I haven't really had much to do with her.'

Frances smiled warmly at Drum. 'Yes, I know Laura. We settled her husband's affairs when he died. She's a very private person, but also very capable and determined. I haven't been in touch with her in months, so thanks for bringing her to mind.'

Leaning down, Drum kissed Frances on the cheek. 'Lovely to see you, Frances. Thank you.'

Feeling lighter in spirit than when he arrived, Drum went down two stairs at a time, emerging into full sun outside the café. He planned to head back to the farm; he had hay to bale, but a glimpse of Harriet serving at the counter made him change his mind. He stopped on a whim and veered into the cafe.

22

And there he is. Drum Murray. Standing at the counter waiting to order. Why did he always make her feel just a little bit awkward? Harriet smiled a greeting, her hand poised to take his order.

'Morning Harriet. Short black please.' Instead of his usual slightly curt manner, he seemed more relaxed. He looked younger when he smiled. Seeming amused by her hesitation, Drum added with one eyebrow raised, 'I'll have a caramel slice to go with it, thank you.'

Knowing her face had flushed, Harriet ignored it, saying over-brightly, 'No problem, I'll bring that right out,' while simultaneously moving to the coffee machine to start his order.

From the corner of her eye, she watched him choose a table near the counter and could feel his gaze on her as she finished making his coffee, then place the slice on a plate. She needed to talk to him about the cottage but felt nervous. Maybe here in the café wasn't the right place for that conversation. She also wanted to ask about Laura, and the bull sale, but Kristen delivered his order as Harriet sorted the payment out for a small group of tourists, just leaving.

Moving efficiently around the café, Harriet greeted customers, took orders, made coffee and cleared tables. Every time she moved past his table, she could feel Drum watching her. What the hell? What was going on with him today?

After almost an hour, he was still sitting there, his coffee and cake finished, the newspaper he had picked up from the complimentary pile near the door barely opened. Harriet wiped her hands on her apron, told Cathy she was taking a ten-minute break, then made another short black for Drum and a long black with a dash of caramel and cream for herself. Carrying them both she approached his table.

'I'm on a short break. May I join you?'

'Of course. Please, sit down' Drum stood, pulling a chair out for her.

Harriet placed the short black in front of Drum. 'I want to ask you something.'

'Well, bribery by coffee will certainly help.' Looking at her, really looking at her, he smiled. Not a half-smile, this one reached his eyes, which crinkled a little at the corners. Harriet drew a breath. He was so, so …. She searched her mind. Handsome. Bloody handsome. Manly. Something primal in her seemed to respond. She felt a flutter in her stomach. She hadn't felt like this for a long time. Not since. Not since before her life changed forever.

'Go on. What is it you want to ask me?' He turned the grin down a notch.

She decided not to mention the cottage straight up. 'It's about Laura Harrison.' He leaned in. She had his attention. What? Really? 'I'm working on a project with her, and we've become friendly.' Hesitating, she looked down for a moment.

Drum touched her hand lightly with his. 'Go on.'

'She's done really well with her first crop of Wagyu bulls, they're ready to sell. Her herd is small, she doesn't have the numbers to attract the right buyers.' Harriet was going to launch into a plea for Drum to include Laura's stock in the bull sale, but he spoke first.

'Let me talk to her. I'd like to have a good look at her stock. From the road they look in excellent condition, she's done a really good job despite the drought. We can make room for them in the bull sale if she's interested.'

Harriet was thrilled. 'Really? Just like that? She thought you …' Biting her lip, Harriet wasn't sure how to continue. Getting her stock into that sale would enable Laura to keep the farm, hang on for rain, keep breeding her herd. And most importantly, keep her promise to Gareth.

Frowning slightly, Drum asked, 'She thought what?'

'Just that… you might not welcome such a small herd to the sale. And the only Wagyu stock.' Harriet spoke quickly, not wanting to tell Drum that Laura thought he didn't like her. He leaned back as she spoke, watching her closely. Harriet had the feeling he knew it wasn't the whole truth.

A group came into the café and Harriet could see she was needed at the counter. She stood, gathering their cups as she did.

Drum stood too. 'I didn't get to know Laura before Gareth died, and only spoke to him a few times, although my father was friendly with him. Since then, she has tended to avoid me. She avoids most people, I understand. I'm not sure if it's grief, shyness or if she's just uncomfortable here. In this town. This area.'

Looking up at him for a moment, Harriet bit her lip. Then opted for the truth.

'It's none of those things. But she should tell you herself. I'm so glad we spoke today, Laura will be keen to talk further, I'm sure.' Not wanting to lose momentum, she added 'Can I ask you to call in? After school perhaps? I'm dropping in there after work. Bring Billie.'

'Good. This afternoon. Four pm. We'll be there.' He strode out as Harriet rushed behind the counter, put her apron back on and smiled at the next customer. Outwardly calm, inside she was wriggling with excitement. Wait 'til Laura hears this! All thoughts of the cottage conversation had fled the minute he agreed to have Laura's bulls in the sale. Now she didn't want to jinx that decision.

'No! Really? Just like that? You asked and he agreed to have my stock in the bull sale?' Laura sat down at the kitchen bench, her expression a mixture of pleasure, amazement and a little doubt.

'It was even easier than that.' In her excitement, Harriet spoke quickly. 'I didn't ask Drum to put them in the sale. I just said you had stock ready to sell, but not enough to attract the right buyers. He jumped right in and offered to place them in the sale. He even said he had admired your stock from the road and would love to inspect them up close. Or something like that. He said he'd been wanting to speak to you, but thought you were shy, or grieving, or stand-offish. I told him none of those things really, but further conversation should be had with you directly.' She paused, watching the information sink in. Laura's doubtful expression changed to one of hope.

'You're brilliant Harri. In just three weeks you've changed my life, the future of this farm.' Finally realising the possibilities of selling her stock this way, tears sprang to Laura's eyes. 'Bless you. You make it seem so easy.' Laura wiped her eyes with the back of her hand. 'But perhaps I've been making it hard … and wallowing. Gareth's death, then the drought. On their own I may have done better, but all at once. Well, it was hard. I made it hard. Thank you.'

Harriet glanced at the clock, already three pm. 'He'll be here at four, I've got banana bread for afternoon tea. He …'

Laura sprang to her feet. 'What? Today? Four? I need to bring some of the stock a bit closer, throw them some hay. I need a shower.' Pausing she glanced around the kitchen. 'Sweep the floor …'

Laughing, Harriet said, 'Stop. Stop it right now. He's a farmer. You're a farmer. He will likely be happy to walk or drive down to see the stock where they are. He'll have his little girl with him, Billie. I can entertain her and get afternoon tea ready while you do farmer stuff. Have a quick shower if you must, but he's here to see farmer Laura, not getting-dressed-to-go-to-the-opera Laura.'

Relaxing slightly, Laura said, 'You're right. We're neighbours, I won't fuss. I'll just throw some clean jeans on and brush my hair. Can you sweep the kitchen, maybe the veranda? We can have afternoon tea out there.' Harriet nodded, grinning from ear to ear with happiness for her new friend. Laura strode from the room, then turned back and threw her arms around Harriet. 'I can't thank you enough Harri, this has made my day. Week. Year. If the bulls sell well my future here is secure. Thank you.'

Harriet hugged her back, then pushed her away. 'Go. Change your jeans. I'm sorted here. You don't have to thank me for anything. Look at you, working with me on the Evans Real Estate project. It's all good. It's what friends do. And it's now three twenty, so go!'

23

*D*riving slowly up the hill to Laura's home, Drum looked around with interest. While small, her property was well looked after, the fences straight and no obvious noxious weed infestations. He'd heard she used a lot of organic farming methods. He was interested to learn more.

Billie chattered all the way from school. About her new friends Emily and Tiffany, about the book she was reading and how far she'd hit the ball playing rounders at lunchtime. He loved having his daughter with him. They had settled into a routine, and she took a bright interest in all he did. Not just the farm. He chuckled inwardly. She had asked him about the Council meeting earlier in the week. She had commented that he was in his 'town clothes' rather than 'farm clothes.' Full of surprises, his sweet daughter often seemed wise beyond her years.

They parked at the homestead gate. Laura strode out to greet him. Tall and lean, she held the garden gate open as Drum and Billie approached. Smiling, Laura held out her hand. He smiled back as he shook it. Firm, capable grip. He suspected everything about Laura Harrison was capable. 'Thank you for having us over Laura. This is my daughter Billie.'

'You are very welcome, Drum. Hello Billie. Harri is making some afternoon tea, would you like to help her in the house or come with your dad to see my cattle?' Drum noted Laura spoke directly to Billie, not directing her question through him. He liked that. So did Billie.

'I would love to see your cattle Laura, but I'll go and help Harri. I'm quite hungry, you see.'

Laura and Drum laughed, then looked at each other, laughing louder. 'Of course. Perhaps you can have something with Harri while you wait for us. She just told me she's hungry too.'

'Thank you.' Billie was already running along the path to Harriet, standing at the front door. 'Harri, Harri, what are we having for afternoon tea? I'm going to help you.'

Harriet leaned down as Billie ran full pelt into her, throwing her arms around her waist. Drum watched with amusement, until he noticed Harriet wince. He frowned. Was she still sore from the car accident? He carried regrets he hadn't taken her to the hospital that night. About to call out to Billie to be gentle, he felt Laura's hand on his arm, she gave a slight shake of her head.

He looked at Laura, his eyes questioning. Laura turned him back through the gate, speaking quietly as they walked. 'Harriet was injured, some months ago. She has been a long time recovering. Coming here has been good for her. She's working, has some colour in her cheeks and has put on a small amount of weight. She needed to. She was skin and bone. If some things cause discomfort, she doesn't complain. She prefers no one to notice.'

Nodding, Drum looked at Laura. He wanted to ask about Harriet's injury. He could feel there was a story there. But he also sensed Laura would not share it. If he wanted to know, it would have to be Harriet that told him.

Reaching the first paddock, Drum could see a dozen or so Wagyu yearling bulls. Fat and glossy, they were feeding on hay.

'Are they quiet enough to get a bit closer Laura? Can we walk around them?'

'Sure. They're really quiet, and good-natured.' To demonstrate, Laura walked slowly up to the closest one. He raised his head, gave her a baleful look, then continued foraging in the hay. Laura patted his neck, walked around him and looked at Drum from the other side of the bull.

Impressed, Drum walked slowly toward the beast. He didn't even look up, just continued eating while Drum ran his hand along his shoulder and rump.

Together they walked around all of them. Patting most of them. Drum asked a few questions about their pedigree, their feed, how she kept weeds down without pesticide. Laura seemed surprised at his interest but was happy to share her methods.

Back at the fence, Drum paused, looking long and hard at the stock. 'You've done well Laura. I'm impressed. We can put these in the bull sale, and I think they'll sell well for you. We can talk reserve price a bit closer to the day.' He could see Laura was pleased, and almost relieved. He mentally berated himself for not making more effort to get to know her, offer some neighbourly support. He sensed she had many stories to share if one took the time to create a connection.

As they strolled back to the house Drum stopped for a moment. 'Laura, I'd like to pick out two for myself. Would you consider selling a couple of heifers as well?'

'Really? You're interested in Wagyu? Of course, I'd be happy to sell stock to you.' Laura paused, then added quietly. 'Thank you, Drum. For coming here today. For the opportunity to sell my stock at the bull sale. This alone will mean I can keep the farm, continue to breed.'

'Don't thank me, Laura. I should have come over sooner. I

could have been more neighbourly, offered assistance after Gareth died. It's the country way, but I, and others, haven't welcomed you as we should.'

Looking pleased, Laura didn't speak, instead nudged Drum with her arm and nodded toward the house. Billie was standing at the front door, waving. Drum lifted his arm in response.

Laura waved too, then added, 'I'm drawing a line in the sand right here Drum Murray. I'm starting fresh. Harriet has inspired me to make more of an effort, reach out to the community. I don't know how she does it, but she has a way of bringing people together.'

Drum could see Harriet standing with Billie now. She was laughing as she spoke to his daughter. He watched Billie take her hand and walk toward them. 'She is an interesting young woman. For a city girl, she has quickly made a place for herself here.'

He saw Laura glance at him sharply, but she didn't comment. Did he say something wrong? Oh yes, Laura is a city girl too. He was about to apologise, retract his remark, but Billie was on them.

'We've got banana bread from the café, and I helped Harri make scones. From scratch. She didn't use a packet mix or anything. We whipped up some cream and we have Laura's home-made jam and Harri is going to make me a hot chocolate. I've already had a whole piece of banana bread.'

Billie took his hand, leading him inside. He glanced at Laura, she was smiling broadly at Billie. After washing their hands, they sat out on the veranda, looking down the paddock to the river. He chatted further with Laura, Harriet adding a comment here and there. Billie was busy putting jam and cream on the scones, then playing hostess, passed them around. They were still warm from the oven and tasted delicious.

'I'll have to take you to work with me Billie. You're a great waiter.' Harriet ruffled Billie's hair.

'You're not a secret member of the CWA are you, Harri?' Drum finished his second scone. 'These are brilliant. Exceptionally light.'

'No, but thank you for the compliment. My grandmother taught me to make scones when I was about Billie's age. The recipe never fails to make me look good, but I'm afraid the rest of my culinary skills are a bit wanting.' Harriet wiped a splotch of cream from Billie's cheek with a napkin as she spoke.

Laura jumped in. 'That's not true Harriet. That stir fry you whipped up two nights ago was particularly good.' Laura raised her eyebrows as Harriet blushed.

Drum saw the blush. He could feel Laura looking at him. Was Harriet blushing because of him? Surely not.

'Let's clear these plates Billie, you can help me pack the dishwasher.' Harriet handed two plates to Billie, then cleared the rest away, carrying them inside. He could hear her chatting with his daughter and Billie's happy little voice replying.

Standing, he thanked Laura for her hospitality. 'We'll talk some more about the sale in the next few days Laura. We need to get the catalogue sorted, in print and online. We use a Newcastle company, takes a bit of time to get it right. I'll organise a meeting next week with the other sellers and the agents, I hope you can come.'

'Absolutely. Just let me know where and when. I'll be there.' Laura stood, paused for a moment, then held out her hand. 'It's been a pleasure to have you here today, Drum. You and Billie.'

'Same. Thank you.'

Turning, he saw Billie standing on a small foot stool at the sink, washing the mixing bowl and cooking utensils, with Harriet beside her, tea towel in hand, drying them. He stopped for a moment, a lump in his throat. Such a lovely picture.

The moment was broken as Billie dropped a small bowl into the soapy water, splashing herself and Harriet. The child froze and looked close to tears. If Harriet noticed, she said nothing, just put her fingers in the soapy water and splashed a bit more over Billie. Billie's face relaxed instantly. She laughed, then threw her arms around Harriet's waist. Harriet looked at him over Billie's head, her expression unreadable.

Holding out his hand he said, 'Time to go Billie.'

Billie jumped off the stool, ran to Laura and hugged her. 'Thank you for afternoon tea Laura.'

Laura leaned down, planting a light kiss on the top of Billie's head. 'You're welcome anytime Billie.'

Harriet wiped her hands on the tea towel she was holding but didn't step toward him. He nodded to her. 'Thank you for afternoon tea Harriet, and for cooking with Billie.'

'Always a pleasure to catch up with Billie.' Harriet waved to Billie as she walked out with Laura and Drum.

Driving away, Drum felt he had failed some sort of test in Harriet's eyes but couldn't figure what it was he'd done wrong.

24

About a week later, on Saturday, Harriet sensed a slight change in the air when she woke at dawn. Cooler with the slightly metallic smell of rain. *Fantastic, rain is so desperately needed here.* The wind had risen, and she donned an old sweater over her tee shirt and leggings, heading to the kitchen to boil the kettle.

Warming her hands around her mug of black tea, Harriet could see scuds of darker clouds heading south. *No rain yet, perhaps the wind will push it away.* She frowned. *Damn it. The farmers really need rain here.*

By ten o'clock she was back at Laura's to put the final additions to the Evans project, before meeting with them the next day. She could see Laura driving back up in her farm Ute, so Harriet waved and let herself into the kitchen, putting the kettle on.

The laundry door closed heavily. Laura came in wearing her trademark overalls. 'I don't think we'll see rain here today. They may get some further south. But this wind is drying out what little feed there is. It really is perfect weather for bushfires, we must be vigilant.'

'I fear you're right, Laura. It's not looking good at all. Have you moved the stock closer? Do you need a hand?'

'I've got them in two paddocks close to the house. They're a bit unsettled, but okay. I've got firebreaks there, protecting them and the house. Hopefully, we won't need it today, but this wind has me on edge.'

Looking out the window again, Harriet saw Drum's Range Rover go past, heading over Rocky Crossing on the way to town. She couldn't see if he had Billie in the car with him, but she imaged he did. She had learned his estranged wife lived in Sydney.

After a quick morning tea, Laura went out again, intending to slash firebreaks around paddocks further down the hill. Harriet told her she'd head back to town and pick up some items to make dinner for them both, then they could work on the project later.

Shopping quickly at the local supermarket, Harriet was about to return to the farm when she saw Drum's car parked near the café. Perhaps she could speak to him there, over a coffee, and tell him about Bellbird Cottage. The thought made her nervous. Her car would be ready on Monday, and she needed to return Drum's and thank him somehow. She bit her lip. The timing wasn't good. Walking in, she saw Kristen behind the counter and Jamie and Angus sitting with Drum and a group of men and women at a table just inside the door.

Harriet spoke to Kristen, who advised it was a volunteer fire-fighters meeting. The conditions were ripe for a fire. Then she heard her name called. 'Harri! Over here, Harri.' Turning, she saw Billie waving from the table up the back that Harriet secretly thought of as the staff table. She had a book open in her hand and a milkshake in front of her.

Harriet smiled and waved back, taking the coffee Kristen had quickly prepared, she walked to the table and asked Billie if she could join her.

'Course you can Harri, we're friends remember.' Harriet sat and asked Billie what she was reading.

'Famous Five. I found these books in the library at home. They belonged to my Granny. They're very old, but I really like them. Have you read this one Harri?'

Harriet took the book from her hands. 'I have read this one. In fact, I read a lot of Enid Blyton when I was your age. The Secret Seven series too. Great books.'

'Oh, there's more? I've almost finished all the ones we have at home.' Frowning slightly, Billie added, 'there is a library in town. I'll ask Daddy if we can join.'

'Great idea, always good to have another book ready when you need it.' What a gorgeous little thing she is. Harriet enjoyed chatting with her. How well-adjusted she seemed to be, despite her parents' separation.

Drum and his party were standing. He glanced over to Billie, smiled at Harriet but looked a little worried.

'There's a fire on the north side of the Bucketts Mountains. I heard Daddy talking on the two-way this morning. They're watching to see if it gets worse, or if there will be rain to put it out.'

Harriet stood, picking up her empty coffee cup. Billie put her book in her satchel, slurped up the last of her milkshake, then climbed off her chair, slipping her little hand into Harriet's. Drum strode across the room.

'Harri.'

'Drum.'

'Billie, I need to run you out to Jamie and Debbie's farm, I have to go and monitor the fire for a couple of hours.'

Billie squeezed Harriet's hand a little. Glancing down, she saw Billie smiling up at her, her eyes wide and innocent.

Inwardly chuckling, Harriet looked at Drum. 'You've no time for that Drum. I can keep Billie with me if you like. Debbie may not be up for much fun at the moment. I have a few more chores in town, then I'm going back to Barrington Homestead, before heading back to Laura's later this afternoon. Billie can help me, and you can just pick her up whenever you're finished, it's on your way home.'

Drum hesitated, then saw the happy look on his daughter's face. He knelt down and hugged Billie to his chest. 'Alright. You stay with Harri, but be a good girl, mind your manners, and help with her chores. Ok?'

'Of course, Daddy. Thank you.' She hugged him quickly around the neck, kissing his cheek noisily, then placed her hand back in Harriet's.

Straightening up, Drum looked at Harriet. 'Thank you, Harriet. We really need to get out there now so we can contain it before it gathers momentum. The wind keeps turning. I saw Laura has moved her stock closer to the house. That's good.'

And he was gone. It must be serious. Even a small fire could flare up in the right conditions. Hot weather, plenty of fuel on the ground, high winds. Walking outside with Billie, Harriet saw the heavier rain clouds had all but gone. No respite from rain today then.

The local library was in Denison Street, and open on Saturday morning, so Harriet took Billie there. She signed her up for membership, feeling confident Drum wouldn't mind. She helped her choose two books. Billie picked out six, but the librarian suggested two at a time was best, so she agonised over her choice, finally agreeing to another Enid Blyton and a Roald Dahl on Harriet's recommendation.

Back at Barrington Homestead, Billie played with Charlie while Rose and Harriet made a light lunch of quiche and salad. Angus was out fighting the fire too.

'I asked Deb if she wanted to come over, but she's not feeling great again today, decided to stay home. Jill, her mother-in-law, is only a few hundred metres away in the main homestead if she needs her.' Rose sighed. 'I worry about Deb. Her pregnancy was quite smooth up until a few weeks ago. She still has several weeks to go, but she's very tired. More than I remember being.'

Glancing at Charlie, playing a silly game of peek-a-boo with Billie, she added 'I'm more tired now than I was when I was pregnant. Angus Hamilton's son is a handful!' She laughed as she said it, but Harriet could see tiredness in her eyes. Maybe she should offer to look after Charlie some time, give her a break.

Just then Charlie sat down on the floor and wailed loudly. Billie looked startled, standing up she nervously came and leaned against Harriet's leg. 'Why is he crying? We were having fun.'

Rose had already scooped her son up, depositing him in her lap. 'It's a man-thing Billie. He cries if he's hungry, thirsty, wet or tired. I'm guessing he's hungry.' As she spoke, she reached for a banana from the fruit bowl in the centre of the table. Opening it, she broke off a piece for Charlie who stopped crying and immediately grabbed it with his chubby hand, squishing it between his fingers before poking some into his mouth.

Looking at Harriet, then Billie, Rose said, 'See? Hungry.'

Billie grinned at Rose. Harriet took Billie's hand. 'We're going to drop over to Laura's. I don't expect she's finished the work for Evans Real Estate, but I can organise some afternoon tea and maybe help her move the cattle if she needs to. Drum will be able to see the car there as he comes along the road. When the fire is under control. Although that may not be for hours yet.'

'Okay Harriet. Take care. Stay at Laura's tonight if you need to. If the smoke gets any worse, it's best not to be driving.' Rose shared her concern.

BACK AT THE FARM, LAURA WAS PLEASED TO SEE THEM BOTH. Smoke haze hung over the Bucketts Mountains. Billie took delight in pointing out the 'sleeping giant' formation of the range to Harriet, clearly visible from Laura's veranda. As they cleared afternoon tea the smoke haze worsened, and flames could be seen in distant treetops. The wind had not abated and with just a look Harriet knew Laura shared her concern.

Taking Billie inside, Harriet played a board game with her for distraction, while Laura walked around her stock and checked the fences were secure. These conditions could spook them.

Late-afternoon there was still no sign of Drum. Billie asked a couple of times if he'd called. Harriet explained that he would still be busy. The wind had turned slightly, which seemed to have slowed the progress of the fire. Smoke hung suspended over the range, but flames were no longer visible.

Close to dusk Drum drove up the driveway. Billie ran out to the car as he opened the door. He had smudges of ash on his face, which Billie tried to wipe away with her sleeve. He looked exhausted, and Harriet noted a red welt across the back of his left hand. A burn. Not serious but needing attention.

'Come in Drum. Have you eaten? I can fix you a sandwich and a cold drink.' Harriet looked at him expectantly. She saw him hesitate, then he rubbed his face with the back of his uninjured hand.

'That would be lovely, thank you.' He followed her into the house, responding quietly to Billie's chatter and questions.

Drum sat on a stool at the kitchen bench and gratefully took the top off the beer Harriet handed him. While she quickly made a sandwich, Billie wandered into the living room with her book. Harriet retrieved the first aid kit she'd noticed in the laundry, then systematically cleaned and dressed the burn. Touching him, tending him, seemed somehow intimate. There was a slight jolt of electricity when she took his hand in hers, turning it gently to smooth on aloe vera antiseptic. He seemed to feel it too, tensed slightly, but perhaps it was the pain from the injury that made him twitch. Head down, wrapping a clean bandage around his hand, she felt him looking at her. She didn't want to look up, meet his eyes. She was afraid he would see the affect he had on her. Finally finished, she packed the items back into the first aid kit, still not meeting his gaze.

'Harriet.' He spoke quietly, but his tone was commanding, more so by using her full name. She looked up. He was staring at her. It felt like the oxygen had left the room and they were in a bubble. Just the two of them. His hazel eyes deepened. Darkened. She held her breath, although wasn't sure why. Her eyes never left his. They were pulling her toward him. Or perhaps he leaned toward her.

The moment was broken as Laura returned. She banged in through the laundry door, greeting Drum as she stepped into the kitchen.

The three adults spoke quietly as he ate the sandwich. Harriet noticed Drum finished the first beer quickly but seemed to savour the second one, taking his time as he spoke.

'If the wind had continued in the same direction it would have been worse. It was heading this way. It took one of Saunders's outlying hay-sheds. It was nearly empty, thankfully. That's how I burned the back of my hand, an ember from the rafter of the shed.'

Laura poured home-made lemonade into two tall glasses and a smaller one for Billie, still in the other room. Harriet sipped hers while Laura spoke with Drum.

'It's just the start of the season Drum. If we don't get rain, there will be more fires. Bigger, hotter ones you won't be able to contain. It worries me.'

'You're doing all you can. Your fire breaks are good. But you're right. With no rain we could be in for a bad summer season. I'm going to head home and check my own stock, hopefully they haven't pushed through any fences today. The smoke will have agitated them.' He sighed as he stood.

'Thank you, Harri. For today. Taking care of Billie. The sandwich, cold beer, dressing my wound. For a city girl you seem to know what's required in these situations.'

Harriet knew Laura gave her a sharp look, but perversely did not want to explain her rural origins to Drum in that moment. He had made assumptions based on her car, her clothes, her manner perhaps. Let him discover the truth in his own time.

'Just what anyone would do Drum. And Billie is a delight. Anytime.'

Taking Billie's hand in his as he walked through the living area, Drum looked back from the front door as he put his boots on. Harriet felt the intensity of his gaze for a moment, then waved to Billie as they walked out to the car.

2 5

Frowning to herself, Harriet tidied the kitchen and pondered her reaction to Drum while Laura went out to check the stock again and take a quick drive around the fence line. She still hadn't mentioned the cottage. It hadn't been the right time, it was obvious Drum was exhausted. Shaking her head slightly as she wiped down the kitchen bench, Harriet berated herself. She'd tell him tomorrow.

Laura returned, looking tired. The smoke haze had lifted, drifted to the south. She would let Laura rest, the work for Evans real estate could wait, she'd left chicken and salad in Laura's fridge and returned to Barrington Homestead for the night. Feeling tired herself, she did a mental inventory of her little kitchen as she drove away. Cheese, crackers, a bottle of wine and a block of chocolate. 'Health food of a nation,' she muttered aloud as she pulled in beside Rose's car.

As she stepped out of the car, the young dog barked from the veranda. Stopping, Harriet gave him a pat. As she did, Rose opened the front door.

'Hi Harri. I'm pleased you were able to get back. Angus says they have the fire under control.' Stepping out, she leaned down to pat the dog, who had abandoned Harriet the moment Rose appeared. 'He's had a shower and is crashed out on the couch with Charlie.'

Nodding at the dog, Harriet smiled. 'Dropped me like a hot rock. He knows the hand that feeds him.'

Rose chuckled. 'Poor Woof. He seems to spend a lot of time avoiding Charlie, who has taken to pulling at his tail.'

'Woof?'

'It's meant to be Ruff, after his grandsire who died a couple of years ago, but Charlie can't say Ruff and calls him Woof instead. It seems to have stuck.'

'Ha. Cute one.' Harriet loved the way Rose took everything in her stride. 'I was going to stay longer at Laura's, but she looked like she needed a rest too. Drum came by to pick Billie up, he told us they lost one of the hay sheds at Saunders' place. Good the wind turned and there wasn't more damage.'

'I know. We're all concerned. Summer has barely begun and unless the rains come as predicted, there will be more days like today. It may get a whole lot worse.' They both glanced toward the retreating smoke haze.

Harriet understood. She'd grown up in an area requiring flood irrigation to maintain feed and crops. The weather was a constant concern. And not just rain. Rain at the right time.

'They're still forecasting La Nina conditions, but so far the reality hasn't proved them right.' She sighed.

'You're a country girl too, aren't you Harri? Where did you grow up?' Rose cocked her head on one side.

'Ha, ha. Got me. Yes. First eighteen years on a dairy farm in the Riverina. I always get back a few times a year, but this year it was a bit longer. Recuperating at home after, er, an accident. Long story. Needs a glass, or two, of red for the telling.' Smiling at Rose, Harriet realised in that moment that she hadn't avoided the answer or found it hard to speak of. In fact, she really *wanted* to tell Rose. Instinctively she knew that by sharing her story she would give a measure of trust to Rose, and just as instinctively she felt confident her trust would be returned.

'No pressure, and it's not my intention to pry. But if you're up for a chat, I'm a good listener.' She reached out, touched Harriet gently on the shoulder. 'In fact, I have a story too. Part romance, part mystery. If you stay around long enough, you'll hear various versions, but I'd prefer to tell you mine.'

'Deal. Let's do that.' Harriet found herself agreeing enthusiastically, warmed by Rose's confidence.

In a change of pace, Rose asked. 'Do you have anything in there for dinner? You're welcome to join us, I've made soup.'

Harriet smiled at Rose, before bending to pat the dog once more. The genuine warmth and welcome in Rose's voice brought tears to her eyes. Gosh, she was turning into a bloody sook.

Harriet looked up, grinning at Rose. 'Thanks Rose, but I've got a feast in my rooms. A bottle of red plus cheese, crackers and a block of chocolate for dessert.'

Rose snorted. 'It doesn't get any better than that. I'm jealous.'

'Well, you're welcome to join me if you like. It sounds like your two men are out for the count.'

Sniggering a little, Rose wagged her finger at Harriet. 'Be careful what you wish for Harriet. I expect Angus will eat then go straight to bed. He's on call from three in the morning to check the firebreaks on this side with Jamie Tait. Seriously, if he takes Charlie to bed with him, I'll join you in an hour or so. I'll have eaten, but happy to share your wine and chocolate.'

'Perfect. See you then.'

Smiling to herself Harriet stepped into her rooms. She felt a kinship with Rose. Country girls who had made a life in the city. Rose had transitioned back to the country. Harriet could too. She felt smoky and grubby. Walking through to her bathroom, she turned the shower on.

After a quick shower she towel-dried her hair, before standing in front of the large bathroom mirror, naked. Only four weeks in Barrington and Harriet could see she had colour, not just on her face, but her arms and legs were slightly sun-kissed from her afternoons at the river. She didn't think she'd gained any weight, but she looked healthier. She felt healthier. Stronger. This place was good for her. Touching her old wound gently, she could see that some of the redness had faded. Yes, there was no missing the scars, but Harriet felt less conscious of them for the first time since leaving hospital. Was it just over four weeks ago she believed she would never be free of these wounds? The physical wound and the damage it had done to her emotionally. Somehow it seemed less important here.

Just as she slipped into yoga pants and a loose t-shirt, Rose knocked on the door.

'It's open.'

Harriet walked from the bathroom to see Rose with a bottle of wine in one hand and a bag of salt and vinegar chips in the other.

'I was going to bring over some soup. But I had these tucked away in the pantry. Goes perfectly with cheese, crackers, wine and chocolate.' Rose waggled her eyebrows a little and Harriet laughed.

'You are my people Rose Gordon. I'll get the glasses.'

'*I* don't know what to say Harri. I'm so sorry you went through that. First the stabbing, then finding your husband was cheating. And not just on you, but in your business. My gosh, so much to contend with.' Raising her glass, Rose clinked with Harriet. 'Here's to you, girlfriend. What doesn't kill you makes you stronger.'

'At first it was too much. Multiple surgeries, the pain, over-thinking Tim's lack of interest, how little he came to the hospital. He's always avoided illness, and at first that's what I thought it was. But I had time to think, and I started to piece together where he was, and even worked out who he was with. Mum came up from the farm, stayed in our apartment, to be close to me at the hospital. That's when I realised he was cheating. Mum caught him out in a lie and just cornered him. Wouldn't let him go until Tim told her the truth. She'd been suspicious too.'

Harriet poured the last of the red into their glasses and popped a piece of dark chocolate into her mouth. 'Now when I look back, thinking it through, I don't believe he was faithful more than the first six months we were married, if that. Three years of marriage. I feel stupid. How did I miss the signs?'

'Well, if you ask me, it sounds as if you were doing all the work setting up the business, pulling long hours. When did you have time to see the signs?' Rose harumphed, as she sipped her wine thoughtfully.

'So where does that leave you now. Your marriage? The business?'

'The marriage is over. Not divorced yet, have to be separated a year. He's already 'engaged' to the woman he was seeing behind my back. A member of staff. At first, I was pissed with her, but now I just feel sorry for her, and a little bit contemptuous. He's got form. How secure will she ever feel, knowing he cheated on me? Every time he's late home she'll be wondering if he's cheating on her. '

'Don't be soft Harri, she deserves whatever she gets.' Rose gave Harriet a steely look. 'You're too nice. But I can see you've let go of your feelings for him, and that's healthy. It means you're emotionally free to start over, whenever and wherever that may occur.'

'Start over. Definitely in business. Personally, I'm not sure I will ever go there again.' Harriet hesitated, then changed tack. 'But the apartment sold while I was recovering at the farm, so I have money in the bank. Not a huge amount, but enough for a decent deposit and to start a new business. I've extricated myself from our business in Sydney. He didn't want to pay me out, but I told him it was either that, or wind it up. We were both Directors. He didn't have much choice. Just as I was making a move to leave Mum and Dad's and head north, I heard from a mutual acquaintance that he isn't doing well with the business. Only six months in and he's already in trouble if my source is correct. I'm glad I'm out of it.'

'So, is it something similar you're looking to start here? I'm really curious.' Rose had curled her legs up under her at one end of the couch. Harriet was at the other end, cross legged. A tray of cheese, crackers, chocolate and chips sat between them.

'It is in a way. But smaller, and really designed for the country, rather than the city. I'm not quite ready to share the plan, Rose, I hope you don't mind. I'm chatting with Ben Evans, both of them,' she giggled 'and if all goes to plan, I will tell you in a week or so. But it's good, I think. Good for me, for the Bens', for the area.' Harriet sat back, flushed from the wine and excited about speaking of the business she had been germinating for weeks, months, while she recovered.

'In fact. It all came about because I decided I would, from now on, use my power for good instead of evil!' She waved her arm around, almost spilling the wine as she did.

Rose snorted. 'Your old business wasn't evil. It was smart. I won't push you, but I'm keen to unravel your plans. It sounds like the only thing evil in your old business was your partner. That bloody cheating husband of yours. The bastard!'

'Yeah. Bastard!' Harriet chugged the rest of her wine and looked at her empty glass. She picked up the bottle. It was empty too. Stretching her legs, she was about to ask Rose if they should open the other bottle in her fridge.

'Don't move. Here's one I prepared earlier.' Rose reached down beside the couch, then held aloft the bottle of red she'd arrived with. 'Voila!'

Laughing, Harriet held her glass out for Rose to pour. 'I don't think I've laughed like this in ages. Not since before. It's cathartic.'

'You betcha. I can't wait for Deb to deliver Jamie Tait's sprout and be able to join us for a girl's night. You're our people too, Harriet.'

They each sipped, and simultaneously lowered their glasses with exaggerated 'aah's,' which started them giggling again.

Harriet laughed with Rose but felt there was something else she should tell her. She frowned for a moment, then put her glass down carefully on the floor. Sitting up straight, she said, 'That's not all Rose. I've left out the best news. I was going to wait until I told Drum, but I'm really, really excited!'

'Told Drum what?' Rose put her glass down too and leaned forward in happy expectation.

'I've bought a house. Well, a cottage really. I'm moving in. For good.'

Picking her glass up, Rose held it toward Harriet while she scrambled to pick up her own glass.

'That's the best news. But what does it have to do with Drum? And congratulations!'

Harriet paused. Drum was obviously a friend of long-standing. Will Rose be upset that she'd bought Bellbird Cottage? Would she know Drum wanted to buy it himself? She took a breath.

'Bellbird Cottage. I've bought Bellbird Cottage.' She waited, watching for Rose's reaction.

Rose put her glass back down carefully and stood up. Harriet watched her nervously.

'Give me a hug! Bellbird Cottage. Are you kidding? Someone needed to buy it. It would be perfect for a B&B, but it's well equipped to be a fabulous home for you. And it's just up the road. We're practically neighbours!'

Relieved, Harriet stood up, allowing Rose to hug her. After a moment Rose held her by the shoulders, looking down at Harriet. 'You're crying! Don't cry Harri, it's brilliant news! Why are you worried about Drum?'

They settled back on the couch. 'Ben Evans told me it used to be part of Drum's family property, but it was gifted years ago to their old nanny. He said Drum wanted to buy it back but wasn't in a position to, with the drought and his personal situation.'

Rose frowned. 'That may be the case. I didn't grow up with Drum, he's older than me and went off to boarding school when I was quite young. But our families are friends and I know his younger brother Fergus. We used to play tennis together. But we've become re-acquainted in the last couple of years, really through Angus, who does all his Vet work. I'm not aware he wanted to buy it back. Yes, it makes sense. But he already has the house on his property that he and Annabelle lived in, plus the homestead. He moved in there when his parents died.' She paused, obviously thinking. 'You need to tell him, of course. It's the right thing to do. Honestly, I'm not sure what his reaction will be. Disappointment perhaps, initially, but then to have someone make it into a home again, rather than holiday accommodation which is the more likely scenario, I think he'll be pleased.'

Harriet was relieved. If Rose was ok with it, then its likely Angus would be. And Angus and Drum are friends.

Leaning forward, Rose added, 'He bloody well should be pleased. Yes. He will be.' Leaning back, she gazed intently at Harriet for a moment. 'But you must tell him. And soon. You don't want him to hear it from Little Ben at the saleyards on Monday.'

Still feeling apprehensive, Harriet sipped her wine. 'I'll see him tomorrow. Let him know. My car will be ready on Monday, I need to arrange to take his back to him. Thank him.'

2 7

Billie ran to the window again. 'Here she is. It's Harri, she's driving up to the house now!'

Before Drum could stop her, Billie was out the front door, running down the steps and on to the path, nothing on her feet. Standing at the top of the steps, he watched as Harriet stepped out of his old car, parking it exactly where it was when he gave it to her.

Harriet turned in time to see Billie skipping with excitement at the garden gate. He had told her not to go outside the garden and wait. Harriet smiled broadly as she walked to the gate where Billie launched herself at their new friend, throwing her arms around her waist. Harriet threw back her head and laughed; loud and infectious, then bent to kiss Billie on the top of her head.

Taking Harriet by the hand, Billie led her up the path to the steps where he stood, partly in shadow on the veranda.

'Good morning Harri. Nice to see you.'

'Morning Drum.' She smiled at him warmly.

'We've made morning tea for you Harriet. I've squeezed six

oranges and we have some caramel slice from Debbie's 'cos Daddy says you like that.'

'Thank you, Billie. I've brought something for you too.'

Holding the front door open, Drum waited for the two of them to step inside before following them down the hall. He could see Harriet glancing from side to side, taking in the long high-ceilinged hallway, family portraits and property photos on the walls as she followed Billie to the large sun-drenched kitchen.

'Would you like a tour of the homestead Harriet? I promised you one when you picked the car up.'

'I'd love that Drum, thank you.' He glanced at Billie, hopping up and down on the spot, who was delighted when Harriet added, 'Perhaps we should have morning tea first, Billie has gone to a lot of trouble.'

At that news Billie led Harriet to a large kitchen table, set for three, with a jug of orange juice in the centre, three glasses and plates and a small wooden serving board laden with caramel slice, cut into odd-shaped pieces.

'This is just lovely Billie, thank you so much.' With a cheeky glance at Drum she added, 'Did your dad cut the slice up for you?'

'Oh no. I'm a big girl. I cut it up by myself. I help Daddy with all the cooking, you know.'

'Your Dad is very lucky to have such good help in the kitchen, and on the farm Billie.'

'Thank you, Harri.' Drum poured juice into the three glasses and passed the platter of slice to Harriet, who took a large piece.

Before eating, Harriet lifted her tote bag onto her lap. 'I have something here for you Billie. Let me see. What have I done with it?' He watched Billie, sitting up straight, trying not to look too eager. He smiled to himself. His girl has nice manners.

'Ah, here it is.' Harriet passed a copy of Roald Dahl's Matilda to Billie, whose eyes widened.

'Ohhh! A book. Is it from the library Harri?' Billie had it open on the table beside her, looking first at the flyleaf, saying 'Matilda' in a quiet voice, before looking back at Harriet.

'Not from the library Billie. This is yours to keep. Perhaps you can add it to your library here.'

Billie scrambled down from her chair, ran around the table and threw her arms around Harriet's waist. 'Thank you Harri, thank you very much!'

'It's my pleasure.' He saw genuine warmth on Harriet's face as she hugged his daughter back. Turning to him, she added, 'Thank you Drum. So much. For helping me with my car, lending me yours.' She paused and he wondered what she would say next. 'And for introducing me to Billie.' He saw affection, and something else, in her eyes. Sadness?

Unaccountably moved by her words, he said brusquely, 'All good Harri. My pleasure.' He kept his eyes down while he sipped his drink.

Billie chattered away and they both laughed and responded to her for the time it took them to enjoy morning tea. He took a breath as he watched Harriet and Billie discussing books in serious tones. What is wrong with him? There is something about this woman...

'Would you like the tour now Harri.' Standing, he began clearing their plates.

'I'd love that, but we can wash these up first.' Harriet stood, reaching for her empty glass.

'I'm clearing,' Billie said firmly. 'Daddy will show you the house. Did you know we have a ballroom? There are no balls in there at all, but Daddy says it used to be for dancing.' She screwed up her little nose as she spoke.

Harriet laughed and gave Billie a quick hug. 'You're a wonderful hostess Billie, thank you. I'd love to see the ballroom.' Turning to Drum, she smiled up at him. 'Shall we?'

'Step this way, your tour is about to commence.' Drum led her back to the hallway, just inside the front door. 'The house was built in the eighteen-eighties. Fourteen-foot ceilings with pressed metal, actually a similar pattern to Rose Gordon's house, although I think theirs pre-dates this by a dozen or so years.

'Three main bedrooms off the left side of the hall and a formal sitting room and lounge room to the right.' He opened the doors to the rooms. The master bedroom was obviously his, and all rooms had French doors, made from richly hued Australian cedar, leading to the wrap-around verandas. The verandas were wide, with solid cane occasional furniture strategically placed.

'Most of the furniture belonged to my grandparents and great grandparents, although my mother added a few pieces here and there. She found antiques from time to time, which fitted with the period of the house.' He walked on.

'There is a smaller room between the two largest bedrooms. It was a dressing room and nursery at various stages. When my brother and I were old enough to have our own rooms further away, my parents turned it into an ensuite. Modern facilities but in a style sympathetic to the era of the house.'

Back in the hallway he stopped at a series of wedding photos on the walls. His grandparents, parents and his brother Fergus. There was a picture of Drum with Annabelle on their wedding day, too. He watched with interest as Harriet studied each picture. Annabelle was tall and striking in a form-fitting strapless sheath. A simple gown, but designer made. She was a beautiful woman, but looking at the picture over Harriet's head, he could see a calculating coldness in his wife's eyes. Or was that only because he knew it was there, in her character? Billie was tall for her age, like her parents, but her face was lively and good humoured. She reminded him of his own mother.

As if she could read his mind, Harriet looked at him over her shoulder, 'Billie seems to have more of your family in her features. She is not unlike your mother, if you don't mind me saying so.'

'I think so too. She is like my mother in more than looks.' Turning, he led Harriet further into the house, through the open kitchen, the formal dining and lounge and then the sunny living area. 'This was the back veranda of the original homestead.'

Then another door opened into a large bright room, obviously Billie's. White timber furniture and pastel quilts, cushions and curtains gave it a youthful, feminine feel. The window seat to one side, with a built-in shelf filled with books, looked well used. Billie ran into the room, nipping between the adults to hop on to the window seat. Harriet was charmed by the way she settled in with her back propped up by pillows, her new book in her lap. 'I read here all the time Harri, It's my favourite spot. And we keep Chippy, that's my horse, in the paddock just beyond the yard, so I see him every day when I get up.'

Harriet walked to the window seat and sat down, leaning against the opposite side. 'What a perfect spot to read, Billie. What a beautiful room.'

'My Nanna made this room for me when I was little. I love it!'

Harriet stood and turned in a circle, taking it in. 'It's perfect Billie, I love it too.'

Drum's heart warmed as he saw Billie smile at Harriet's words. He remembered another conversation after his parents died. Annabelle had called the room 'hideously old-fashioned.' Glancing at Harriet again, as she leaned down while Billie pointed out favourite books on her shelf, he saw what a contrast this woman was to his ex-wife. Smaller in stature, and perhaps not as striking in a formal sense, but warm and genuine. And pretty. Really pretty. A bit too thin perhaps, but positive and optimistic. He could sense that she knew the value of work too. He doubted Harriet had been handed anything on a silver platter.

'Daddy. Daddy!' Billie drew him from his musings. Harriet glanced out the window, but not before he saw a smile hovering around her mouth. Caught again!

'And on to the ballroom.' Billie led the way into another hallway, with a small room off each side. 'Men's and ladies cloakrooms, in the day,' he said. He was pleased to see Harriet's pleasure in the old homestead.

Billie pushed open the large cedar double doors to the ballroom. Even though he'd seen it himself thousands of times, it still impressed. Polished timber floorboards in the centre, occasional tables and chairs around the outside, which was carpeted in a heavy navy carpet.

He grinned when Harriet cocked an eyebrow at him. 'Axminster?' He nodded. He saw her silently mouth 'Wow!' as she looked around the impressive room.

'My grandfather put the bar in at the other end, and there's a galley kitchen back there too, on the other side of that door. There have been balls, dances, weddings, birthdays, tennis parties, land care meetings, you name it, this room has seen it all. Fergus and Moira had their wedding reception here – with a marque out on the tennis court too.' Glancing at Billie, who was now running in a big circle around the room, he added, 'I hope we hold Billie's important birthdays here, and perhaps one day her wedding.'

Harriet looked at him. Her eyes, usually a lovely blue, seemed darker. The raw emotion on her face moved him toward her, then Billie barrelled into them, and the moment was lost. Looking down at Harriet as she listened to Billie, he wondered if his instinct was correct, that she had untapped depth. Not a question for today. Yet still he wondered.

They left the room, returning to the large, bright kitchen area. Billie wandered back to her room, her new book still in her hand.

Standing at the kitchen bench, Harriet thanked him for the tour. 'You have a beautiful home, filled with precious things. Not just things. Memories. History. As Billie grows you'll create many more memories. How special.'

He could see she meant every word. He felt the same. His parents had felt it too. Fergus also, but perhaps to a lesser extent. Yes, it was his job to preserve this heritage.

'Um, Laura is going to pick me up shortly. We'll be back at two for the sale meeting. I hope you don't mind me coming back with her, but she's a bit nervous, and perhaps I can help with the marketing or brochures …' she looked up at him, a slight frown creasing her forehead.

'That's great Harri. Happy to have your expertise and I definitely want Laura to feel comfortable. It doesn't matter that her offering at the sale is small. In comparison, I mean. She has the only Wagyu stock and I really think that's a drawcard.' He saw relief on her face, but then she frowned again.

'Is there something else Harri? You look worried.'

2 8

---

*H*arriet glanced out the window, then looked at Drum.

'I've bought a house. A cottage really. Here. In this region.'

His expression changed from one of surprise, to a slow smile of pleasure. Good, she thought. Keep that feeling.

'Really? You're planning to stay?'

'Yes. I was looking for an area, a town or region, to start a new business. Booking into Barrington was just to give me a rest for a couple of days on the way. I've had, er, a busy few months.' She had his attention, now she just had to tell him where she had bought.

'But spending a few weeks here.' She looked at him. 'Getting to know Rose and Angus, Debbie and Jamie, you and Billie, Laura, the Bens ....' She stopped for a moment.

'Yes.' He nodded, encouraging her to continue.

'I realised that although the area is smaller than I planned for, it has all the ingredients I need to make a fresh start. I have to be out of my accommodation at Rose's just after Christmas, and well, I just found something I really like. And I bought it. It's nothing like this of course. Small. A cottage. But sweet. Perfect. It's just me, I don't need much.' She realised she was rambling. He was leaning back against the kitchen counter, his long legs crossed at the ankle, his arms folded. Damn him, he was smiling. Was he enjoying her discomfort?

'That's great Harri. I am surprised. A city girl like you choosing to buy in the country. But I'm pleased. I really hope it works out for you.' He raised an eyebrow.

Damn him. Making assumptions. Just because I came here from Sydney doesn't mean I grew up in Sydney. He hasn't even asked, just assumed. Not sure if she was angry because of his assumptions or needing to give herself courage.

Almost defiantly she looked him in the eye. 'Bellbird Cottage. That's what I've bought. I'll be your neighbour.'

He was shocked. This was not what he expected. Harriet cringed internally. This man had been nothing but kind. Maybe she should have looked for a different place. But damn it, he's had years to buy it himself. It could have been bought by anyone.

His relaxed posture changed in an instant. He looked confused and cranky. He straightened, arms still folded, staring at her.

'Bellbird Cottage?' He repeated it. She nodded, squaring her own shoulders slightly. Any hint of friendliness between them vanished. His tone was icy.

'Was that what you were doing when I saw you driving with Ben Evans? He didn't say a word.'

Trying to soften the blow, Harriet spoke in Ben's defence. 'Ben told me you had mentioned buying it back one day. That it used to be part of your property. But Drum, you haven't done that. Ben is acting for the seller. He's contracted to seek the best offer for the property.'

Drum turned, his back to her, ramrod straight. 'Damn!' he

spoke quietly. 'He's my friend. My father's friend. He should have told me. I would have tried to buy it myself.'

Hearing the tone in his voice, Harriet stepped toward him, placing her hand gently on his back, 'I asked him not to. I didn't want to get into a bidding war. By law he didn't have to tell you.' She wanted to add that isn't it better to have her living there permanently, than to be rented for short term accommodation, but he turned, his face dark with anger.

'I think that's Laura's car outside. You'd better not keep her waiting.'

Harriet had expected him to be disappointed perhaps. But not this angry. Shocked, she nodded and picked her bag up from the back of her chair.

'I'll just find Billie, say thank you …'

'Just leave Harriet. I'll tell Billie you had to go.'

Turning, Harriet strode toward the door, tears filling her eyes. Damn him! Perhaps she should have talked to him first. But if she hadn't fallen in love with the cottage, she may not have decided to stay. Perhaps she shouldn't stay anyway. It's not too late to get out of the contract.

Out on the veranda she went quickly down the steps, the presence of Drum standing behind her sending shivers up her spine. The man was red hot angry. Cripes. Is there another side to him? Is that why Billie was so frightened when she dropped the bowl in the sink at Laura's?

Laura was stepping out of the car as Harriet approached. She raised a hand to acknowledge Drum. Harriet didn't look back but said to Laura over the roof of the car, barely concealing the tears ready to spill out, 'We need to go Laura. Please. Can we just go.'

Glancing from Drum to Harriet, Laura nodded and slid back into the driver's seat.

29

'I've stuffed it. Really stuffed it.' Harriet was crying and wiping her eyes with a tissue at Laura's kitchen bench.

'I was so confident the cottage was perfect. Ben tried to tell me. But he's a good real estate agent and is obliged to sell if he gets an offer. Now, the friendships I've made here may be lost. Locals stick together. If Drum is set against me, they may all turn.' Taking a breath, Harriet turned her tear-ravaged face to Laura. 'And you Laura. What have I done to you? What if Drum now refuses your cattle in the sale, because of me?'

Laura waited patiently as Harriet vented. 'What will be, will be. I'm no worse off if that happens. But Drum is a businessman too, and I think he really wants my cattle in the sale. Let's leave emotion to one side, as I think Drum will too. We go back at two for the meeting. There will be others there, including Ben Evans. Maybe this will be okay. But if not, it won't damage our friendship Harri. And I really don't think Rose will buy into Drum's issues either. Or Debbie for that matter.'

'But I don't want to cause ruptures in these friendships. I shouldn't have rushed in. I will speak to Ben privately after the meeting today, withdraw my offer. I'll stay on for a few days, finish the work for Ben Evans, then head north like I planned.'

'Gather yourself Harri. We will be united and professional when we go back after lunch.' Nodding, Harriet sipped the iced tea Laura put in front of her. She knew her business concept was reliant on local support and now doubted she could make it work in this town. Why did she have to rush in and buy the cottage. She may have found something just as suitable if she'd waited – stayed at a motel for a few weeks. If she withdrew her offer, would Drum's trust be restored? She shook her head, smiling wanly at Laura's questioning look.

'I just don't know what to do. Perhaps you should go to the meeting alone, it may be better for you.'

'No.' Shaking her head, Laura set the salad bowl between them, offering the servers to Harriet. 'Getting my cattle in the sale was a long shot. The opportunity would not have arisen but for you Harri. You've given me a boost of confidence. I'm not keen to face Big Ben Evans by myself. I need you with me.'

Taking a deep breath, Harriet lifted her head. 'You're right Laura. I owe it to you to be there. Maybe Drum has thought about it since I left. The shock may have worn off.' Speaking with more confidence than she felt, she reached for her laptop and notebook.

'What do you know about the sale Laura. How do they usually market it?'

'They printed and posted out colour catalogues in years gone by, and a page on Evans Real Estate website with all offerings and details listed. I looked at it last time. It's very basic. They also had a couple of pieces in regional and ag papers, like The Land and Weekly Times. On their own websites too. Honestly Harri, it could be done better. Branding, dedicated social media, engagement with buyers and sellers.' Laura served herself from the salad bowl.

Aware that Laura was watching her, Harriet shook her head slightly. 'What if...'

'Yes?'

'What if part of the deal, for you to have your cattle in, is that you help with the branding, social media and engagement? Offset some of the costs you would normally have to pay for the auctioneer and so on.' Harriet grinned. 'They would have paid for everything in the past. Brochures, printing, advertising to support the editorial in the press. Now they have someone with graphic design skills. And Laura, anything you can't do, I can help with. It might get me back in Drum Murray's good books. What do you think?'

'Great idea. I am a bit worried about some of the costs. This arrangement may help me with that. But also help the other sellers. I know they won't be financially strapped like I am, but who doesn't want to save money and have more control of their messaging?'

Glancing at the clock on the kitchen wall, Laura began clearing their plates. 'I'm going to have a quick shower and change.'

'I'll wash up. You get ready. I'll make a few notes to take with us. But I don't want to be pushy. Let's hear what they have to say, generally, before we show our cards.'

'Good. Be strategic. Focus on the benefits for all concerned. That's smart.'

Opening her laptop, Harriet did a few google searches on previous sales, finding editorial, ads and some references on social media. All a little bit ad hoc. Could be more cohesive. No real branding, just a list of logos for the various breeders involved in the sale.

At one forty-five they were back on the road to Drummond Murray's. They had seen Ben Evans' car go by thirty minutes earlier, and now there were two vehicles in front of them, moving slowly toward the Murray homestead.

They parked beside the other vehicles. The group gathered on the front veranda turned, almost as one, to watch as Laura and Harriet walked toward them. Drum Murray came down the steps, his hand held out to Laura.

'Thanks for coming Laura, pleased you could make it.'

Shaking his hand Laura smiled. 'Thank you for having me here, Drum.'

Harriet stood back a little, waiting for Drum to acknowledge her. Turning to her he nodded. 'Harriet.'

'Drum.' So, this is how it's going to be? Civil but not friendly? And using her full name. At least he welcomed Laura warmly. She watched as Drum introduced Laura to the group.

'You know Ben Evans of course? And his son, Little Ben?' Little Ben shook Laura's hand then continued down the steps to Harriet.

'How are you, Harri?' He took her outstretched hand, then leaned in to kiss her on the cheek. She blushed, hoping no one noticed.

'Good, thank you Ben.' Not sure if she should mention Drum's reaction to her contract on Bellbird Cottage, she decided to discuss it with Big Ben, if she could speak to him privately during the afternoon.

'Laura, Harriet, this is Jim Fraser. He has Julie with him, she's just taken some afternoon tea through to the dining room. You know Angus Hamilton and Jamie Tait, of course. And the Bain brothers, Logan and Wiley.' The men towered over Harriet, all of them over six foot. But they smiled, shook her hand, made comments on the likelihood of rain and included both women in general small talk as they followed Angus through the house to the large dining room.

Julie Fraser stepped forward, hand outstretched. 'Laura. We met at the saleyards a while back. Nice to see you again.' She was dressed in jeans and boots and a chambray shirt with the Fraser logo embroidered on the pocket, like her husband. Turning to Harriet, she smiled warmly. 'We haven't met, but I've heard a lot about you. Welcome to Barrington.'

Taking her hand, Harriet relaxed at the easy warmth in the woman's tone. 'Thank you, Julie, it's good to meet you too.'

The table was set with water and juice jugs, a plate of fruit cake and a cheese board. 'Anyone for tea or coffee?' Drum stood as everyone found a seat. Harriet hesitated, not sure if she should join them at the table or wait to one side. Little Ben pulled a chair out next to him, indicating Harriet should sit.

'Too damn hot for tea today mate.' Wiley Bain, the older of the brothers, spoke as he sat. 'How about we talk business, then knock the top off a cold one.' Nods all around. Drum passed jugs of water and juice around as they took their seats, chatting informally.

Drum barely glanced at Harriet, but she noticed he was quite attentive to Laura and sat her to his right. Disappointed for herself but pleased for Laura, Harriet listened to the general discussion as they settled.

'We've only eleven weeks to the sale, so it's the business end as you all know.' As Drum opened his mouth to continue, Billie burst into the room.

'Harri! Harri! You're here too!' She flew around the table and climbed on to Harriet's lap, giving her a huge hug as she did.

Drum frowned at his daughter briefly. Or perhaps at Harriet. She couldn't tell.

'You all know my daughter Billie?' Smiles and murmurs of

acknowledgment filtered around the table. 'Billie, you were going to read in the other room while we have our meeting.'

'But that was before I knew Harri would be here.' The last bit sounded slightly petulant. Drum looked over Billie's head at Harriet.

Unsure what to do, Harriet said, 'Er, would you like me to come and read with you Billie?'

'That's a good idea.' Drum spoke quickly, but at the same time Ben Evans said, 'No, I'd like you here Harri, we could do with your marketing expertise.'

'Oh.' That was Billie. Harriet leaned down and spoke quietly to her. 'How about you go and read for a bit, then come back in for afternoon tea. We can have a better chat then.'

Drum stood, perhaps thinking he would have to take Billie to the other room. But she slid off Harriet's lap, giving her a little pat on the cheek. 'Come and get me when it's time for cake please Harri.' She skipped from the room to various chuckles and Drum's obvious relief.

Sitting back a little, Harriet listened to the discussion around the table. Drum kicked it off, with a welcome to Laura, which she acknowledged with a shy nod of her head. He ran through the logistics of bringing the animals in, a couple of days before the Auction as some buyers like to inspect the day before. Angus would check all sale animals were healthy upon arrival. Most of them would be trucked in, but Laura's farm was close, and Drum offered to walk them in using horses and dogs.

'Thank you, Drum. The cost of transport for such a short distance does seem unnecessary. I'll assist, and perhaps Harriet if she has capacity on that day.' Laura looked across the table at Harriet.

'Yes of course, happy to help you, Laura.' From the corner of her eye, she saw Drum raise an eyebrow. Arrogant. He believes I am without any rural experience. Well, hasn't he got a surprise in store.

Logan Bain cleared his throat. All turned toward him. A man of few words, he looked directly at Laura. 'We haven't had

Wagyu in the sale before. The right buyers may not be there for you. You should set a decent reserve and be prepared to pass them in if the interest isn't there.'

Laura stiffened, but Big Ben, seated next to her, touched her gently on the forearm. Harriet saw surprise flit across her friend's face.

As Logan finished, Ben spoke. 'Drum tells me he has already negotiated to buy a couple of heifers and a bull from Laura. There will be other buyers there who may be keen to diversify their herd or begin a Wagyu line of their own. Yes, Laura will have a reserve, just as you all will, but don't be surprised if her stock brings in some new buyers too.'

Jamie and Drum nodded. Julie Fraser glanced at Jim before adding, 'We're pleased to have your cattle in the sale Laura. It's not a competition, it's about having a good selection to bring the right buyers to us. Your stock won't detract from ours, and we agree with Ben, they enhance the overall offering.'

Looking relieved, Laura relaxed, smiling and murmuring thanks to everyone. Harriet had expected resistance but was pleased Laura had found allies instead. The most supportive appeared to be Drum, as Harriet expected, and Ben Evans, which she did not foresee.

They moved on to costs. Firstly, the feed and care of the stock while they were at Drum's and for the few days it may take for all sold stock to be delivered to their new homes. All the farmers offered hay and grain from their own stores, to be pooled. Laura agreed, but Harriet knew her reserves were far smaller than the others.

Then the conversation turned to marketing and advertising, and Harriet pulled her chair in closer to the table. Julie Fraser had been making notes as they went, and Harriet wondered if she should pull her laptop out of her bag to take notes too.

When Julie read the notes from the last sale, six months prior, the advertising figure seemed very high to Harriet. Laura paled slightly. Even shared between them, it was a large amount.

'May I ask a question?' Harriet glanced at Ben, then looked at Julie, who nodded as Ben murmured assent.

'What is the breakdown of the costs for marketing and advertising for the last sale? I'd just like to understand in case there are more cost-effective ways of achieving the same end.'

Reading from her notes, Julie advised the biggest costs were a printed sale catalogue, and postage and the hire of a firm in Newcastle to manage editorial and advertising for the six weeks prior to sale. They had used this company for the last four sales, with quite good results.

'Harri, this is not very different from the work you are doing for us, at Evans Real Estate. Do you have any suggestions?' Little Ben smiled as he spoke.

'If I could ask some more questions first. The catalogue. Is there a reason you have one printed and posted, rather than, say, a website with email newsletter updates?'

Wiley Bain had not spoken, but now he leaned forward. 'The buyers are farmers, like us. Not all are comfortable with websites and such. And a catalogue can be physically brought with them. They like to mark the lots off as they sell, noting the prices. Some bring catalogues from previous sales, to compare genetics and so on.'

'Do any of you here, today, use the internet for your business on a regular basis?' Harriet looked at each of them, noting the nods as she went around the room.

'So, if you all do, it's likely your buyers do too, wouldn't you think?' She had their attention. 'A website can be built for a fraction of the cost of designing, printing and posting catalogues. It can be used again for the next sale, uploading new stock details.

If there is a last-minute withdrawal of stock, or replacement animal, that can be done quickly as well. It can be set up in a format that looks familiar, like a catalogue. If any buyers want a printed version, they can print it themselves. Ok, it may not be as glossy, but they could even choose to print just a selection of lots.' Some seemed surprised, but were taking it in. Little Ben was smiling fondly at her, which threw Harriet off for a moment. Laura was nodding and looked keen to contribute to the conversation.

'Put this together with editorial and ads in the usual places, supported by strong social media, plus personal emails to your buyers with a link to the website. The website could be monitored too, so real-time conversations about particular animals can be directed to individual sellers. It would give buyers an opportunity to make decisions before the day, so they are ready to bid for what they want.' Harriet paused looking first at Laura, pleased to see a glint of amusement in her eyes, then to Ben, the other sellers and finally Drum.

Little Ben spoke first. 'It's brilliant. Would definitely keep the costs down and engage our buyers. But we still need to get the website built and monitored, the email campaign developed, and the social media presence established. We could see if the firm in Newcastle could manage this.'

'Yes, good idea. If we all agree, let's get some prices.' That came from Jamie Tait. He looked at Julie Fraser. 'Can you chase up some quotes Jules?'

'I can do it.' Laura spoke up but looked a little uncomfortable when all eyes turned to her.

Julie spoke first. 'Happy for you to chase quotes Laura, thank you.'

'I don't mean chase quotes. I can do it. Build the website.' Surprise was evident on the faces around the table.

'Go on, Laura.' Drum spoke quietly.

'I'm a graphic artist. I have a whole Mac system set up. I still do a bit of work for old clients in Sydney.' Pausing, she looked at Ben Evans directly. 'I did the new logo concepts for your re-branding Ben.'

'Well, I'll be!' Big Ben threw back his head and laughed, slapping the table at the same time. 'Aren't you full of surprises! Now I know how Harri turned those designs around so quickly. That's excellent news.'

Laura continued, with more confidence. 'I've built websites before, but I know Harri has experience there too. We can use the existing branding but change it slightly with the new sale date. Harri would be better placed to write the editorial and ads and build the social media platforms. Manage the email delivery too.' Pausing again, she looked around the table. 'Let Harri and I quote on this work. You will be surprised how cheaply it can be done, by comparison to your regular costs. Further to that, could I offset my share of feed costs by doing some of this gratis?'

Leaning back, Laura looked flushed, but pleased with herself. The others began talking to each other, and asking questions, until Ben held up his hand. 'One at a time. Is everyone happy for Laura and Harri to quote on this, show us the savings and how it could work?' Smiles and nods of agreement from all. 'Anyone worried about making this change?' All seemed keen, except the Bain brothers.

Wiley spoke first. 'Could we create a few good quality catalogues, from the website, for anyone who requests it? This sale could be a transitional one. If it works for most buyers, we could go catalogue free at the following sale. We just don't want anyone to not attend because they have trouble getting the information.'

'Absolutely. We can do that.' Laura spoke with a measure of authority and beamed at the group. Harriet sensed the relief Laura felt, being able to offset the costs.

Drum stood. 'A toast is in order. Beer? Wine?' He looked around the table, his eyes momentarily resting on Harriet. She turned her head as Billie ran into the room. 'Is it time for cake now Daddy?'

'Yes Billie, you can bring it in if you like.' Drum watched Billie as she dashed to the kitchen, then he brought a bottle of red wine to the table and a few bottles of beer. 'Mid-strength lads, most of you are driving.'

Laura chose to drink a beer, while Harriet had a glass of wine with Julie and Big Ben. Billie climbed on to Harriet's lap again, a glass of juice in front of her and a big piece of fruit cake.

Little Ben moved his chair closer to Harriet engaging Billie in a funny conversation about her horse Chippy. Enjoying their banter Harriet laughed out loud, giving Billie a hug as she did. Glancing up, she felt, rather than saw, Drum's eyes on her. She turned to Little Ben who was demanding he be allowed to ride Chippy next time he came, with Billie telling him he needed a bigger, fatter horse to ride. She caught his eye and they laughed together, delighting in Billie.

'Billie. Leave Harriet be. Come and sit here for a moment.' Drum beckoned his daughter, who reluctantly, but obediently, slid off Harriet's lap to stand beside her father on the other side of the table.

Big Ben and Laura were standing a little apart from the group, holding their drinks and speaking quietly near the window. Laura was almost as tall as Ben, and just as lean. She touched him gently on the arm. He smiled at her and shook his head, then patted her shoulder for a moment. A slight flush and a relieved look passed across her friend's face. Harriet would ask later what that exchange was about.

Moving across to Angus, Jamie, Jim and Julie, Harriet answered questions about the marketing and advertising. They were keen on the idea and Julie said she'd drop previous catalogues and the budget to the café next morning. Drinks finished, the Bain brothers left first, with the Frasers shortly after. Laura and Harriet were saying their goodbyes when Jamie's phone rang.

'The little missus.' He grinned and answered the phone, moving out to the veranda as he spoke. His grin changed to a look of concern. 'Don't move, I'll be right there. Don't move Deb!'

Turning to the group now assembled outside the front door, he drew a breath. 'It's Deb. Waters broken. Gotta go.' Visibly shaking, he pumped Drum's hand. 'Thanks Drum. Good meeting, thanks.'

Angus stepped in. 'Hang on mate. We came together, remember? Give me the keys. I'll drive. We'll be at your place in ten minutes. Is her mum with her? or Jill?' He waved to them all, walking down the steps, one arm around Jamie's shoulders, who was back on the phone now to his mother.

'Mum's going to her now. Come on Angus, get me there.' Jumping into Jamie's Ute, Angus gave a quick wave and backed around, heading quickly out the driveway.

Big Ben frowned. 'She's early. Not too early. It might be a blessing, she's been really unwell these last few weeks.' Putting an arm around Harriet's shoulders, he gave a squeeze. 'Thank goodness you blew into town when you did Harri.'

The sudden display of affection unsettled her, tears welling in her eyes. Blinking a couple of times, she glanced at Drum. He was looking directly at her, frowning. Glancing away, she said goodbye to both Bens. As Laura was thanking Drum, Harriet stood behind her. Billie had wandered back inside at some point. Finished, Laura began to head down the steps. Harriet watched her for a moment, then stepped toward Drum, holding her hand out. 'Thank you, Drum, this has been a great outcome for Laura, and for the sale itself.'

Holding her slim hand in his large one he looked down at her, his expression unreadable. 'And for you Harriet.'

'For me what?' she tried to pull her hand from his.

'A good outcome for you.' He released her hand.

Waving once more, as the last of the vehicles pulled away from the homestead, Drum turned to check on Billie. He would see if she wanted a quick ride on Chippy, then brush him down and feed him.

Walking inside, he thought again about the meeting. It had been better than he expected. All were very accepting of Laura's inclusion. The Bain's had initially put up some resistance, but he and Ben had talked them around a few days before. They'd been happy enough when they left.

Back inside, Billie was carrying plates and glasses to the sink. 'Good girl, thank you.' Leaning down, he kissed the top of his daughter's head.

'Was it a good meeting? I thought Harri might stay and read with me afterwards.' Disappointment flit across her face, before she smiled again. 'Nice cake Daddy. Mrs Fraser left the rest of it for us. She said it's lovely if you warm it up and put some ice-cream on it. A bit like Christmas pudding she said.'

Laughing, Drum knelt down and hugged her tightly. 'Dessert

for tonight then. Would you like a quick ride on Chippy before we feed him?'

'Yes please. I'll put my jeans on and be right back.' Planting a kiss on his cheek, she scampered off to her room, back moments later in jeans with her riding boots in hand.

As they walked to get Chippy's bridle, Billie chattered away. He wasn't paying close attention but heard 'Harri this' and 'Harri that.' What was it about this woman that had his daughter so entranced? He struggled to work her out. City girl but seemed to fit in well here. That surprised him. And smart. She was definitely smart. Not lazy, she was doing business with Ben and now planning to do some work with Laura. And she was still helping out at the café. But she'd bought Bellbird Cottage and he was annoyed he hadn't bought it himself. Bloody Ben Evans and his ethics. If he'd given Drum a heads-up, he would have found the money and bought it himself. He shook his head. No, he couldn't do that. He had to sort Annabelle out first.

Sighing, he walked beside Billie as she selected Chippy's bridle from the stable, then walked confidently into the paddock. The horse came straight to her, taking the small apple she pulled from her pocket. Clever girl. She fed him regularly, so he was never hard to catch. While he ate his apple, she slipped the bridle over his head, barely able to reach his ears to settle it into position. Chippy lowered his head for a moment, sniffing at her pockets and she quickly put the bridle in place, doing up the cheek strap.

Glancing over her shoulder, she looked at him with a triumphant smile. 'I can catch him myself now. It's easy.' Billie walked toward him, the reins in her hand and the horse following quietly.

'Good girl. You've done well. Would you like me to get your saddle?'

'I can do it. You watch.' Billie grinned at him, placing the reins in his hand while she skipped through the gate into the stables, coming back with her pint-size stock saddle and a saddle blanket tucked underneath. She held it with both hands and was struggling a bit, her face red from the effort, but he didn't move to help her. Drum could see she wanted to do it herself.

Billie walked around and set the saddle down on the ground, taking the saddle blanket and positioning it gently on Chippy's back, crooning to him softly the whole time. She gave the horse a couple of gentle pats on his withers, then retrieved the saddle and with a big heave, got it onto his back. The saddle blanket dislodged a bit and seemed to be bunched up. Drum was about to step forward and straighten it for her, but she looked at him, her face a mixture of determination and concentration, and standing on tippy toes she lifted the front of the saddle enough to adjust the blanket. She ducked under Chippy's chin, around to his other side, and did the same there. Satisfied it was all straight she came back around and reached beneath her horse, bringing the girth strap through.

She did it up as tight as she could. Drum knew it needed at least one more notch. Then, standing on tippy-toes again she held the leather girth tightly, gave Chippy a gentle poke in the tummy and while he breathed out, she slipped it into the next hole. Drum laughed out loud.

'Where did you learn to do that Billie? That's a good trick.'

'From Pa. He showed me when I was little, and he was teaching me to ride on Sparky. Do you remember that? Pa said Sparky was a 'little guts' and liked to hold his breath when you put the saddle on, so he would poke him in the tummy to surprise him, then do it up quickly. I don't think Chippy is a guts like Sparky, but I'm not as strong as you, so I thought I would try Pa's trick.'

Memories of his father teaching five-year-old Billie to ride flooded back. Sparky was a little Timor pony he had bought for Billie when she was two, and he had been a guts, and pig headed and hard-mouthed. Drum had sold the little horse when Annabelle took off to Sydney, preferring Billie to ride Chippy, a small stock horse with a better temperament. He was moved that Billie had such a special memory of her grandfather.

Billie led Chippy to an empty feed bucket, turned it upside down and stood on it to get her left foot in the stirrup and throw herself confidently up into the saddle. With Billie safely mounted, Drum saddled his own, larger stock horse, Jack. He was impressed with his daughter's confidence and capability, considering she had only been back on the farm a short while. She was a natural. A warm glow of pleasure settled in his chest.

They walked the horses down the front driveway and along the creek. Not sure what made him come this way, he stopped. Bellbird Cottage was on the other side of the creek, nestled among overgrown roses and fruit trees. It was a pretty cottage, and he would like to see the yard trimmed and weeded. It looked a bit rough and uninhabited. Perhaps he had over-reacted to Harriet buying it. At least it would be permanently lived in, not rented out for holiday makers or turned into a hunting lodge for weekend warriors. He shook his head at the thought.

Billie gazed at the cottage. 'The little house looks a bit sad don't you think? There was a very old lady there, a long time ago. Gran took me to visit once. We gave the lady some home-made cake and a carton of fresh eggs and she gave Gran a big bunch of flowers from her garden. Has she gone away?'

'That lady was a schoolteacher for a long time. She taught Pa when he was a boy and even taught me and Uncle Fergus when we were young. She lived in this cottage for a long time, and Pa gave it to her when she retired. But Billie, she was very old and died some time ago. And now her family have sold it.'

'Oh. If it was Pa's cottage, shouldn't she have given it back?'

Drum studied Billie for a moment. She had such a keen sense of justice.

'Well, maybe she could have. But she gave it to her own family, who live in the city, so they've sold it now.'

They looked at the cottage in silence for a moment, then Drum turned his horse toward home, expecting Billie to do the same. After a moment she trotted up beside him.

'Do you think a little girl about my age will move in there? It would be nice to have someone to play with.'

Drum glanced down at her hopeful smile. 'Well Billie, I just heard today that you know the person moving in there.'

'Oh really? Who is it?'

'Harriet. She told me today she's bought the cottage and will move in quite soon.'

Billie laughed. 'Harri? Really? That's wonderful!'

'I thought you wanted someone your own age to play with?'

'But Harri's even better. She loves reading and horses and she talks to me like a grown up, not a little kid. She's already my friend. I can even ride Chippy down here and visit her some-times. And we can go swimming together … and you can come too Daddy. You can visit her too and come swimming. She's your friend too.'

Billie's enthusiasm was contagious. Drum silently resolved to speak to Harriet. Apologise. It would be good to have her here. Billie likes her. The Bens' like her. She stepped in for Debbie and brought Laura into the sale, effortlessly. Yes, he should speak to her.

Thinking of Debbie, though, he thought it was time they went back to the house, checked on her progress. He'd call Jamie. Or perhaps Rose, Jamie would be busy. He glanced at Billie, a look of concentration on her face as she held Chippy firmly. Even the quietest horse liked to head home at a cracking pace, but she knew and was sitting deep in the saddle. Definitely a natural. Looking up at the sky for a moment, Drum silently thanked his father for giving Billie those early riding lessons.

3 2

*P*ausing at the door of her room, Harriet turned and knocked on the door to the main homestead. She needed to check on Debbie. It would be too early for the birth, she thought, but Rose may have some news.

The door opened quickly, Rose would have seen Laura drop her home.

'Any news yet?' Harriet noted the concerned expression Rose wore.

Sighing, Rose shook her head. 'Not about the baby. But Debbie wasn't doing well, so they've airlifted her to the John Hunter Hospital in Newcastle. Jamie is driving there now with his Mum for support. Deb's parents are also on their way.' She stepped aside to let Harriet in. They walked back to the kitchen, where Angus was holding a sleeping Charlie on his lap.

'Hi Harri.' Angus looked worried. Little Charlie made a snuffling noise in his sleep and Angus held him close to his chest, anguish on his face.

'Angus.' Harriet spoke quietly.

'He can't lose her. Either of them. Jamie can't go through that.' Angus shook his head, raw emotion blazing in his eyes.

'She's in the best place. She'll be all right. And the baby. She has to be.' Rose looked close to tears but began making a pot of tea while Harriet perched on a high stool at the kitchen bench, beside Angus.

They drank their tea, chatting quietly while Charlie slept. Angus and Rose had their phones on the kitchen bench, in easy reach if there was news. Angus stood as Rose refilled the kettle. He handed the sleeping child to Harriet.

'I'm just going to check the horses, throw some hay to them.' He slid his phone into his back pocket. 'Call me if you hear anything.' Rose nodded wordlessly, as he strode toward the door.

'Do you want me to take him Harri?' Rose reached for Charlie, but his little body was warm and heavy in Harriet's arms, and she wasn't ready to surrender him. She looked at Rose, shaking her head. 'I don't want to wake him.'

They sat together, not talking at all for the most part, each lost in their own thoughts until a shrill beep from Rose's phone startled them. Rose grabbed the phone. 'Jamie' was all she said.

Charlie woke with a start at the noise and began crying loudly. Harriet stood and stepped away, whispering soothing words while rocking him gently. His crying subsided as Rose laid the phone back on the bench.

Harriet placed the child in Rose's arms, watching as she rested her cheek against his, closing her eyes for a moment.

'They're taking her in now for an emergency C-section.' Rose shook her head, tears in her eyes. 'Jamie said they almost lost them on the way. It's touch and go. They may not be able to save them both. He's been told to prepare himself.' Her voice broke as she sobbed, 'how do you prepare for that?'

Little Charlie was patting his mother's face. She held him

against her again, but he hollered and began wriggling in her arms.

Harriet reached for him automatically, 'I'll give Charlie some fruit. Rose, go down to the stables and update Angus.' Rose agreed wordlessly and still crying, walked to the door. Harriet let her breath out. She wasn't aware she'd been holding it. With Charlie on her hip, she reached for a banana, breaking off a piece for him, smiling sadly as he gurgled and grinned and shoved it into his mouth, totally unaware of the drama around him.

Rose and Angus returned together, less than an hour later. Harriet had moved to the living room and was playing a game of blocks on the floor with Charlie. He toddled to his parents when they came through the door, arms outstretched. Angus scooped him up, hugging him tightly, as Rose sat down next to Harriet.

'She's delivered a baby boy. He's doing well.' Her voice trembled. 'But Debbie's weak, the next twenty-four hours are critical. If she can get through this, she'll be okay. They've got to get her blood pressure down. She's a fighter. She has a son. She has everything to live for.' Rose leaned toward Harriet, who automatically put her arms around her.

'You're right. She is strong. She'll get through this. Keep the faith, Rose.' Patting her back, Harriet kept her own tears at bay. Her emotions were in turmoil, but nothing compared to Rose, who had known Debbie her whole life.

After a few moments Rose clambered to her feet, leaning into Angus, still holding Charlie. Harriet tried to keep her voice even, wanting to leave before her emotions came to the surface. 'I'm going to leave you now, please let me know if you hear more news.' Rose nodded sadly. Harriet walked down the long hallway to the door through to her suite. Once there, she lay on the bed, thinking about Debbie and her child. About her husband Jamie and the family and friends, like Rose and Angus, who will keep vigil while she fights for her life. About the wonderful people who will be in this new baby's life, regardless of the outcome for Debbie.

Hoping and praying that Debbie will get through this, Harriet cried. Relief that the baby boy was safely delivered, fear for the health of her new friend and a strange feeling of belonging, that she had the right to share the emotion with this community. It was something she hadn't felt since leaving home at eighteen. Her tears subsided and Harriet thought about the day's events. Despite Drum's reaction to her purchase of Bellbird Cottage, she felt, instinctively, that she had found her home. Her people. That Barrington was her future. The picture was still unclear, but she knew she would stay.

33

It was dark when she woke. Harriet checked her phone. Rose had left a message asking her to come through to the main house when she was ready. Checking the time, Harriet realised the message had only been sent twenty minutes before. She washed her face in the bathroom, then went through to the house.

She found them in the kitchen, Rose's eyes were red from crying and Angus looked grim. Preparing for the worst, Harriet placed her hand over Rose's, resting on the kitchen bench. Rose turned her hand over and gripped Harriet's fiercely. 'She's fighting, Harriet.' Tears welled in her eyes. 'But she's had a stroke. We don't know how bad just yet. Jamie's with her.'

'Oh Rose.' Harriet squeezed her hand, then turned to Angus.

Angus put his arm around Rose, pulling her on to the seat beside him. 'Charlie's in bed. He went without a whimper, first time ever. I think he knows.'

'They've called him Warwick. Warwick James Tait. Deb was holding him when she had the stroke. They're assessing her, doing all they can to prevent further strokes.' Rose drew in her breath. 'Jamie is doing well. His mum, Jill, called us. He's been brilliant with Deb, with the baby, with the doctors. He's positive she'll make a full recovery.' She shuddered. 'Oh God, I hope he's right!'

'Is there anything I can do?' Harriet knew Deb's needs would be covered by her own family, and Jamie's, but she had to ask.

'There is Harri.' Angus nodded at her. 'Keep the café going with Cathy. I know Kristen is there now, but just oversee things for Deb, support the staff, maybe answer customer questions. Cathy will be upset and would rather be in the kitchen than deal with customers. Jamie asked if you could step in for a bit longer.'

Harriet agreed swiftly. 'Of course, I'm happy to stay on. Happy to help in any way I can.' Her heart swelled, she felt included, part of Team Deb.

OVER A QUICK COFFEE WITH ROSE NEXT MORNING, HARRIET learned that Debbie's stroke had not been as severe as first thought. The left side of her face had dropped, and her speech was slurred, but she had movement in all limbs. The prognosis was more positive than they'd heard the night before. The danger of further strokes had receded overnight.

Feeling optimistic, Harriet was at the café just as Cathy was unlocking the front door. They hugged, rejoicing in the better news, and began setting up for the day.

As Angus had predicted, a steady stream of locals dropped in, asking after Debbie and baby Warwick. The local grapevine was on fire. Harriet fielded questions and set some room aside in Debbie's office for cards, flowers and gifts. Jamie's father was heading to Newcastle in the afternoon, he would take them with him, hoping the outpouring of kindness from the community would aid Debbie's recovery.

Around mid-morning, Harriet dashed down to the mechanic's workshop to pick up her car. Angus had driven her in earlier, and Joe Daly had messaged that her car was ready to pick up. Insurance had covered most of the cost.

Running her hand over the new bonnet and bumper, Harriet marvelled at the repairs. The car looked brand new. She grinned at Joe. 'Good work, no one would even know it's been in an accident. And you've washed the exterior and vacuumed the interior. Thank you.'

'All part of the service Harriet. It's a great little car, you must enjoy driving it.' Wiping his hands on a clean rag, he shook Harriet's before handing her the keys. 'Now that we know our way around it, we can do the regular services on it too. I hear you're staying in town. Bought Miss Boxshall's old place.'

Harriet raised her eyebrows, smiling as she did. 'Word travels, I only signed the contract last week.'

'My niece is the cleaner.' Joe chuckled. 'I hope it wasn't meant to be a secret.'

'Not at all. I'm excited about moving in just before Christmas.' Thanking him again she drove Alfie to her usual car park behind the town hall. As she got out of the car, Little Ben pulled in beside her in his large white Landcruiser, dwarfing her vehicle.

'Hi Harri.' He walked around her car, giving a low whistle. 'Wow! Is this yours? I had no idea what you were driving when you hit the kangaroo. I'd love to take a spin in it sometime.'

Harriet looked from the admiration clearly present on Little Ben's face, to his large, tall frame. He stood over six foot four inches. Alfie was 'low slung,' as Drum had described. She started giggling, trying to picture Ben folding his legs into her car. He looked at her, then back to the car and laughed out loud. He leaned against the sleek Italian bonnet in a proprietary manner. This set Harriet off again until she was laughing-crying, pointing to him, to her car, to his height. He threw his head back and guffawed, making a couple getting out of a car on the other side of the carpark pause for a moment, look at them, and wave. Harriet tried to say something but couldn't get the words out.

She stepped toward Ben, who reached out, drawing her into his arms for a bear hug. He held her for a moment, while their chuckles subsided. Harriet looked up at him. He really is a warm, good-hearted man, she thought.

'Harriet. Ben.' She spun around, stepping out of Ben's arms. Drum had stopped in front of them, two bags of groceries in his hands. 'I see you have your car back. Looks good Harriet.'

'Yes. Thank you. Just picked it up.' She blushed, wanted to explain why they were laughing, hugging, but Drum nodded at Ben and walked toward his own vehicle, parked a short distance away.

'I have to dash Ben, needed at the café.' Harriet smiled, grabbed her wallet, and walked briskly away.

Driving home, Drum felt unaccountably pissed off. Seeing Harriet in Ben's arms had annoyed him, but more than that, he had seen them laughing like a couple of kids as he approached, and he felt, what? Envious? Shaking his head at the thought, he drove across Barrington bridge faster than he intended. Sure, he liked her. He liked the way she was with Billie. He liked the way she'd brought Laura into the bull sale. He could even admit he admired the work she was doing with Ben Evans Real Estate. The new branding was brilliant. Just right. She obviously had some really good marketing and people skills. Stepping in for Debbie at the café, taking everything in her stride. What's not to like.

Not wanting to continue this train of thought, he slowed as he neared Laura's property, glancing up at her house on the ridge. About to continue on his way, a movement halfway up Laura's paddock caught his eye. A heifer was calving, her tail was up, and she was moving around more than usual. Without giving it much thought, Drum turned sharply to the right, heading up to Laura's gate. He stopped by the side of the road and leaving the car, stepped through the fence toward the heifer. Now he could clearly see two little hooves poking out. Knowing how tame and easy to handle Laura's animals were, Drum spoke quietly as he approached. 'There you go. Having a bit of trouble? This might be your first calf, eh lovey?'

The heifer looked at him balefully, then promptly dropped to her knees, flopping on to her side. She let out a mournful bellow. Patting her gently, Drum kneeled behind the animal. He could see she was pushing, the little feet retreated a little, then came out with each push. But she wasn't making progress.

'I'll give you a hand, lovey. I'm going to grab your little one's feet and pull, just a little, when you push.' He knew he was talking nonsense. To a cow. But he didn't want to scare her back to her feet. He took a firm hold of the little hooves, slick with membrane, then as the cow pushed, he pulled firmly. The head came out, but the little animal's eyes were closed and its tongue protruding, with no sign of life.

'Damn.' Drum spoke aloud, Laura did not need to lose a valuable calf. The cow pushed again, and this time Drum managed to pull the whole body free in one slithery movement. He cleared the mucus from the calf's mouth and rubbed it briskly on the chest. The young heifer stood and turned to her baby. Putting her head down she began to lick it, removing some of the membrane around it.

Watching for a moment, disheartened, Drum remembered something his father once told him. A story about swinging the calf around by its back legs to help cough up any mucus in its throat. It might be an old wives tale, but the calf wasn't breathing, he had nothing to lose. Standing, he took the calf by the back feet, lifting it free of the ground, then turned in a circle, swinging the calf outward as he did. Once. Twice. Three times around. He stopped and gently laid the calf down, checking to see if it was breathing as he did. A moment passed, then it opened its eyes and gave a bark-like cough. The mother nudged and nuzzled her baby as Drum took a step back, grinning broadly at the cow and calf.

'Halloo,' Laura was walking rapidly down the paddock from the house. He waved, waiting for her to get to him.

A tall woman, she nearly knocked him flat when she threw her arms around him, hugging him hard.

'You did it! I saw the whole thing from the house. It was dead, wasn't it? What a thing! I would never have believed it!' Drum stepped back, but still wasn't sure the calf would be ok. Turning, he laughed out loud to see the little thing already standing on shaky legs, tottering around its mother.

'It's a bull Laura. A valuable addition to your herd.' He knew he was grinning at her, but he felt so chuffed his efforts had worked.

'A bull hey? I might have to name it Drummond.' Laura punched him lightly on the shoulder.

'If you do that, I'll buy him from you when he's weaned.' He laughed again, thrilled to see how pleased Laura was with his efforts.

'Come up to the house Drum, I'll make us a cuppa, if you have time.' Laura smiled as she waved toward the house.

'Sure, thanks. I might need to wash up a bit first.' Drum held his hands up, sticky with afterbirth. Stepping beside Laura he matched her long strides as they walked up the hill to the house. At the top they turned and watched the heifer and calf for a moment. The little one had his head under her belly, clearly getting his first drink.

Grinning at each other, Drum followed Laura into the house, taking a moment to wash up in the laundry trough before entering her cosy kitchen.

~

Sitting at the kitchen bench, a cup of tea and home-made scone in front of him, he told Laura what he knew about Debbie's condition and the birth of little Warwick.

Laura pushed the jam closer to Drum. 'Harri called me last night, told me she was staying on at the café for a bit to help out. At Jamie's request. They're hopeful Deb will make a full recovery, but it will take time.' Laura bit into her scone. 'And Harri. What a breath of fresh air she is.' Her eyes narrowed a little as she looked at him. 'I heard you aren't happy about her buying the old cottage.'

Drum took a sip of tea, followed by a huge mouthful of scone. Not wanting to answer straight away, he closed his eyes for a moment. Opening them, he smiled sheepishly at Laura. 'Great scones, Laura.'

'Harri made them with Billie last time. I put a few in the freezer and pulled these two out this morning. Perhaps I knew you'd drop by to save my calf.' She winked.

Throwing back his head, Drum laughed. 'You got me. The woman can cook, I'll give you that. And she's great with Billie. Actually, she's great with everyone.' He leaned forward a little. 'And here's a news bulletin for you, fresh from the source. You're right, I wasn't happy she bought the cottage. It was my father's, and grandfather's, and I always thought I'd buy it back. I reacted badly when she told me, irrationally even.' He picked up his tea.

'Easy to do Drum. It's part of your family, your history.' Laura looked him in the eye. 'But it's been empty for close to two years. You would have bought it already if you could. If it was a priority.'

'I know. I've had time to think about it. I just thought it would be there when I was ready.' Looking straight at Laura, he added, 'you probably know I have some competing priorities. Having Billie full time now.' He cleared his throat. 'I'm sure you've guessed, if you haven't already heard, but I need to deal with my wife. Soon to be ex-wife. Make a settlement. I couldn't buy the cottage right now anyway.'

'You should speak to Harri, now you've had time to gather your thoughts. She was talking about not going through with the sale. Not staying in Barrington. She felt that if you were against her, it might be hard to establish her business here.' Reaching across the bench, Laura touched Drum's hand for a moment, adding quietly, 'We need her here Drum. She's good for this town. She's certainly been good for me. And now she's stepping in a bit longer at the café. And she needs to find her place, she hasn't had it easy.'

Drum nodded, sitting back a little. 'What is her story, Laura?'

Laura picked up their empty cups, taking them to the sink. She shook her head, chuckling as she did. 'You won't get it from me. It's something Harri will tell you when she's ready. Talk to her Drum. Make her feel welcome.'

Drum passed the plates to Laura at the sink. 'I will Laura. I'll speak to Harriet, and I will make her welcome. You're right. This place could do with more people like her. Such a community spirited person, unusual for a city girl, in my experience.'

'Don't judge her by the city girls you know, Drum.'

'Like Anabelle you mean? My wife?'

Laura paused. 'I don't know your wife, but I've heard she didn't like it here. Didn't try to fit in. Chalk and cheese, Drum. Chalk and cheese.'

Drum didn't answer, but Laura's words resonated with him. He would make an effort to talk to Harriet. Soon. It seemed she was forming a relationship with Little Ben Evans, who he considered a friend. Drum nodded to himself. He would make an effort.

Walking outside they stopped for a moment to look again at the cow and calf. They had moved closer to the small herd in the paddock, the calf now laying by her mother's side.

'A well-earned rest, I'd say. Just happy it worked out.' Drum turned to open his car door.

'Drum. Stop.' Laura looked him in the eye, her voice gruff with emotion. 'Thank you. Truly. I wouldn't have thought to do that. I would have lost this one.'

Drum patted Laura on the shoulder. 'We're neighbours. We help each other out. I'm glad I stopped when I did.' Grinning, he thrust his right hand out. 'I'm definitely buying Drummond the bull calf when he's weaned.' Laura put her hand in his, shaking firmly.

'It's a deal.'

35

Two weeks passed quickly, the café busier than ever and Christmas now only a week away. Debbie's recovery was slow, but steady. Rose had been to Newcastle to see her and said she brightened every time she held the baby and was feeding him herself. Locals dropped by the cafe daily for an update on Debbie and baby Warwick, most of them buying coffee, cake and even takeaway meals in a show of support. Harriet, Cathy and Kristen were run off their feet, with customers sometimes waiting for their orders.

There were no complaints from locals. One slightly exasperated tourist, asking loudly why his order was not on the table yet, was firmly put in his place by the tennis ladies at the next table. Regulars cleared their own tables and when Angus Hamilton dropped by to get coffee, and saw how busy they were, sent his assistant Melanie in for an hour to help during the lunch rush on several days.

Melanie didn't mind, she'd told Harriet that her daughter Tiffany is Jamie and Debbie's niece. She's family and happy to help. Harriet knew, from Rose telling her own story, that Melanie was raising Tiffany on her own and her ex-partner, Jamie's older brother, was still in prison on domestic violence and other charges. It can't have been easy for her, yet she was well known and obviously liked by the locals. It confirmed Harriet's belief in the strength of the local community.

Ending each day hot and tired, Harriet had made little progress with her plans to move into the cottage. She had arranged for her personal items to be delivered from the storage complex in Sydney in a removal pod. She had a small collection of original paintings, eclectic, but each one held meaning for her. Boxes of books, an armchair she had always had in her bedroom, a dinner service and other kitchen items, bed linen and towels and her clothing and shoes. The pod was arriving in the afternoon, sometime after lunch. The driver would call her when he arrived, and she had a couple of hours to get everything out of the pod and into the house.

Shouldn't be too hard, she thought, and maybe the driver would help her with any heavy items. Harriet had ordered a queen bed ensemble to be delivered that afternoon too, and Cathy had assured her they would be fine at the café and to just go when she got the call.

Harriet picked the keys up from Ben Evans, the contract was now unconditional, she could move in. The cottage was hers, despite settlement still being a couple of weeks away. Driving out there just after two, her suitcase and personal items from her stay at Barrington Homestead in the rear of the car, she was pleased Alfie had no trouble, even with the gravel road and driveway. 'So there, Drum Murray, my little Alfa Romeo is perfect for these roads.' She spoke aloud as she pulled up in front of the cottage. The truck still hadn't arrived, the driver had called and said he was still an hour away, but Harriet thought she'd open the little house up, take her personal items inside, and air it a bit. And walk through to decide where she would place her paintings and decide where other bits and pieces should go.

Thinking about Drum Murray, she'd been pleased when Laura told her the week before that he'd confessed he'd overreacted to her purchase and was planning to speak to her. But he had been strangely absent from the café and Harriet still felt nervous, but less so. The crisis with Debbie had helped her decide to stay. She felt part of the community, even in a small way, and her attachment to the area, the cottage, the locals, was growing.

Walking through the front door, she again felt sponginess in a couple of the veranda boards at the front. She'd definitely need to get those replaced. She chuckled to herself, imagining Little Ben jumping up and down a couple of times and falling right through! She couldn't have that.

The cleaners had done a brilliant job, everything was dust free and smelt fresh. They'd removed the dust cover from the dining table and polished it. Harriet ran her fingers over the rich dark wood, then turned in a circle. Home. This was home now. Very different to the modern place in Sydney she'd shared with her husband, but this felt good. Better. More her style.

The rumble of a truck changing into low gear had her rushing back through the open front door. She watched as the driver performed a series of turns, finally backing the vehicle up close to the front garden fence. Climbing out of the cab, he walked purposefully toward her. A stout man, almost as round as he was high, Harriet revised her earlier thoughts of asking him to help her unload.

'Hello love. Are you,' he looked at his clipboard, 'Harriet Russell? I'm Dave.'

'Hi Dave. Yes, I'm Harriet.'

'Good, good. Well, I'll just run the ramp down from the back of the truck here, and open the pod for you, then you can take your time unloading.' He looked at his watch. 'I've got to get moving in just under two hours.'

'Fine. Thank you, Dave. Yes, that's perfect.' Harriet watched as he set the ramp in place and walked up, opening the pod. There were four other pods on the truck, two the same size as hers and one large one sitting on top of them.

As the doors opened, Harriet could clearly see it was completely full, everything packed neatly, some items with blankets around them. Harriet took a deep breath. She really wasn't supposed to lift heavy items yet. She wondered if Dave might be inclined to give her a hand if she offered him some cash. As soon as the thought came into her head, he spoke.

'I'm just going to sit myself under your lovely apple tree over there and have my lunch.' He reached back into the truck and brought out a small esky, taking it with him to the shady spot.

Harriet could do nothing but walk up the ramp to commence unloading. She found some of her paintings, each one bubble-wrapped, wedged between larger items. She pulled out three lots, taking them inside where she leaned them against the master bedroom wall.

The next item was her bedroom chair. An overstuffed armchair she loved to curl up in when reading, or sometimes sit in cross-legged with her laptop. Drawing the blanket off, she folded it neatly, then looked from the large chair to the ramp, to the front of the house and back to the chair. She glanced over at Dave, but he was leaning with his back against the tree, looking away from her, a sandwich in one hand and a bottle of coke in the other.

'Damn. He's deliberately not looking. He doesn't want to help me.' She muttered the words to herself and was surprised when she got an answer.

'That's what I'm here for Harri.' Turning, she saw Laura standing at the garden gate in her usual overalls, hands on hips.

'I didn't hear you drive in.'

I'm not surprised, you were buried in that pod muttering to yourself!' Laura laughed and walked briskly up the ramp, looking keenly at the chair.

'I'll take the bottom and lean it over, you take the top.' Laura was already lifting as she spoke, and Harriet hurried to get into position. Laura took most of the weight, walking backwards down the ramp. Once on the ground, they continued into the house.

'First on the right Laura.' They rested the chair for a moment in the front doorway, then carried it through to the main bedroom.

It was hot, and both were sweating from the heavy chair. Laura looked at it longingly, 'it's very inviting, I bet this is your favourite.'

'It is.' Harriet looked at it too, then turned to leave the room. 'Thank you Laura, I appreciate you coming over to help.'

'Least I can do for my new neighbour.' They grinned at each other and headed outside, walking back up the ramp. The next layer of boxes was lighter. Mostly kitchen items and linen. Harriet had completely forgotten about the two heavy oak bookshelves, and the large hallstand, also heavy timber. She'd had them in storage for a long time, as they hadn't worked in the modern apartment, and she'd been too attached to sell them.

With each load they took into the house, the spectre of the heavy timber furniture looming closer had her frowning. She was already sore, some of the boxes of books had really strained her healing abdominal muscles. Harriet didn't want to complain, she could see Laura was choosing to take the heavier items as it was. Harriet glanced at Dave again, he was now laying back in the grass, hat over his face, snoring loudly.

When they had removed everything but the timber furniture,

they stood at the door of the pod, sipping on the cold-water bottles Harriet had pulled from her fridge.

'Well. We should get the bookshelves out first. This one here I think.' Laura strode to the closest bookshelf.

'You know they're a pair? They're exactly the same.' Harriet raised an eyebrow as she spoke.

'I'm telling myself this one is the heaviest, and the rest will be easy.' Laura took one end and began shuffling it sideways. Harriet rushed to get the other end.

'Stop right there! Both of you. Now!' Drum Murray strode up the ramp, looking mildly miffed. 'You're kidding me? I'm not letting you lift that. Either of you. Step aside.' Laura and Harriet let go and looked at Drum in surprise.

'Well, you can't lift it by yourself Drum, it needs two people.' Harriet was amused by his macho display. 'Why don't Laura and I take one end, and you take the other?'

'Damn you woman. You're not lifting it.' He jerked his head toward Dave, still laying under the tree. 'What's his name?'

'Dave.' Harriet looked over. Dave hadn't moved.

Drum walked to the back of the truck, shouting, 'Dave! Mate. Get up here and help me with this. Now!'

Dave sat up, then looked up at Drum, who was now glowering at him. He stood and walked over. 'I don't get paid to unload. Mate.' He crossed his arms over his chest.

'So, if we pay you, you'll get your lazy ass up here and help these ladies?'

Dave looked at the ground, then shrugged. Harriet opened her mouth to speak, intending to offer the driver some cash, but as she did, he slowly walked up the ramp and into the pod, taking one end of the bookshelf.

'Good man.' Drum nodded at him and took the other end of the heavy piece, walking backwards down the ramp. 'Show me where this goes Harri.'

Hurrying in front of the men, Harriet led the way through to the living area. 'Against this wall, thank you. The other one beside it please.'

They positioned the piece, then walked back to the truck together, bringing the second one in without any conversation. The hall stand was the last piece. It was big and awkward, and Harriet and Laura rushed up the ramp to help the men. Dave straightened, looked at Drum, then Harriet. 'It's all right love. Let the men do it. You've worked hard enough today.'

Harriet glanced at Drum, could see he was trying not to laugh. 'Alright then. Of course. Thank you Dave, it does look a bit heavy for us.' She elbowed Laura, who snorted, then coughed. 'Absolutely. Thank you, Dave.'

Less than ten minutes later Harriet had signed the delivery docket and Dave was on his way, having refused the fifty dollar note Harriet offered. 'All in a day's work love.'

Harriet and Laura laughed, then hugged each other before Harriet turned to Drum. 'You came just in time, thank you.'

'Sorry I wasn't here earlier, I had a mob of young stock break through the fence up in the high country, only saw the truck here on my way down. Had I known, I would have organised my day differently.'

Harriet blushed. She hadn't spoken to Drum since the day of the sale meeting almost two weeks ago, and she was now struggling to know what to say. Here she was, moving into his ancestral property, against his wishes.

'Harri, I've got to go, need to feed the cattle.' Laura smiled. 'But you're welcome to come up to the house for dinner tonight, I don't think you'll have time to prepare anything.'

'Thanks Laura but you've done enough. I would still be unloading if you hadn't turned up when you did. I think I'll just nip into Barrington and grab a pizza later. I'm still waiting on the bed for my room, so I can start unpacking while I wait.' Laura nodded and walked toward her Ute, glancing at Drum as she left.

'Bye Laura.' He turned to Harriet. 'I've got to go too. Billie has a tennis lesson after school, but I need to fetch her now.' Drum started to move away, but Harriet reached out and touched his hand.

'Thank you, Drum. For helping.' She wanted to say more, clear the air about the cottage but there was no time.

'There'll be plenty of time to chat Harri.' It was like he could read her mind. 'We're neighbours now. And friends, I hope.'

The use of her nickname and the warmth of his tone brought a lump to her throat. Glancing back toward the road, she could see the furniture truck heading their way. Her new bed was arriving. Taking a breath, she turned back to Drum. 'Of course. Friends. Thank you.' She tried to convey a deeper meaning, grateful he was no longer angry, into the words. If he understood, he didn't say, just gave her a brief smile, then strode toward his car.

36

$\mathcal{E}$xhausted, sore and hungry, Harriet sat on the front step for a moment. The sun was sinking, but it was still hot. She raised the bottle of water to her mouth, wondering if she should have a shower and drop up to Laura's anyway, she was sure to be welcomed, and a glass of wine would be lovely. A mosquito buzzed near her ear. Standing, she stretched, feeling the muscles pull in her lower right abdomen. At least she had muscles there now, perhaps a bit of soreness was a good sign.

Harriet knew she was stronger and fitter than when she had landed in Barrington almost six weeks ago. Her old wound hardly bothered her at all and the scarring, although still noticeable, had faded from angry red to a puckered pink.

Walking into the cottage, her cottage, she paused for a moment. The hall stand was perfectly proportioned and created a beautiful entry statement. Stepping into her bedroom, she'd made the new bed up with crisp white sheets and a cream cover. Harriet loved the autumn tones in the dark green throw and russet, orange and deep yellow cushions she'd placed on the bed and in the large bedroom chair, itself a dark cream.

Impulsively she stripped off her clothing, throwing it into the wicker laundry basket behind the bedroom door. Wrapping herself in a thin robe, she padded on bare feet to the main bathroom. Looking at the large claw foot tub, she tossed up whether to have a luxurious soak, then shaking her head she walked to the rear of the cottage, to the second bathroom and turned the shower on.

After a shower, she would spend another hour or two unpacking the kitchen boxes. Perhaps she could order a pizza, if the local shop delivered. She'd put a bottle of wine in the fridge earlier, in case Laura dropped back.

Standing under the shower, she revelled in the water pressure for a few minutes, then washed her hair. Stepping out, Harriet wrapped a large bath sheet around herself, scooping her thick hair up in a smaller towel. She never scrimped on bath towels, the bigger and softer the better. And good bed linen. And nice underwear. Giggling to herself, she admitted she did like quality over quantity, with just about everything. Wine, food, clothing. Even people.

Walking down the hall toward her room she paused. Was that a car door? Voices. Picking up pace she rushed the last few metres, only to find herself poised at her bedroom door, still clad in nothing but a towel, when there was knock at the door, and it opened inward at the same time.

'Harri!' Little Ben filled the door, a pizza box in one hand and a six pack of beer in the other. Harriet clutched the towel tighter as he stepped inside, grinning, seemingly unaware of her state of undress.

Before she could reply, Rose squeezed past Ben. 'Step aside you great lump of a man, there are people here with champagne.'

'Harriet! We've surprised you. Get dressed, there's more of us out here. We've come to feed you. A sort of surprise house-warming if you will.' Rose stepped forward, laughing, gave her a pat on the shoulder and a gentle push toward her bedroom.

Grinning back, Harriet stepped inside her room, closing the door. She wiped her eyes with the back of her hand. There were more voices. Angus, little Charlie. Perhaps others.

Thankful she'd unpacked some of the clothes she'd had at Barrington Homestead, Harriet pulled on underwear, a pair of navy capri pants and a sleeveless loose shirt, white with tiny pink rosebuds all over it. She ran the brush through her damp hair, then tied it on top of her head in a loose bun. Mascara and lip gloss and she was good to go. Rose was similarly dressed, so Harriet had a quick look in the mirror, then followed the happy sound of chatter and laughter to her kitchen and living area.

Pausing at the door, she drew in a sharp breath. Rose was setting champagne glasses on the kitchen bench, while Angus was prizing the cork from a bottle. Three pizza boxes sat on the dining table and Laura was laying out paper plates and napkins. Little Charlie was on the rug in the living area playing with wooden blocks, while Big Ben supervised. Little Ben, beer in hand, looked up, one hand on the nearest pizza box.

'Harri! You didn't think we'd let you starve on your first night, surely? We'll eat, drink and then help with any unpacking, moving of furniture, hanging of paintings and so on. Welcome to your new home!'

Flushed with pleasure Harriet stepped forward, and on tip toes kissed Ben on the cheek. 'Thank you. Was this your idea? So lovely.' She looked around at her new friends. 'All of you. Thank you.'

'Actually, it was Drum's idea. He called me this afternoon and told me how hard you and Laura had worked getting your stuff unloaded and thought we should meet here with food and drink and welcome you properly.' Rose handed a glass of champagne to Harriet. 'He should be here any minute, Billie is making something special to bring.'

'We're here! We're here now Harri!' Billie walked slowly into the room, Drum behind her, concentrating on the platter she held in both hands. A large, slightly lop-sided cake covered in chocolate icing was perched in the middle. 'I baked you a cake. A welcome cake. From scratch. We're late because it had to cool before I could put the icing on!'

Harriet set her champagne glass down on the dining table and took the platter from Billie's hands. She looked at the cake and grinned at Billie. 'It's the best-looking cake I've ever seen. And it smells delicious, thank you.' Handing the cake to Angus, Harriet knelt down and opened her arms to Billie, who leapt into them, hugging her fiercely. Billie's cheek against her own, Harriet glanced up at Drum. His eyes were dark with emotion. Pride for his daughter perhaps? Harriet blinked a couple of times to keep her tears at bay.

'Come in, come in, we need to eat this pizza before it gets cold.' That was Little Ben, opening the pizza boxes, the smell wafting out. Harriet was hungry, really hungry. Big Ben had opened the doors to the back veranda, and they all found their way out there, some sitting on the steps, Laura and Big Ben in a pair of wicker chairs that had seen better days, the rest on the floor, backs against the wall. Rose drank her champagne, then held Charlie while he drank his milk from a sippy cup. His eyes fluttered and Angus reached down, taking his son gently from Rose, holding his little body against his shoulder, patting his back every now and again.

Harriet was on the top step, her back against the veranda pole, half-turned toward the cottage. Billie was beside her and Drum leaned against the pole on the other side of the steps. Little Ben had set up a portable speaker in the kitchen, playing

Spotify through his phone. Country and blues songs created a relaxed atmosphere as they sat and chatted together.

Drum and Billie got up to cut and serve the cake. Harriet patted the spot next to her and Rose sat down. 'It's a lovely cottage Harri. I've never been inside, Miss Boxshall didn't entertain visitors much, but my grandparents used to come and help prune her roses every year. I really love what you've done with it already. You've got a bit of style, my friend.' Rose nudged Harriet with her shoulder and Harriet leaned back into her. 'I suspect this may become the venue of many a girls' night, especially when Debbie is well enough to join us.'

Laughing, Harriet glanced around at the small group of friends. Neighbours mostly, although she didn't know where the Bens' lived. 'I think you're right Rose. Definitely a good spot for a girls' night.'

Billie returned, large chunks of chocolate cake and gooey icing on paper plates, handing them to Rose and Harriet. 'Hmmmm, this looks so good Billie. Maybe you should ask Debbie for a job at the café.' Rose picked up her piece and took a giant mouthful, chocolate around her lips and on her teeth.

Billie giggled. 'You look funny Rose.' Harriet took a piece and did the same and Billie laughed again.

Mumbling through her piece of cake, Harriet said, 'we're going to need napkins Billie. Lots of napkins.'

Billie jumped up and dashed inside, returning moments later with a roll of paper towel. 'This is what Daddy and I use when we get messy in the kitchen.' She tore off sheets and handed them to everyone.

'Always very elegant at your place, Drum Murray.' Angus grinned as he handed another beer to Drum and Little Ben.

'Oh mate. You don't know the half of it.' Drum gave Billie a wink, who giggled.

Harriet wiped her mouth, her eyes following Billie as she

walked among the adults, offering paper towel and picking up empty plates. What a gorgeous girl. She drew her breath. If only. Looking up, she met Drum's eyes. He looked at her for a long moment, then back at his daughter. Harriet watched him and he turned to her again, this time his eyes had softened, love for his daughter evident.

Angus laid Charlie, now asleep, on the rug in the living area, and returned with more champagne, topping up Harriet, Rose, Laura and Big Ben. Little Ben, Drum and Angus were drinking beer, although they seemed to be taking it easy, just enjoying the company and some easy-going banter. Harriet noticed that Big Ben and Laura had sat together most of the evening. Laura had told her she had apologised to Ben at the sale meeting for the way she'd spoken to his wife when she dropped by after Gareth died. Ben had shaken his head, saying Rosemary had never mentioned it to him, so there was nothing to forgive. Harriet glanced at them and wondered if a deeper friendship was developing between them. She couldn't be happier for her friend if that was the case.

Getting up to go with Billie to the bathroom to wash her hands, Harriet looked back over her shoulder. She'd found a place for herself. A community. Billie tugged on her hand, and she let the thought slide for a moment, although it continued to warm her long after.

Returning to the veranda her friends were beginning to pack up. Ben snapped a garbage bag open and gathered up the disposable plates and utensils and empty pizza cartons, while Drum had stowed the empty champagne and beer bottles into another. Laura was washing up the glasses, and the cake platter. They'd eaten it all.

Harriet cleared her throat. They all paused, looking at her expectantly. 'Thank you. Drum for thinking to do this, to all of you for coming. It's been a huge day and it's ended on the best note. Ever.' Turning to Billie she reached out and hugged her to her side. 'And you Billie, making a welcome cake. From scratch. Thank you so much.' Billie cuddled into Harriet for a moment.

Rose packed away Charlie's toys as Angus scooped him up. 'Goodnight Harri. Cathy said to tell you to stay away tomorrow. Come in on Monday. She'll be fine with Kristen, and you can get yourself set up here, properly.'

'Thank you. That's lovely of Cathy. I have to go into town tomorrow anyway to stock the fridge, so I'll drop by, check on them. But it's good I won't need to rush.' Touching Rose on the arm, she said more quietly. 'And Debbie? Is there any more news of her and the baby?'

Rose nodded, her face brightening for a moment. 'They're sending her back to the local hospital next week. If she continues to improve, she and baby Warwick will be home by the end of next week. It's good news. Really good news.'

'Oh, how wonderful. I can't wait to see her and meet her baby.' Harriet reached up and hugged her friend, who gave her a tight squeeze in return.

Drum and Billie were the last to leave. Little Ben had hesitated when saying goodnight, finally hugging her tightly and kissing her lightly on the cheek. Harriet blushed but reached up and kissed him back on the cheek with a resounding 'schmak' making everyone laugh. She felt Drum watching but wasn't game to glance at him.

The Bens had picked Laura up, so they followed Rose and Angus down the driveway in their vehicle. Harriet hugged Billie goodbye and watched as Drum helped her into the car, ensuring she put her seatbelt on although they had only a short distance to drive. Only five hundred metres if they'd walked across the paddock and had a way to get over the creek.

Harriet moved to the bottom step of the veranda and Drum walked back to her. She was surprised when he reached out and took her in his arms, hugging her briefly. 'Welcome to Bellbird Cottage Harri. I am happy you're here. And I'm sorry I reacted the way I did when you told me. I was rude and you didn't deserve that.'

Looking up at him she smiled, 'I nearly didn't you know. I was close to relinquishing the contract under the cooling off period. But I'm happy I'm staying, and it means a lot that you're okay with it. You're my neighbour and the father of one of my favourite people in the whole world, so, you know, it might have become awkward.' She was grinning now, enjoying his sheepish expression.

'Oh, *father* of one of your favourite people? What does one have to do to become a favourite person in their own right?' He was laughing now, all tension between them forgotten.

'Hmm. Bake a chocolate cake. From scratch. With icing. That might do the trick.' Grinning broadly she waved to Billie as Drum walked to the car.

Harriet ambled back through the cottage and after closing the doors to the back veranda she poured herself a glass of water to take to her room. She imagined the echo of happy chatter and laughter remained in the living room and she turned around twice, taking it in. They hadn't done any more unpacking, or hung her paintings, but it had been a relaxed, happy night and she felt welcome. No, more than that. She belonged. Climbing into bed in her undies and tee shirt, she drifted off to sleep, a happy smile playing around her lips.

3 7

The night was warm, but Harriet slept soundly, waking at dawn to the raucous laughter of three kookaburras on the front garden gate. Sitting up, she contemplated her body for a moment. Her arms, back and legs were aching from lifting and carrying yesterday. But she thought of these as the 'happy' aches of physical activity. Nothing like the deep-seated pain that had crippled her for months. She also had a slight headache. Too much champagne. But what a fun night.

It was early and she didn't have to go to the café today. She should try to get some more sleep. But shaking her head, she stepped out of bed and peered out the window. There was only one kookaburra now. Perhaps startled by her appearance, it flapped its wings and flew up and over the house.

Wide awake now, she threw on some clothes; shorts and the sleeveless top she'd worn the night before and walked through the cottage to the kitchen. Her kitchen.

They'd tidied up well from last night's party. A handful of washed glasses were turned upside down on the bench beside the sink. Harriet turned the jug on, a cup of tea would get her going.

She didn't enjoy instant coffee, so it would have to be tea until she could buy a coffee in town later. Maybe she should get a coffee maker for the cottage. Turning in a circle, she looked at the bench space and opened the pantry. There was room. She'd definitely get a small coffee machine.

Holding the fridge door open, she peered inside. Not much for breakfast. She hadn't really thought about it the day before. Sighing, she closed the door and pulled her phone from her back pocket, tapping a shopping list into it as she walked around. She'd head into town when the café was open and have breakfast there, then pick up what she'd need for the next few days.

Tea in hand, she stepped out to the back veranda. She could hear the creek gurgling away at the bottom of the garden. It was peaceful here. On the other side of the creek, up a slight slope, some young cattle grazed. Something startled them and they turned, almost as one, and trotted away from her. She could almost feel the vibration of their hooves as they disappeared amongst the trees. A flash of grey caught her eye. She watched as Billie trotted out from the trees toward her, riding her small grey stockhorse on the other side of the creek. Seeing Harriet, Billie waved madly.

Harriet waved back and walked through her garden to the fence, leaning on a little wooden gate. Billie gamely set Chippy at the creek, which the horse crossed in a series of lunges, splashing water over himself and his rider. Harriet held her breath for a moment, but Billie kept her seat as the horse almost jumped up the creek bank, then trotted the few metres to where Harriet waited.

'Good morning Billie. You're up early, and you're a good rider, I held my breath for a moment when you put Chippy into the creek.' Harriet rubbed the horse's cheek as Billie slid off, throwing the reins over the gatepost.

Climbing up the wooden gate to sit on the top rail, Billie

removed her riding hat and grinned at Harriet. 'We had to check the heifers. Dad's just over that rise, on his horse Jack. He said I could come as far as the creek and that I wasn't to make any noise because you're a city girl and city girls sleep in.'

Harriet put her arm around Billie, giving her a quick hug. 'Well, this city girl is an early riser, and I'm glad I was. I've had several visitors already today.'

'Really? Who?'

'Three noisy kookaburras and Norah of Billabong.' Harriet winked at Billie.

'Ha, kookaburras don't count and I'm Billie of Montrose, not Norah.' Harriet was about to explain the Norah reference, when Billie continued, 'she's my favourite character in the Mary Grant Bruce books. I have the whole set, they belonged to Nanna.'

'I'll have to get up much earlier in the morning to trick you, Billie Murray.'

'Yes, you will.' Billie said this clearly, but her eyes were twinkling. Laughing together, they turned to watch Drum ride toward them on his large bay stallion, two cattle dogs trotting behind. His horse paused momentarily on the other side of the creek, then at a word and nudge from Drum, gathered himself and jumped the whole creek, trotting the last few metres up to the gate.

'Harri was already awake Daddy, she was out on the veranda when I rode down to the creek.' Billie sounded a little defensive.

'Morning Harri.' Turning to Billie he added, 'I can see that Billie, thank you. How did you get across the creek?'

'Chippy just charged right through it. My boots are wet.' Billie stuck her legs out to demonstrate.

'So I see. I'm not keen on you doing things like that when I'm not there to watch you. What if you'd fallen off?' Drum spoke quietly, but firmly to his daughter.

'But Harri saw me. She waved from the veranda, so I knew it was okay.' Billie spoke equally firmly.

Drum glanced at Harriet, who was trying not to show her amusement. Looking up at him, her eyes wide and innocent, she chimed in. 'I did see her Drum, from up there on the veranda.'

'Hmm. Thank you, Harri.' He looked at the empty mug in her hand. 'I told Billie we'd ask you to breakfast if we saw you up and about.'

'Yes, please come to breakfast Harri! I'm making fresh orange juice and Daddy makes the best scrambled eggs. With green stuff.'

No longer able to hide her amusement, Harriet laughed loudly and looked up at Drum, still astride his large horse. 'Green stuff? Well, that does sound tempting.'

'Chives and parsley.' He was laughing too. 'G. O. P.'

'G.O.P?' Harriet was bewildered.

'Grown On Property!' Billie and Drum chimed in together.

'Oh, I see. Well, I couldn't turn down an invitation for that.' Harriet laughed.

'We noticed last night. That is, Billie noticed, when she put the cake in your fridge last night, that you hadn't had a chance to go shopping and she thought you might be hungry when you woke up.' He winked.

'I'm always hungry when I wake up, so I was worried you would be too Harri.' This from Billie.

'You're right. I was making a shopping list just now, I need to stock my fridge. And pantry. And yes, breakfast would be lovely.' Looking at their horses, she added, 'do you want to go back the way you came, or would you like to bring the horses through my yard, and we can walk around to your place together, without going back through the creek?'

'Billie, why don't you take Chippy through and head home with Harriet. I'll go back over the creek, there are a few heifers in the next paddock I need to check quickly, but I'll probably beat you home anyway, it's shorter this way.' Harriet and Billie waved as Drum turned his horse, and barely touching him with his heels went straight into a canter and in a few strides gathered himself and jumped the creek clearly, not missing a beat as he cantered up the other side and out of view.

'I'll be able to do that when I get a bigger horse. But I love Chippy and he'd jump it if I asked him to. Daddy says he's a very game little horse.' Billie jumped off the gate as she spoke, and Harriet unlatched it, swinging it inwards so Billie could lead Chippy through. Latching the gate again they walked toward the back of the cottage.

'Why don't you walk Chippy around to the front and out of the garden, and I will come through the house and meet you. I'll just put some shoes on.' Harriet watched as Billie confidently led Chippy around the side of the cottage, then dashed inside, changed into linen pants and canvas runners, then popped out through the front door. Billie was standing outside the garden gate, holding Chippy's reins and her helmet.

Harriet joined her and they walked down the drive together with the little horse, chatting about mornings, horses and books. They were at the homestead in fifteen minutes and Harriet went to the stables with Billie, watching as she unsaddled her horse, quickly brushed him and gave him a small apple before turning him into the paddock with Drum's horse, already grazing on some hay.

'Your Dad must have been quick.'

'It's really close if you go through this paddock here. You can just see the top of your chimney through those trees.' Harriet looked where Billie was pointing. She was right, it was just a few minutes across the paddock, and creek, to her cottage. But the trees and slight undulation of the paddock gave both houses privacy.

'Come on Harri, I'm hungry. We can go in through the laundry and wash our hands. And I'd better get changed, my socks are wet.'

Harriet wandered from the laundry to the kitchen when Billie shot off to get changed. Walking in she saw Drum whisking the egg mixture, a tea towel over his shoulder.

She giggled. 'What can I do to help? Although you look right at home in the kitchen.'

Glancing up, he chuckled. 'Needs must. Is my daughter getting changed?'

'Yes, she is. Without being told to. Although she did mention she is *prodigiously* hungry.' Harriet bit her lip to stop from laughing out loud.

Drum thew back his head and laughed. 'It's the reading. She comes out with some cracker sayings, and if I question her on big unfamiliar words, she generally knows their meaning and context.' He shook his head, his pride obvious.

'Best not to do the juice, that's Billie's job. And she sets the table. But you can get some toast started if you like. And if you want coffee, there's an espresso machine in the butler's pantry, just through there. And you know how I like mine already.' He nudged her with his shoulder.

Nodding happily, Harriet found the coffee machine, listening to Billie's cheerful remarks to her father when she returned as they bustled around in the main kitchen together. Pausing for a moment, Harriet felt a sharp pain in her chest. A tightness. Tears came to her eyes. She wasn't sure what she felt for Drum. But Billie. Well, Billie she could love. Did love. She drew a breath, blinked back her tears, then stepped back into the kitchen, a coffee in each hand.

'Toast is ready too.'

'Harri, we're ready. Come and sit here.' Billie patted the chair beside her.

38

'What are your plans today, Billie?' Harriet placed the damp tea towel on the drying rack by the stove.

'I think Daddy wants to visit Mummy, but it's too early to call yet. I don't mind, I got to ride Chippy and have breakfast with you Harri.' Drum had left them to do the dishes, claiming he had matters to deal with in his study. Calling his wife was clearly one of them.

'Well, I need to head home Billie. I have to go shopping and fill my fridge and pantry so I can invite you for a meal next time.'

'And Daddy. He can come for a meal too, can't he?' Drum had appeared in the doorway. Harriet looked at him over Billie's head. He looked slightly annoyed. She hoped it wasn't at her.

'Yes, Daddy too. Of course.' Harri watched as Drum walked in, picked up Billie and held her tightly against him.

She laid her face against his for a moment. 'Is Mummy awake yet. Are we going to see her?' Billie seemed keen, and Harriet turned to walk away.

Glancing at Drum to say goodbye, she saw anguish in his

eyes, and stopped. He set Billie down and dropped to one knee, his face level with hers. 'Mummy's not up to a visit this weekend, Billie. But we're making plans to see her soon.'

'Oh.' Billie deflated a little, then brightened. 'That's okay Daddy, we have a lot to do here. We were going to move the weaners to a new paddock, and Tiffany said I could come to her house for a sleepover if I wasn't going to Sydney. Can you call Tiffany's Mum please?'

'Sure. I'll do that right now. We could ask if Tiffany can come here instead, if you'd like that?'

'Maybe next time. She has a new puppy, so I'd really like to go there.' Billie was almost jogging on the spot, a day of playing with a friend and a puppy swiftly erasing her disappointment at not seeing her Mum.

Harriet gave Billie a hug. 'Your weekend sounds fabulous. Perhaps we can catch up for a swim tomorrow afternoon, when you're home from Tiffany's, and you can tell me all about it.'

'Oh yes please Harri, a swim would be wonderful. I'll see you then.' Turning to Drum she announced, 'I'm going to pack my bag now.'

'Hold on young lady. What about moving the weaners?' Drum was barely keeping his laughter in check.

Billie looked uncertain for a moment. 'Sure. Can we do it now? Right away?'

Drum gave her a gentle push, 'It's fine, I'll move the weaners this afternoon, you go and pack your bag.' Billie bolted for the door. 'Don't forget your toothbrush. And pyjamas!' Drum called out but she was gone.

Harriet walked to the front door with Drum, wondering if she should ask about his conversation with Billie's Mum. But it really wasn't any of her business. Except she felt invested in Billie and hated to see her hurt, if only briefly.

'You're probably wondering what the deal is with Annabelle?' Drum spoke quietly.

'It's none of my business.' Harriet stepped out the front door, then turned. Her cheeks flushed, she blurted out, 'But how can anyone NOT want to see Billie. How can she stand being away from her! She's her mother!'

Drum shook his head sadly. 'I don't know Harri. It's beyond me. I wonder …' He trailed off, looked straight into Harriet's eyes. She could see anger there, and pain. Before she could respond Billie came galloping along the hallway, wearing a backpack and a huge smile.

Harriet stepped off the veranda. 'Thank you both for a lovely start to the day, and the best orange juice and scrambled eggs. With green stuff.'

They all spoke at once. 'G.O.P!'

'Bye Harri. See you at the river tomorrow!'

'Bye Billie, have fun tonight!'

Harriet walked briskly back to her place, the day was going to be hot, and she still had a lot to do. The cottage was cool when she stepped inside. Harriet put a load of washing in the machine then double-checked her grocery list.

Driving into town she decided she would call in at Ben Evans Real Estate. It was time to float her business idea past the Bens'. It was already nine, they should be open. Harriet dropped into the café first. Cathy and Kristen were busy but managing okay. There were no groups booked in and they assured Harriet she should have the weekend off to get her place sorted.

Walking down to the real estate office, coffee in hand, Harriet glanced around the main street. Most of the street parking was full, although the Council parking behind Town Hall still had plenty of car parks available. She mused over the difference between locals and out-of-towners. The locals were scurrying along the street, in and out of shops, with a purpose. Some stopping to chat with friends and neighbours in the street as they went about their Saturday chores.

The visitors were more leisurely. Window shopping, pointing out the big clock on the Town Hall, studying the windows of the real estate offices. Carrying a coffee or juice from Debbie's café, a gift bag with the branding of a local store. Asking where the best place for breakfast would be. Harriet pointed out Debbie's café to a middle-aged couple who had stepped out of a very new four-wheel drive vehicle with interstate number plates, when they asked where to go for coffee.

A bell tinkled when she pushed open the door to the real estate office. Big Ben was at his desk, a coffee from Debbie's in front of him. Harriet held hers up. 'Cheers. And good morning.'

'Cheers to you too. I would have bought a coffee for you, had I known you were coming in.' Standing, he walked around the desk, leaning back against it as she approached.

Harriet laughed. 'I almost bought you one just now. Then I remembered you would have been in when they opened, had a coffee with your breakfast, then bought another one to bring to the office.'

'I'm a creature of habit Harri. You know me too well.' He sat back in his chair, indicating she should take a seat on the other side of his desk.

Sitting, Harriet placed her coffee on the desk, then reached into her bag, pulling out her business plan. 'Thanks again for last night, it was the best house-warming. Ever!' She beamed at him. 'How busy are you, Ben? Do you have time for a chat?'

'I'm manning the office. The young bloke is showing a prospective buyer the old courthouse. It's on the way out of town in an old goldrush village. Needs a bit of work but would make a good bed and breakfast.' Ben took a sip of his coffee, looked at the cup briefly and tossed it in the bin under his desk. 'Finished. Do you want to wait for Ben, he'll be less than an hour I expect.'

'Actually, I'd like to run this by you first. And if you're keen on my idea, we can share it with Ben when he returns.'

Leaning back in his chair, he smiled encouragingly. 'Fire away. I'm very curious.'

Straightening her back, Harriet took a breath. 'Here goes. You've seen the Escape programs on TV? They do it in the UK. Escape to the Country?'

Ben nodded. 'They did one here recently called Escape from the City. Probably couldn't use the UK name because of copyright.'

'That's it, that's exactly it.' Harriet nodded. 'But my plan is a slight variation on this concept. Bringing city people to regional areas is one thing. Not for television, of course. The real deal. A common factor with these programs seems to be, generally, they need to be within commuting distance from the city if they're still working, or they're already retired.'

'Yes. That's true. And Barrington is too far for a city commute. Go on.' Ben had leaned forward, his face lively with interest.

'I want to target working age people. More than that, younger people with families. Those who haven't been able to get into the housing market in the city. And those that have but are looking for a lifestyle change. A slower pace perhaps, but a real sense of community.' Harriet grinned. 'This place oozes with community spirit. Look at me, only six weeks and I have enough friends to throw me a surprise house-warming party!'

It was clear Ben was taking this in, thoughts, and questions, flitted across his face. 'It's a great idea Harri, but where will they work? There's not a lot of jobs here.'

'That's just it. If the last year or so has taught us anything, it's demonstrated that people *can* work from home. Remotely. In a lot of businesses. In a lot of industries. There's already a housing boom just outside the cities, for such people trying to find affordable housing for their families and working from home much of the time. But the outer city suburbs, some of them, have less to offer than country towns like this one. A beautiful region, great community, good schools, plenty of sport and activities for children. Only an hour and a half from the beach.' She could see he was taking it in. 'If you live in the outer city suburbs, you'd drive an hour and half to get to the beach too.'

'Yes. That's right. Go on. I'm still not sure they'd want to be this far from their work.'

'You're right. Some won't. But many will. And they're who we want.' Harriet drank the last of her coffee. 'Think about it Ben. In the city they'd be looking at a three-bedroom brick and tile home, no character, on a small block in a western suburb far from work. They could work from home some days, but there would be an expectation they would attend the office once or twice a week, because they still live in the city.

'Compare it to here. Barrington. For the same investment they could buy a bigger home, or build, on a large block, or even small acreage. They could have a lifestyle, a community, for themselves and their families. The beauty of it is, they are too far from the city to be called in for just a day. They can work from home most of the time. No commute. Take the kids to after school sport, put the time they save into their family, their property, the community. If they need to attend the office, they can arrange to be there for a couple of days at a time, but less often. Recent research indicates that companies allowing such working arrangements have happier, more productive staff.'

'It's great. You're right Harri. It won't be for everyone, but if you target market, you will find the right people. I like it.' He smiled. 'I can also see the synergy with our business. Finding the right properties. Some might even want to move here and rent for six months before buying. Just to be sure.'

'Yes. And I'm not talking about a mass influx of newbies.

Half a dozen the first year would be brilliant. I've got a couple of corporations who want to collaborate with me, offer it to some of their staff. They're keen to downsize their city footprint. I would be paid by them, actually, to develop a program and an offering for a few employees. The good thing about doing it this way, is that these people already know each other. Their partners and children may know each other. If we get more than five from one corporation in the area, they are keen to set up an office in town here. Where they can hot desk, take meetings. Have all the technology they need to link in with head office. It's decentralised but can also be a hub.' Harriet paused to let her ideas take shape for Ben, who nodded thoughtfully.

'Ben. I need an office in town myself. Bellbird Cottage isn't big enough, and I need to be able to meet with people, talk to them, show them around. Would you consider letting me rent the spare desk from you, use your office as a base?'

Standing up, Ben walked around the desk. 'I don't need to consider it. It's the best concept I've heard in a long time. It's great Harri. Let's talk to Ben when he gets back, work out the details. When do you want to start?'

Harriet tried to contain her excitement. 'Straight away really, but I've got to keep on at the café, at least during the morning and lunch rush. I've committed to stay as long as I'm needed.'

Ben walked to the rear of the room. 'Come with me Harri, you haven't seen the rest of the office.'

Harriet followed Ben through the rear door, where she already knew there'd be a kitchen, and probably a bathroom. Standing inside the door, she was looking down a long hallway. The building went a long way back. Following Ben as he pointed out a spacious kitchen and eat in lunchroom to the right, then a meeting room to the left, with a table and eight chairs. Harriet had no idea there was so much space. She'd thought it was just a small shop, with a kitchen out the back. Moving down the hall there were another two offices to the left, both equipped with large desks. Finally, to the right was a bathroom, again bigger than she expected, then out the back door was off street parking for three cars. Ben's Landcruiser was already parked there and as they watched, Little Ben pulled his car in beside it.

39

*B*en grinned as he hauled his frame out. 'Nice to see you Harri. Recovered okay from last night?'

'Sure. Thanks again for a brilliant night. Best house-warming ever.' Harriet smiled in response and hid her surprise when he leant down and brushed her cheek with his lips.

'Harriet has filled me in on her business concept this morning son. Have you got time for a chat?'

'Really? Excellent. I've got time. The old courthouse didn't suit my buyer, and I have no other stock to show him today.' They walked back into the rear of the building, Big Ben holding the door open for Harriet to go first.

Harriet gave a brief overview to Little Ben, who quickly understood the concept and saw the synergies between their businesses.

'I have questions, Harri. It's nuts and bolts stuff, so you may not have all the answers yet.' Big Ben drew a large notebook from his drawer. 'How much time do you think you need to put into the business in the beginning? Is it full time? I know you have committed to more time at the café, but if you were finished there?' He let the question hang in the air.

'I've thought about it quite a bit. It's unlikely to be full time, ever. It's just not a big enough township for that. But I'm okay with it. I can supplement my income with marketing and branding work. I'm hoping the work I've done for you, with Laura's help, will generate interest from other businesses.

'I need a place to work from and a main street presence would be good. Renting a desk and maybe some window space from you, for my own branding, will be far cheaper than taking an office of my own, although I note there are a few empty shop fronts I could secure at a reasonable price.' She had their attention, so she continued. 'Sharing with Evans Real Estate means I could also have a landline, have my phone answered if I'm out with buyers or in the city with clients. Have my clients greeted and looked after if they walk in without warning. And of course, fast internet capability, the meeting room, the kitchen. And a more substantial presence. The benefit of your listings and local knowledge, relationships with potential sellers. Street Cred if you will.'

Looking them both in the eye, she added. 'I would, of course, provide the same service to you. Answer your phones and greet your clients if you're out. Quid pro quo.'

Little Ben leaned forward. 'We've had a couple of conversations about working with you Harriet before we knew the extent of the potential collaboration between our businesses.' He glanced at his father, who nodded encouragement.

'We could offer you the desk, use of all facilities, room for your own branding.' He paused. Harriet waited, almost holding her breath. 'If in return you could provide, say six to eight hours per week on our website, listings, window cards and general marketing. We're considering starting a rent roll again, and will need a property manager once we build it a bit, but if you could cover that in the beginning …'

Harriet stood, speechless. She was afraid she'd cry if she spoke, this arrangement was perfect. She held out her hand. Big Ben reached over, took her hand and shook it firmly, before draping his other arm around her shoulders and hugging her to his side. 'You're a breath of fresh air Harriet. I can't wait to have you share our space.'

She turned to Little Ben. Grinning from ear to ear, he held his arms open. Harriet shook her head, laughing at the same time. In one small step she was enveloped in his huge arms and received a resounding kiss on the top of her head.

'Sealed with a kiss!' He threw his head back and laughed, releasing her at the same time. 'But Harri, I'm curious about your branding. What are you calling your business?'

Glancing at her watch, Harriet realised it was lunchtime. 'Come to the pub with me for lunch, both of you. I'd like to have a glass of wine and a meal with my new ….' Hesitating, she looked at each of them in turn. 'What are we? Partners? I'm your tenant really. Colleagues?'

'Friends Harri. We're friends and we're doing a little business together. Sharing some space. Helping each other.' Big Ben slipped his phone into his pocket. 'Let's have lunch. Lock up son, divert the mainline to my phone and put the 'out on inspection' sign on the door. If anyone wants us, they'll call.'

Ten minutes later, a beer and two red wines on the table, Little Ben asked the question again. 'Your branding Harri?'

'I've tossed around a few ideas, but my personal favourite is ***Barrington. A Place to Start Over.***' Harriet picked up her glass, taking a sip while she watched their reaction.

4 0

'Bloody perfect Harriet. A place to start over indeed.' Little Ben nodded enthusiastically, a little foam from his beer nestled on his top lip. Grinning broadly, he raised his glass. 'Cheers. Here's to Barrington. A Place to Start Over.'

Harriet laughed and noisily clinked her glass with his, then his father's. 'Cheers to you too. Ben Evans Real Estate.' Noticing a few people had stopped eating their own meals and were watching with interest, possibly amusement, Harriet lowered her voice. 'Thank you. Both of you. Really. You've made it so easy for me. I'm really excited to work with you both.'

'Our pleasure Harri. You're a catalyst for change. In a good way. For us. For Laura. For Deb. Even Drum. You're smart and hard-working and really, really good with people. You'll be an asset to us, I'm sure of it.' Big Ben smiled at Harriet, while beginning to stand. 'Lunch? What would you like Harri?'

Harriet got up quickly. 'No. My treat. Please. Let me buy you both lunch.' She looked at Little Ben. Always hungry, it seemed, he was quick to answer. 'Steak sandwich Harri. Thank you.'

'Chicken burger please Harri.' Big Ben spoke quietly, looking

213

at her fondly. 'The chicken is local, organic. They do a great lunchtime schnitzel too.'

'That's me then. Love a schnitty.' Harriet headed to the bistro end of the bar, placed the order, paid, returning with a table number. 'Eight. The money number. Also good luck.' She was tingling with happiness. It felt right. She was moving ahead and making decisions. Doing business with good people. Not only that, despite their brief acquaintance, she instinctively knew the Bens had her interests at heart.

'Ha! I don't go in for all that Harri, but it sounds good.' Little Ben said as his phone began ringing. Standing, he pointed to the phone, now at his ear, making 'excuse me' signals as he walked out into the beer garden.

Ben leaned in. 'It's good Harri. Good business. You're not overcapitalising by setting up your own premises and you'll have additional income from working with us. And the cafe while they need you.'

'Oh Ben. You're not paying me. I'll work for rent reduction, window space, internet access.' Harriet looked him in the eye. This needed to be a business arrangement.

'Honestly Harri. You will cost us nothing. The internet is unlimited. The desk and other offices are spare. Even the window space costs nothing, and you will sort out your own branding for it. But in return you will actually provide marketing support we have a budget to pay for.' He leaned back as the bartender arrived with their meals. Little Ben was returning too. 'We can talk about this more on Monday. We'll think it over.'

'Think what over Dad?' Little Ben pulled his chair in, took a sip of beer, cut his steak sandwich in half and picked it up in his hands, taking an enormous bite, while nodding happily.

'The arrangement with Harri.' Big Ben picked up his knife and fork and cut into his chicken burger.

'Harri. We were going to speak to you this week about

coming in part-time. We'd be taking advantage if we let you work for free. There will be a lot of benefits for us, for very little outlay.'

Her heart warmed at their faith in her business concept. And in her. She looked down at her plate. The schnitzel looked great, golden brown with a fresh salad and a few home-cut fries. Taking her time, she cut a piece, popped it into her mouth and chewed for a moment. She was about to speak, to thank them, but Little Ben jumped in first.

'There are another four main street real estate agents here Harri, and two others without a main street presence. We all know each other, share listings and work together. You could have teamed up with any of them and got the same deal. Maybe even a better one. But you came to us. We're thrilled to have you join us. It will give us an edge.'

'We'll always collaborate with the other agents. It's a small town. But this cements our standing as the premier agency, for want of a better term.' Big Ben looked at his son and smiled at Harriet.

'Dad, we've always been the premier agency. You've been on Council since forever and the Evans name is well known, not just here, but in the rural sector throughout this region, and further afield.' He paused, taking the last bite out of his sandwich, before wiping his fingers with his serviette. 'But we've not been strong in residential and lifestyle properties. Our association with you will lift our profile there. There's more benefits for us than you, Harri.'

Surprised by his forthright manner, Harriet nodded, looking at them in turn. They were a lot savvier than she gave them credit for. And they'd had conversations between them about how they might harness her expertise. 'Then it's just good business. Transparency and honesty will be the foundation of our relationship. Thank you.' Her voice caught on the last words. They believed in her. They had no doubts at all. And while she was firm in her own convictions, having it reinforced meant more to her than she could express.

Little Ben pushed his chair back. 'I'm heading to Drum's place to look at his heifers. I've got a buyer looking for stock.' He put his phone in his pocket, smiled at Harriet and walked out.

'He works hard in the business, doesn't he? You've raised a good man there. He's a good agent and he's great with people. And he's honest.' Harriet pushed her plate away. She'd finished her lunch, her plate was bare. It was delicious. She honestly couldn't remember enjoying a meal more.

Big Ben looked wistful for a moment. 'I'd like to take the credit, but he is his mother's son. Sure, he's learnt the business from me, and he went away for a couple of years to Queensland working on a large station. Real estate agents sometimes have a bad rap. But he's proud of our business, respects my position on Council and in the community, and ensures we are scrupulously transparent with our clients, colleagues and community. He'll be Mayor one day, Harri, I'm sure of it. Maybe after he finds the right girl.' He winked at Harriet, and she laughed out loud, delighted at his cheekiness.

'Don't play cupid. Please don't. Ben and I, we're friends. I don't know if there's anything more for us. But having Ben Evans, both of you, as friends suits me just fine.' She winked back and he chuckled.

'Touché Harriet. I'll keep my thoughts to myself on the subject. Now, let's go and pick out an office for you, shall we? I'm thinking you could work from the front desk at times, but you should have one of the offices in the back for your client meetings, paperwork and so on. Come and have a look, let me know what you might need.'

41

---

*D*rum watched Ben drive away. He had picked out a dozen heifers for his buyer, they'd send a truck for them on Wednesday. Just as well, Drum thought, the conversation he'd had with Annabelle earlier in the day had made him realise how hard it might be to hold on to the whole place.

The phone call that morning just after Harriet left, before he took Billie to her sleepover, had taken him by surprise. He'd already spoken to Annabelle, but she'd had time to think. Or perhaps scheme. Annabelle had been calling Billie on Monday evenings, and he generally let Billie answer the call herself when he saw it was Annabelle's number. They never spoke for long. Billie told her what she was doing at school, but as soon as she began to chat about the farm, the horses or the swimming hole, Annabelle generally finished the call.

He rarely listened to the conversation but had registered Billie mentioning Harriet and her party last night and the breakfast they'd made together. He'd hoped Annabelle would see how happy Billie was here with him. But after a few minutes Billie stopped talking, her face stricken, then turned to Drum, holding the phone out.

'Mummy wants to speak to you.' He took the phone from her and waited until she left the room.

'Annabelle.' He knew he sounded curt, but seeing his daughter's face drop, obviously chastised by her mother, annoyed him deeply.

'Drummond. What's going on there? Wilhelmina said someone has moved into Bellbird Cottage. A friend she said. Why haven't you mentioned this? Where are the funds from the sale?'

'Funds from the sale? Annabelle, the cottage was owned by Miss Boxshall. The funds will have gone into her estate for distribution.'

'What?' Her voice rose. 'You said you were buying it back after the old lady died.'

Sighing, Drum gritted his teeth. 'I didn't buy it back Annabelle. I knew I would need funds for settlement with you. As I've explained previously, we don't have a lot of cash on hand at any given time. It's all tied up in stock and crops.'

'Well, you'd better liquidate a few assets Drummond, because my lawyer is sending a settlement proposal to yours.' She paused for a moment, then spoke in a lower tone. 'I don't know who this Harry is that has made friends with our daughter, but I hope you're ensuring she isn't mixing with anyone unsavoury. What do you know about this man who's moved into the cottage?'

Drum almost laughed, but perversely did not want to explain that Harry was actually Harri, and a woman. Annabelle's care of Billie had been lackadaisical, to say the least. She was in no position to cast aspersions.

'Harri is fine. Don't concern yourself. I will speak to Barlow when your lawyer's paperwork arrives.' He paused for a moment, then added, 'Billie is happy here. She's settled at school and doing well. I don't want our divorce to upset her. Goodbye Annabelle.'

Now, as Ben drove out, Drum needed to gather his thoughts. Maybe speak to Fergus too. Put a plan together that will make Annabelle happy. The last thing he wanted to do was drag it out. Best for all of them if they could reach an agreement and move forward. Sighing, he admitted to himself that Billie needs regular contact with her mother. But damn, he just didn't trust the woman. Not with Billie's feelings and not in terms of the forthcoming property settlement.

After the call with Annabelle he'd found Billie curled up on the window seat in her bedroom, book in hand. But she wasn't reading, and when she turned her face to him as he walked in, he could see she'd been crying.

Across the room in two strides, he sat on the window seat and opened his arms to his daughter. Billie climbed on to his lap and sobbed into his shoulder.

'I'm, I'm, sorry Daddy. I didn't mean to upset Mummy.' She looked up at him, tears on her cheeks and anguish in her eyes.

Holding her close he rested his chin on the top of her head for a moment, willing evidence of his anger at Annabelle from his features. After a moment, when her sobs subsided, he gently set Billie on her feet in front of him. Taking her small hands in his large ones, he looked gravely into her eyes.

'You've done nothing wrong Billie. Nothing at all.' Taking a deep breath, he hoped Billie was mature enough for him to be honest. 'You know that Mummy and I haven't lived together for a long time now. We have been talking and think it best if we make that permanent.' He watched his daughter process what he'd said.

Billie nodded, frowning. She glanced out the window at Chippy then looked back at Drum. Speaking very quietly, she watched his face as she asked the question. 'A divorce? Are you and Mummy getting a divorce?' She looked close to tears again.

Drum's heart was breaking for her, but realising she understood, he pushed on. 'Yes Billie. We think it's best that we get a divorce.' Billie drew her hands from his, holding them over her face, again sobbing loudly.

Damn. It's too much for her. He tried to gather her back into his arms, but she stood firm. Looking up at him she almost shouted, 'are you sending me back to Mummy! Don't you want me here anymore?'

Close to tears himself, Drum spoke quietly, but firmly as he reached for her hands again, holding them against his chest. 'No. That's not going to happen. I want you here with me. Always.' He was amazed as her anger changed to relief and she threw herself against his chest, sobbing and laughing at once. 'I can stay here? With you? Always?'

Wrapping his arms tightly around her trembling body, he shuddered. What the hell had Annabelle done to this sweet child to make her so fearful of returning to her? Murmuring into the top of her head he said, 'Yes, always.' Rubbing her back while she absorbed his words, he contemplated other conversations with Annabelle. Often telling him Billie was a handful. Had she ever hurt the child? Struck her? Or was Billie's desire to be with him drawn more from neglect and disinterest on Annabelle's part. He suspected that was largely it. His wife was selfish. Always had been, but he, and his parents, had felt Billie needed to be with her mother. He wondered if he should have fought for Billie when Annabelle left two years ago. It may have saved his sweet girl from heartbreak.

He'd fight for her now. He'd make sure Billie felt safe. Loved. Settled. What every child deserves.

Climbing back up on the window seat, Billie looked sadly out the window. 'I do love Mummy, really I do. And I try so hard to be good for her. Quiet. Not ask too many questions. Read in my room if she's tired.' Turning to Drum, she added, 'She's always tired. I get on her nerves, so she likes me to stay in my room. But Daddy, I get so bored sometimes. School was okay, and I like going to friends' houses after school sometimes. But at our house, the Sydney house, there's just not much to do…' she trailed off, turning back to watch Chippy grazing outside.

'I'm sorry Billie. I didn't know how hard it was for you there. I know now, and it will only be short visits there when you want to see Mummy, or she can come here to see you.' Billie brightened visibly at his words, and he mentally berated himself for not checking into her welfare more thoroughly while she was with Annabelle. Assuming she wanted to be with Billie, he wondered how easily Annabelle would have given her up at the time.

Then he recalled their argument when she was leaving two years ago. She had taken Billie, he realised now, not because she wanted her daughter, but because it would hurt him not to have her. She'd used Billie as a pawn to get what she wanted. More money. Better terms. Well, that would stop. He would be fair in his settlement offer, but Billie was non-negotiable. She's been through enough. She needs love and stability.

Billie nudged him. 'Are you okay Daddy? Are you sad about the divorce?'

He smiled at her and took her small hand in his large one. 'I'm sad that it didn't work out Billie, but very happy to have you with me. I'll make sure Mummy is okay and of course you can see her, but this is your home. Here. With me.' Taking her hand, he added, 'How about you get your gear and I drop you off at Tiffany's house to see that new puppy.'

Jumping to her feet, Billie grinned. 'I'm ready!'

4 2

Harriet carried her groceries in, stocking the pantry and fridge. She spent a further hour or so fully unpacking the kitchen, moving a few things around until it looked just right. Setting a large old-fashioned glass bowl of fruit on the end of the kitchen bench she stepped away and admired it from the dining area. While it wasn't a large kitchen, it had everything she needed, and she could picture herself hosting a girl's night or a dinner party here. Vastly different to the home she'd had with her husband in Sydney, she realised she was more at home in the cottage already.

Back in the master bedroom she contemplated the large stack of paintings leaning against the wall. Moving over to them she lifted each one up, separating them until she had four large acrylic canvases, two large timber-framed charcoal drawings of girls with long, windswept hair, and ten timber-framed water-colours of varying sizes leaning against the wall and bed. She set the 'wild sisters' as she thought of the charcoal pictures on each side of the bed. They'd work well in the main bedroom.

Carrying the smaller watercolours two at a time, she decided seven of them would work in the hallway, three on the side where the large hallstand stood, and four on the other side. They were all of heritage style buildings in country towns. Several were painted by a watercolour artist from Queensland, active on Instagram. Harriet had five of her paintings and had become friendly with the artist, who had framed the paintings in timber especially for Harriet and were a great fit for the little cottage.

Three smaller 'chook' paintings went to the kitchen. A perfect setting for them. They were also by one artist. Walking back to the large acrylic paintings, she studied them. They were vibrant, modern Australian landscapes. While they were too modern, really, for the cottage, Harriet decided she'd make them 'work.' Art was subjective, after all. She knew her collection was eclectic, to say the least, but every painting told a story and she wanted them all hung. Two large ones in the dining area and two in the lounge. The bright colours popped against the subdued, heritage colours of the walls and while not traditional, Harriet spent a happy couple of hours hanging them all and was pleased with the results. Setting the hammer and left-over picture hooks on the kitchen bench, she stood back, arms folded, and looked between the two main rooms. A few bright cushions on the couch and a bright bowl on the dining table might be needed to tie it all together. Walking back up the hall, she nodded her approval of the pictures hanging there. Stopping for a moment she swapped two around. Perfect.

As the day wore on, Harriet pottered happily around her home. A knock at the front door startled her. As she hurried down the hall, she could see a tall shape through the stained glass. Drum she thought. Suddenly flustered, she glanced at herself in the mirror set into the hall stand. Her face was flushed with exertion, she had just hung out a load of washing, and her hair was escaping its high ponytail, leaving wavy blonde tendrils around her face. Oh well, he'd seen her at the river, hair completely wet.

Opening the door Harriet was surprised to see Little Ben standing there, awkwardly holding a dark red ceramic pot with a healthy plant growing out of it, so tall it almost hid his face.

'Ben! Hello.' Harriet chuckled to herself as he held the pot plant toward her.

'A house-warming present Harri. It's a Happy Plant. Mum used to give them to home buyers, she always said it brought luck, love and happiness into a home.'

Taking the plant, Harriet beamed at him. 'Come in. I'll find the perfect place for this.' Ben followed her down the hall, pausing to look at her paintings as he went. Stopping at the edge of the living area he looked around and gave a low, appreciative whistle. 'Love what you've done already Harri. Gosh, your art really pulls it altogether. You should be a stylist, my friend.'

Placing the plant under a window in the dining area she stepped back. 'Good colour choice Ben. I was wondering what colour throw I need on the couch over there. I'll match it in with this beautiful pot. Perfect, thank you.' She turned and impulsively hugged him, standing on tippy toes she planted a kiss on his cheek. He gave her a quick squeeze and moved back, just a touch.

Hmmm. I don't think he's that into me after all. I might have been reading his signals all wrong. But he is a great friend. Harriet walked to the fridge, smiling over her shoulder. 'Can I interest you in a beer Ben, or a glass of wine?'

'Beer please if you've got it.' Harriet handed him a bottle. The same brand the men had been drinking the night before.

'Good job Harri. My beer of choice.' Ben smiled and leaned against the kitchen bench.

Harriet opened a bottle of red and poured herself a glass. 'Come out to the veranda, it's starting to cool a little.'

They sat on the top veranda step, each leaning against a veranda post. 'So, tell me a bit more about yourself Ben. I know you're local and a partner in the agency, but what about personally? Hobbies? Girlfriend? What keeps you up at night and what gets you up in the mornings?'

'Ha, you know how to ask the right questions Harri. Sure you're not an investigative reporter?' As Harriet laughed, Ben took a long swig of beer, then settled himself more comfortably. 'Hobbies. I still play a bit of football, rugby union. I'm in an old boys team now, they run a masters competition. Myself, Drum, Angus and Jamie. You probably know some of the others too. We're not as quick as we used to be and we don't scrum quite as hard, but it's fun. I'm also keen on tennis. You've seen that Drum has a tennis court up at the main house? We've had some hilarious tennis parties there. We're probably due for one soon. Do you play Harri?'

'I do. I'm not great. Used to have a good strong first serve. It's been a while. I could get on board with a tennis party.' Harriet sipped her wine waiting for him to go on.

'I read, mostly biographies. And I like the cinema. It's a shame we don't have one here anymore, we have to go to Taree or Forster these days. I guess everyone streams their movies now, but I really like the big screen experience.'

'You're so right! I always said I wouldn't live in a town without a cinema, yet here I am.' Harriet waggled her eyebrows, laughing, 'if we do well out of our mutual business, we should build a small cinema. Two screens, one gold class style and one for the kids and teens. We could run classics once a month, like 'To Kill a Mockingbird' and 'It's a wonderful Life.' What do you say?'

Ben was laughing and nodding. 'Good plan, lure a few more

people here Harri, increase our economic standing and there will be an opportunity. Love it! You're an ideas girl.' This was said drily, and she laughed along with him. He was such easy company, already becoming a good friend.

'And girlfriends Ben. You've got to be the most eligible man in town. I've seen the way some of those girls looked at you in the pub the other day.'

'Ha.' Ben took another mouthful of beer. 'Are we joking around now Harri, or do you want the truth?' Ben's expression had sobered, and he spoke quietly.

Not sure what he was about to say, but sensing this was important to him, Harriet smiled encouragement. 'The truth Ben. We're friends, aren't we?' Even as she spoke, she wondered if he was going to profess feelings for her, and her stomach turned over, knowing she didn't reciprocate them. Although she liked him enormously and felt sure he would be a great partner, husband and father, for someone else. She almost held her breath, watching his face as he collected his thoughts.

'There is someone. I've cared for her, since, well since she was in her senior year at school. I'm a few years older.' He sighed.

'Go on.' Harriet went inside, returning with another beer. He took the top off and sipped. Then put it down beside him.

'I was keen to ask her out, but she started seeing a mate of mine. Even when I thought it was over, well, I couldn't go there. She finished school and moved to Sydney. My mate was there too. He hinted that he saw her sometimes. I'm pretty sure he knew I had a thing for her.' He lifted the beer to his lips, took a long swallow, then put it down again. 'Mum knew her, knew how I felt. Didn't really approve, thought she was a bit, you know, easy. She had a reputation. This was more due to what my mate said about her than anything she actually did. So, with Mum's encouragement, I went north. Worked on a cattle station for a couple of years, then in a stock and station agency up there. I did date a couple of girls while I was away, may have even stayed there. But Dad wanted me home, wanted me in the business with him. I came back.'

'Do you regret that, Ben? Is that what keeps you up at night?' Harriet spoke softly, sensing he was unburdening himself for the first time in a very long while.

'No, I don't. I love working with Dad. With Mum too when she was alive. I just haven't moved on from my crush. My first love. Sure, I've dated, but no one I really connected with.' He looked sideways at Harriet. 'Until you came to town, Harri.'

'Oh!' Harriet blushed, speechless.

'Don't worry, I explored my feelings, my attraction to you. Nearly kissed you that time.' He grinned, and she let her breath out.

'But Harri, you're not her. She's here again you know. Been back in town a few years. She has a daughter, she's a single Mum.' He held his beer in front of him, seeming to study it for a moment. 'She's had a rough time. Domestic violence. Emotional abuse too. He's in jail now, that old mate of mine.' His face hardened for a moment. 'I could kill the bastard! He's ruined her for anyone else. She's timid, doesn't trust, says she'll never re-partner. The best I can hope for is being her friend. To her and her daughter. She's a gorgeous kid, about Billie's age.'

Harriet nodded sympathetically. 'That's such a shame. For her, you and her daughter.'

'You may know her. Melanie. She works at the Vet Clinic with Angus. Her little girl is Tiffany. I think Billie is over there tonight, Tiff got a new puppy this week. They're both recovering from all they've been through. Mel and Tiff. I drop in sometimes, help her around the house with any handyman jobs. She trusts me. Feels safe. She has no idea how I feel about her. How I've always felt about her. Pretty sure she looks upon me like a big brother. If only I'd asked her out before Greg did, when she was finishing high school. Perhaps we'd be married now with three or four kids.'

'Melanie! Of course, I know Melanie. She helps in the cafe at lunchtimes when we're hammered, and she drops by almost every day to get coffee and lunch for herself and often for Angus.' Harriet frowned. 'Tiffany served me the very first morning I came to town. Deb is her aunt, I think.'

'Greg Tait. Jamie's older brother, Debbie's brother-in-law. Football star. Big mouth. Con artist. Abuser of women and children. I had no idea, always considered him a mate. Looked up to him when I was young. He could talk to women. You know. Smooth, charming. He lied a lot. Whereas women treat me like a big friendly giant. Someone safe. They don't look at me as a potential partner. As a lover.'

'I don't think it's over Ben. Keep doing what you're doing. Being Melanie's friend. She has reason to trust you. Be a positive role model for Tiffany. I think you'll find an opportunity to let Melanie know you care, let her think on it. Don't give up Ben, stay the course.'

'Do you think so? Really? I'd hate to scare her, lose her friendship and trust.' Ben took a deep breath, a small smile on his lips.

'I really do. I know Melanie is part of Rose's friendship group. I'm going to get to know her too.' Harriet gave him a light punch on the arm. 'You should've asked her and Tiff to my house-warming last night. Missed opportunity big man, missed opportunity.'

Ben laughed. 'You're right, I should have asked her last night. I've just been so sure I'm firmly in the friend zone, you know?'

'Well, maybe you have to change her perception of you just a little.'

'And you Harri? Boyfriend? What keeps you up at night?'

'Okay. You've got me.' Harriet relaxed, comfortable with the conversation. 'Separated. Soon to be divorced. I suspect my ex-husband wasn't faithful for very much of our three-year marriage.' She smiled, somewhat sadly 'I had an accident late last year. My own fault really, I argued with a bag snatcher and was stabbed, here.' She indicated her lower abdomen. Ben looked shocked, but indicated for her to continue.

'My recovery was long. Complicated. Additional surgeries. I thought a lot about what I want in life while I recovered. Where I want to be, what I want to do. The sort of people I'd like to have around me. It became clear that Sydney was not my place.' She glanced at Ben, he was completely focussed on her.

'I'm from a small country town, further south. Smaller than this one. I left at eighteen. At the time said I'd never live in a country town again. I wanted a career, the big smoke. And it was good. For more than ten years it suited me. But when I was down, unwell, marriage over, I realised I had no real community around me. Friends, sure. But my biggest support was from my parents, my brother, my hometown.

'So, I started thinking about a new business concept. It wouldn't work in my hometown, just too small. I planned to head north once I could travel. I left Sydney the day after my thirty-first birthday. Hit a 'roo on the way here … and, well, here I am.'

'Wow! Harri, you've been through so much. Everyone has a story when you take the time to ask. Thanks for sharing.' He leaned back, took another sip of beer, then grinned at her. 'But you didn't answer the boyfriend question. You're getting divorced. Not all men cheat. Surely you'll have another crack, you know, at some point.'

'Ha, ha. Who's asking probing questions now?' Harriet looked away for a moment, past the back garden to the creek and trees beyond. 'I haven't shared this with anyone Ben, not even my parents.' She paused, then looked up at him, tears in her eyes. 'The stabbing. The surgeries. It's unlikely I can have a child. The damage …' she waved a hand around her stomach. 'Knowing that, well, it makes me wary of getting involved. A relationship, marriage. Most men will want a family and it's not something I can offer. I think I've reconciled myself to it. I'm focussed on the business, this community. My family and friends, of course.'

Ben nodded, reached over and touched her arm gently. 'That's hard Harri. I'm sorry. But family isn't a deal-breaker for every man. For myself, I'd be happy to be married to Melanie and raise Tiffany with her. I'd like children of my own, but if she didn't want that it wouldn't stop me from loving her.' He stood, his beer empty.

Harriet smiled sadly, got up and walked to the kitchen with him, where he wrapped his huge arm around her shoulders. 'Just be open to the possibility. Who knows what the future holds for any of us?' She nodded and leaned into him for a moment. She felt lighter. Unburdened.

Looking up at him she smiled slowly, her eyes full of unshed tears. 'I know one thing Ben Evans. I've made a true friend in you. Thank you.'

'Me too Harri. So grateful you've come to town. Change is in the air. For the town, the community. Maybe for me too. I'm more excited about the future than I've ever been.' He leaned down, kissing the top of her head. 'And what's said at Bellbird Cottage stays at Bellbird Cottage. I respect your privacy Harri, and I'm honoured you've felt comfortable speaking to me.'

'Thank you, Ben. Same.'

Ben set his empty bottle on the bench. 'I best get on, I'm cooking dinner for Dad tonight and we're off early tomorrow to look at property in Armidale with a buyer.'

Harriet walked him out to his car, reaching up to give him a hug. Movement in the distance caught her eye. Drum was riding Jack toward his homestead, two dogs trotting beside him. He could clearly see Harriet and Ben, hugging tightly by the car.

43

Striding toward the café on Monday morning, Drum noticed Harriet at the front counter, chatting and laughing with Little Ben. He frowned. Wondered if they were becoming an item. He'd known Ben Evans since primary school. A good bloke, Harriet could do worse. But their easy friendship annoyed him. She looks so relaxed in his company. Mentally shaking his head, he smiled at them as he walked in.

'Harriet. Ben.'

'Drum. Your usual?' Harriet moved across to the coffee machine as he nodded.

Little Ben, coffee in hand turned to Drum. 'I was just telling Harri we're already getting enquiries for the bull sale. Quite a lot from interstate. It's going to be cracker year, I can feel it.'

Ben's easy-going tone and positive outlook always impressed Drum. 'I think you're right Ben. A bit of rain would be good, keep the fire danger at bay and kick the feed along, but everything seems to be picking up. We've had a few tough seasons, but a drop of rain and a good sale will start the new year off well.'

'Thanks Harriet.' Drum reached for the coffee she passed

over the counter, tapping his card with his free hand. He glanced at his watch. 'I'll catch you up later.'

Drum walked to the door with Ben. 'I've got a busy morning but will drop by the office later today, I need to catch up with your dad.'

'I'll let him know.' Ben walked toward his office and Drum hesitated for a moment at the downstairs door to the old bank; his Solicitor, Barlow, waiting for him upstairs. He glanced into the café. Harriet was serving an older couple, smiling as she spoke to them. Her face glowed with health, her smile genuine. He drew in a breath and shook his head as he opened the door. Bloody Harriet Russell. Always so bloody nice to everyone. Too bloody nice to bloody Ben Evans. He walked upstairs, wondering why he gave the woman so much thought.

Sitting in front of Barlow, a cup of tea in front of him, Drum shook his head.

'Repeat that please Douglas. She wants what?' Drum's head was spinning. Annabelle's lawyers had sent a settlement request.

'Annabelle is asking for the value of the Sydney apartment, in cash. Not the apartment itself.'

Drum took a deep breath, struggling to keep his anger in check. 'The apartment is worth almost as much as the farm. We've had it for years, my grandparents bought it in the fifties. It's worth a fortune.' He sat back, rubbed his hand across his face, his heart sinking. 'Even if we sold it, half would have to go to Fergus. There's no way I can raise that sort of cash.'

'This is a negotiation Drum. Annabelle's team has made a request. Now we counter-offer. Let's just think about it for a moment. My first question is, why does she want the cash and not the asset? We've already advised she can stay in the apartment for life, or until she remarries, with an allowance. More when she has Billie in the holidays.'

'Why does the bloody woman do anything Douglas?' Drum paced around the room. 'If I knew how her bloody mind worked, we'd probably still be married.' He stopped pacing. 'Or we would never have married.' He looked at his Solicitor. 'Can we ask Frances to come in? I'd like to know what she thinks about this.'

Barlow picked up the phone. 'Can you join us, Frances?'

With Frances sitting at the desk with them, teacup in hand, they went through the letter from Annabelle's lawyers again. Drum looked at Frances in expectation.

'Well. Reading between the lines and having known Annabelle for the better part of ten years, I think she's hiding something.' Frances reached for the document, reading it again, silently, while she thoughtfully sipped her tea.

She laid the document down and looked at her husband, then Drum. 'It's possible she's leaving. Leaving Sydney, maybe even Australia. I think she has another home lined up. A better home. And she wants the cash.' Frances turned toward Drum. 'Didn't Billie say her mother had been seeing someone. Does she know his name?'

'You're on to something Frances. Yes, I think you're right. Billie did say that. But she didn't give me his name. I don't really want to ask her, make her complicit in this...' he paused. 'This negotiation.' He turned to Barlow. 'And if she does have a lover or partner, does this make any difference?'

'It could. Yes, she is entitled to a settlement. But she hasn't worked on the property or been part of the business here. She was happy to stay in the Sydney home and take a generous allowance. I think we can make a smaller cash offer, and an allowance up until she remarries or re-partners. We can factor in the monies she has already received, not to mention the funds she's spent on jewellery, clothes, holidays, spa resorts and visits to her family in England. Without contributing at all. And her care of Billie in the last couple of years has been, well, questionable. You are Billie's primary carer now, and that's what the courts want to know.'

Leaning back, he looked from Drum to Frances. 'Drum, you have friends in Sydney. Friends who mix in the sort of circles Annabelle likes to move in. Make some enquiries. If she has re-partnered, we can offer a smaller settlement. One where you won't have to sell assets to raise the funds.' He smiled. 'Well, maybe a few bulls at the sale in the new year.'

Drum slapped his hand on his knee. 'You're right Douglas! She's kept Billie with her simply to keep the cash rolling in. But I'd say Annabelle has been developing a relationship, and now Billie is getting in the way of that. She's chasing as much cash as she can from me, in a settlement, before she goes public with her relationship.' He roughly ran a hand through his hair. 'How I ever fell for her ...'

Frances leaned forward. 'You were young Drum. Keen to start your own family. And no matter what, you have Billie. And she's priceless.'

'Yes, she is Frances. Priceless.' He looked at Barlow. 'I'll make some calls, see if I can find out the real story. And we need to speak to my accountant, see what we can realistically offer as a settlement. I won't be ungenerous.'

'Does Billie have a passport Drum?' Frances asked the question as she stood. Drum looked at her for a moment, then at Douglas, then back to Frances.

'She does Frances. We took her to England to visit Annabelle's family three years ago.' He paused. 'Do you think Annabelle will try to leave the country with Billie?' Drum frowned. Annabelle wouldn't want the responsibility, he was sure of it.

'Where is the passport? Do you have it, or does Annabelle?'

While Drum could see where Frances was heading, he didn't think Annabelle would take Billie without his permission.

'Actually. Annabelle would have it with her passport. It's certainly not with mine.'

'Taking her a is a long shot. But Drum, what if she does? For leverage?' Douglas walking around the desk. 'Cancel her passport Drum. Just to be sure.'

'Yes. All right. To be sure.' Drum agreed grimly, shaking Douglas by the hand. He waved goodbye to Frances and almost ran down the steps, letting out a frustrated breath when he opened the door to the street.

44

The days seemed to roll into each other as Harriet worked mornings at the café and afternoons at Evans Real Estate, spending some time on their marketing and the rest on her own business. She had hardly seen Drum, and Billie had been in the café twice with Melanie and Tiffany, said she was staying there while Drum was away on business. Harriet had hoped Drum might call on her if he needed help with Billie, but saw she was happy to be with Tiffany. Melanie, if a bit reserved, was a caring mother.

Driving into town on Saturday after a message from Rose inviting her to Barrington Homestead for a late lunch, Harriet slowed when she saw Drum on horseback, behind a small mob of yearlings, two cattle dogs weaving back and forth behind them. She came to a complete stop, waiting for him to get them to the side of the road. It was unusual that Billie was not with him.

Glancing over his shoulder, Drum lifted one hand in a wave of acknowledgement, then touched the brim of his hat as he turned the cattle into a paddock. Moving off slowly, Harriet smiled at him as she drove by. A quick look in her rear-view mirror showed Drum watching her drive away. A tingle of excitement fluttered in her belly. Shaking her head at herself, Harriet crested the small hill and Drum disappeared from view.

Dropping into the café, Harriet was pleased to get a quick hug from Cathy. 'Deb was in earlier, with Jamie's mum, Jill. She can't drive yet, but she looks great, and she had baby Warwick with her. He's a real little charmer.' Cathy's relief at Debbie's recovery was evident and her enthusiasm was infectious. Harriet had hoped she would see Deb herself, but had been reluctant to visit her so soon, she'd only been home from hospital a few days.

'Do you need me today, Cathy? Rose has asked me to a late lunch, but I can help here first.' Harriet looked around. The café wasn't busy, and Kristen gave her a wave from the coffee machine.

'No Harri. We didn't expect you in today and we've done really well. We had a bit of a rush when we opened, but it's just been steady since, so we're under control. Enjoy your day.'

Thanking her, Harriet turned to walk out when Cathy called her back. 'Oi, Harri. I've got some passionfruit cheesecake here, do you want to take it out to Rose's with you?'

'Cheesecake? Passionfruit? You betcha.' Harriet spun around grinning and followed Cathy through to the kitchen.

Ten minutes later she pulled up in front of Barrington Homestead. A grand old home. There were a couple of cars parked to one side that Harriet didn't recognise. She was suddenly grateful for the box containing the cheesecake. She'd thought it was just her and Rose today.

Rose walked down the steps, taking the cheesecake box from Harriet. 'So pleased you could make it Harri. 'You didn't have to bring anything.' She opened the box and had a quick peek. 'Oh well done. Passionfruit cheesecake. This won't go astray.'

'Cathy's idea. Who can say no to her cheesecake?' Harriet grinned happily as Rose laughed. 'Who indeed?'

Rose ushered Harriet through the front door to the main kitchen. There was Debbie, sitting up at the bench, the baby in her lap. 'Debbie! What a surprise! I didn't expect …' Harriet rushed over and hugged her gently before looking at the baby. She kept her head down for a moment, her pleasure at seeing Debbie looking so well, brought her emotions to the surface.

'And I think you know Jill and Melanie. Tiffany and Billie are down at the stables with Angus, feeding the horses.' Harriet nodded and smiled at both women.

'Take him please Jill, he gets quite heavy after a while.' Debbie waited while Jill scooped the baby up, settling him against her shoulder. Turning to Harriet, Debbie held out both hands. Harriet took them. Debbie was smiling, but her eyes were filled with tears.

'Dearest Harri. But for you I may have lost Warwick. May have lost myself too, for that matter. I don't know how to thank you …' Debbie was crying freely now, and Harriet felt tears coursing down her own cheeks, but shook her head murmuring, 'I only did what anyone would do, it was nothing, really.' Rose pushed a box of tissues closer to them before turning to distract young Charlie, who was now asking to be picked up.

Studying Debbie as she spoke, Harriet could see one side of her face seemed to droop slightly, but she otherwise looked well, if a little tired. 'My confidence in you stepping in, helping Cathy, dealing with the customers, took all thought of the café from my mind. And earlier, helping when I collapsed, staying on. Being there. Harriet, you've been a godsend. But more than that. A friend. You are a friend. And now I hear you're staying, you've bought the cottage…' Debbie took a tissue and blew her nose.

Rose patted her back gently. 'Harri knows Deb. I told you from the very start that Harri is our kind of person.' She looked pleased with herself. She took the baby from Jill and rocked him as she spoke. Charlie had wandered off with a biscuit in his hand.

Leaning forward, Harriet kissed Debbie on the cheek, holding her face close for a moment. 'You have a beautiful baby Deb.' They all started speaking at once, oohs and aahs and how gorgeous is baby Warwick.

Debbie looked proudly at her baby. 'Yeah. Good genes, he is pretty cute.'

'Sit here Harri.' Melanie patted the high kitchen stool beside her.

'Thank you.' Harriet slid on to the seat. 'You've had Billie with you for a few days?'

'Yes. Drum was away, Sydney, I think. He's catching up on cattle work today and picking her up tomorrow morning. We love having Billie. She's been great for Tiff. They sit together in class.' Melanie smiled happily.

'That may not last.' This from Jill. 'Miss Grayson told me yesterday that they talk 'all the time' and she may separate them. And apparently Billie has been helping two of the boys in class with their reading, but not always with their permission.' Harriet laughed to hear this. Billie was a wonderful reader and very grown up in some ways.

'Bless her. She's a very special girl.' Harriet shook her head, chuckling, picturing Billie reading to the boys in class.

'She is Harri. She adores you. Talks about you all the time.' Melanie smiled at Harriet, then reached over to take the baby from Rose.

'Give him to Harri, Mel. Can you help me get the lunch things out?' Rose set cutlery and plates on the kitchen bench, as Melanie went into the kitchen, pulling items out of the fridge. Debbie leaned across, intending to help set the table.

'Sit!' the other four women spoke as one and Debbie dutifully sat back in her chair.

Just as baby Warwick was handed to Harriet without ceremony, Rose took off after little Charlie down the hall. Harriet perched on her stool, baby Warwick carefully cuddled in the crook of her arm. Glancing at Debbie, who was laughing delightedly as Rose slithered to a halt on the polished floorboards, her offspring firmly in her grasp. Walking back to the kitchen, Charlie squawking and struggling to get down, Rose held something between her thumb and forefinger. As she drew closer Harriet would see it was a ring. Rose's engagement ring.

'I take it off to wash up, and the little blighter managed to snatch it off the sink.' Shaking her head, Rose put Charlie on his feet before sliding the ring on to her finger. Turning to her son she said 'No!' quite firmly. He looked at her for a moment before wandering off to a mat piled high with wooden blocks. 'It's not the first time. He's taken to dropping things into the toilet. My ring. My phone. His father's wallet. Our son has expensive taste.' Rose sighed dramatically, glanced over at Charlie, then back at the other women.

'Angus and the girls should be back in shortly. He'll take Charlie for a little while so we can chat.' As she spoke, Angus strolled through from the laundry. Charlie ran to him on his chubby little legs and was hoisted high in the air, giggling, before Angus tucked him under his arm like a football.

'Hello ladies. My helpers are washing their hands and will be in directly. There was an incident with a poddy calf and some milk.' They could hear Billie and Tiffany laughing from the laundry. 'I've come to take my son out for a while.' He glanced from Rose to Charlie and back again. 'Should I ask?'

'Just take him Angus. Wear him out. Please.' Rose gave him such a look of pleading that the others laughed loudly.

'Your wish is my command, my lady.' Angus winked at the group before leaving the room, Charlie's giggles floating back to them.

'Oh Debbie. Would a girl have been easier? Charlie wears me out. Not just physically. My patience too.' Rose sighed and plonked herself down beside Debbie before looking across at Harriet, Mel and Jill. 'And it's a dry gig today. You're all driving, and Debbie is breastfeeding.'

'Umm, that's true. But you can have a drink, Rosc.' Debbie urged.

'No. No, no, no. *He* senses my weakness.' Rose shook her head. 'When I'm mellow and relaxed after a glass of wine, *he* does something. Some mischief.' She emphasised the *He*.

'Seriously Rose, you are starting to sound like you think your son is possessed.' Debbie said laughing.

Rose leaned in and automatically the others leaned toward her. In a loud stage whisper she added, 'I'm not sure *he* isn't. Possessed that is. *He* is **very** mischievous.'

Harriet replied, also in a stage whisper. 'Open some wine Rose, we can have one glass …'

Holding baby Warwick, sleeping quietly in her arms, Harriet watched as Rose set down glasses filling them with wine. She poured apple juice into a wine glass for Debbie. A sense of belonging hit her. She was relaxed with these women. She was real. Raw. Herself. How quickly her barriers had come down with them. The affection she felt was genuine. Feeling teary again, she leaned down, gave baby Warwick a kiss on the top of his head. A warm flush of happiness washed over her.

Tiffany and Billie skipped into the room. Billie ran straight to Harriet. 'Hi Harri. Baby Warwick is very cute, isn't he? I've had lots of cuddles this week.'

'But he's not as much fun as the puppy, is he?' Tiffany took Billie by the hand. 'Let's make a farm with Charlie's blocks.'

'Okay.' Billie turned and trotted into the living room after Tiffany.

Jill smiled. 'Those two. Inseparable. And good for each other. Billie wants to teach Tiffany to ride, so I think they're hatching a plan for her to go to Drum's next weekend.'

Melanie looked concerned. 'I don't know. About Drum having them by himself. I know he's great with Billie. But both of them. Could be a bit much.'

'Don't worry Mel. Harri's right there, a few hundred metres away. He can call on her if he needs anything. Right Harri?' Rose looked at Harriet, eyebrows raised, smiling broadly.

'Sure Melanie. I'll be right there. They'll be fine.' Hesitating for a moment, but sensing an opportunity, she added 'so what will you do Melanie, with a night off?'

'Yes Melanie. What will you do?' Debbie added, grinning like a co-conspirator.

'What? Why? I don't know. Get a few jobs done around the house.' Melanie took a sip of wine.

'What sort of jobs?' Jill looked over the top of her wine glass. Harriet could sense something was going on and nodded encouragingly to Melanie.

'Well. I was going to put some shelves and drawers into Tiff's wardrobe. It's all just hanging space and could be better organised.'

'Really? You must be a better handyman than me.' Harriet could see the others agreeing.

'Yes. No. I mean, Little Ben said he'd help me. He's picked up all the shelving already. It's just easier to do without Tiff trying to help.'

'Ben does a lot of jobs around the house for you, doesn't he?' Rose set the quiche and salad on the centre of the bench, nodding for them to help themselves.

'He does. He's a good friend. I've known him since I was at school.' Melanie sounded defensive. She looked at Harriet. 'Anyway, I think Ben's got a thing for you Harri. Drum said something to Angus the other day at the clinic, that he saw you and Ben, um, together.' She tried to brighten her voice, but Harriet detected a hint of disappointment. Hmmm, so she's more aware of Ben than she lets on.

'No. Drum's got it wrong. Ben has become a mate. He's great. But there's no connection between us. Romantic, I mean.' Harriet took a sip of her wine. 'He dropped by with a house-warming present last Saturday. Actually, he talked about you and Tiffany. A lot.'

Melanie blushed from her head to her hair and made an 'O' with her mouth. 'But he's never, you know. He's never. Tried anything. We've always been. Platonic.' Her words were coming out in short-hand, confusion and something else on her face. Hope?

Jill put her arm around Melanie's shoulders. 'Ben knows what you've been through Mel. You and Tiff. He respects you. Doesn't want to scare you. Doesn't want to hurt you.'

Rose leaned in. 'I think he doesn't want to make a mistake and lose what he has with you. Your friendship and trust. Mel, I remember he liked you when we were finishing school, but you were keen on Greg, and well, he was Greg's mate. He wouldn't after that. You know. Mates honour and all that. I wonder if he's burned for you all these years.'

'And what about you Mel? How do you see Ben?' Debbie questioned her gently. Melanie glanced toward the living area where the girls were playing.

'He's Ben. I trust him. He's a gentleman. He loves Tiffany, and he's a great role model. I'm so happy to have him around her. I just never thought.' She stopped, drew a breath. 'Never thought he saw me like that. I even wondered if he was, you know ...'

Rose laughed. 'Really? Gay? Not Ben. I'm sure he's all red-blooded bloke under that amiable exterior. But Mel, if you like him, you know, fancy him, you're going to have to let him know. I think he's too afraid of hurting you to make the first move.'

Melanie looked at each of them, her hand over her mouth, her face flushed, her eyes shining. 'Really? Truly? This isn't a joke?'

Jill smiled, sadly. 'We would never do that to you Melanie. You've been through enough.'

'So, it's up to you girlfriend.' Debbie raised her glass to Melanie. 'If you have feelings for the big man, you need to let him know. And next Saturday night is your chance. Tiff will be at Drum's with Billie. And Harri. Let him help you fit the closet. Offer him a beer. Dinner.'

'Oh yes. Dinner. The man does like his food!' This was from Harriet, smiling encouragement.

Melanie looked down at her glass, then set it firmly on the bench, looking at her friends. 'I'm doing it. I've always cared for Ben, even loved him, I just never thought…' A tear escaped down her cheek. 'I never thought I was good enough for him!' She sobbed the last words out and all the women, with shakes of their heads, said, 'No. that's not true.'

Jill held Melanie's hand for a moment. 'It was our son that hurt you. I'll never forgive him for that. It's not how we raised our boys. And Melanie, we love you and Tiff, nothing would make us happier. Ben Evans is the real deal. He's a gentle giant, but I suspect his feelings run deep.'

Melanie nodded, too overcome to speak. Rose stepped in.

'Lunch girls. Serve yourselves. We have cheesecake for dessert.' Rose nudged Melanie with her shoulder. 'It's the real deal Mel. You and Tiff. You've started to heal, you're ready for this. You deserve it. And he deserves you. And Tiff. I can see he loves that little girl to bits. Let him in Melanie, he's a good man.'

Melanie nodded wordlessly, then looked at Harriet, saying quietly, 'And you Harri? You're sure there's nothing between you?'

'Oh, we have something. Friendship. Honesty. A working

relationship. But no romantic feelings Mel. I couldn't be happier.' She thought about her conversation with Ben the previous week. His feelings for Melanie and Tiffany ran deep, it made her happy to think of them together.

Brightening, Melanie wiped her tears. 'Thank you. All of you. This lunch was meant to be for Debbie and baby Warwick.'

Harriet sat back, enjoying the fun, banter and support of these women, her friends. 'It is Mel. It is for Deb. Cheers.'

Rose raised her glass. 'Here's to you Deb. And the little bloke. And friendship.' They all smiled at each other, taking a sip of their drinks. 'Oh hell, Deb you haven't thought this through.' Rose looked at Debbie, her mouth a large 'O' shape.

Sensing something, Debbie giggled. 'What Rose. Out with it.' The others looked on, waiting for the punch line.

'Warwick. Your beautiful baby. You know he'll get Wazza. By the time he starts school he'll be Wazza.' Rose tried to look serious, but Debbie was having none of it.

'And I'm Deb, and we have Harri, Drum, Billie and Tiff and Mel. And Big Ben and Little Ben. It's what we do here. Warwick will be called Wazza. They'll put it on the back of his footy jersey in High School.' She narrowed her eyes at Rose. 'You're the odd one out. We've never shortened Rose. Or Angus for the matter.'

'My parents thought it through. Just saying.' Rose took a sip of her wine, looking over the rim at Harriet, a small smile playing around the corners of her mouth.

Harriet laughed, delighted by the warmth and fun between these women, her new friends. Who had been friends themselves since they were young. The baby woke, opened his mouth and let out a little cry. Debbie reached for him, as they all began their lunch, chatting comfortably together.

45

*H*ome from lunch and a very special afternoon, Harriet drove to the swimming spot. While she had the creek at her back door, it wasn't really deep enough for a swim. Parking in the usual place she glanced up towards Laura's property, wondering if she would see her and come down too. Harriet had almost called her, but Laura had mentioned the day before it was calving time and was constantly checking her stock.

After a refreshing swim, she sat on the rocks in the middle of the river with the water cascading around her. Leaning back, resting on her elbows, she tipped her head back letting her hair trail in the water. Eyes closed, Harriet blocked out all sounds, just focussing on the water, the sensation of it washing over her lower body.

'Thought I'd find you here.'

Sitting up quickly, heart pounding, Harriet's wet hair flipped over her face. Pushing it aside she saw Drum, chest bare, waist-deep just a metre away.

'You startled me!'

'I can see that. Sorry.'

He didn't look sorry. In fact, he was looking at her, the whole length of her. Flushed, and a little annoyed, she moved quickly off the rocks and let the river envelop her, up to her chest. Her pulse raced. She felt like she'd been caught out.

He raised his eyes to her face, a query in them. Feeling exposed, Harriet didn't want to talk to him about her injuries. She realised she felt okay telling people now, but she'd prefer to be fully clothed during the telling.

Confused for a moment, she splashed him. He raised his eyebrows higher and splashed her back. They flicked each other a couple of times, moving closer during the water play. Suddenly, she was right in front of him, his broad muscled chest at eye height. She stared. Chest, shoulders, arms. Suntanned and strong, she wanted to reach out and touch him.

Glancing up, she looked into his eyes. They had darkened. Anger? Annoyance? Harriet was embarrassed, started to move away, toward the riverbank and her towel and clothes.

'Harri.' She looked at him again. His voice had taken on a deeper, gravelly tone. Just saying her name conveyed something new and surprising to her. A new emotion. Passion? Lust? She hesitated, held his gaze. Her eyes moved over his face, stopping at his mouth. How would his lips feel on hers? She was in front of him. Neither spoke. He was looking at her lips now. She wanted to reach up, pull his head down, feel his mouth on hers.

'Harri.' His voice drew her closer. He moved toward her, pulled her to him. She hesitated for a moment, then reached up, touched his face, trailed her fingers across his mouth. Groaning, he bent his head, his lips touched hers. Gently. Too gently. Without warning she was on fire. Feeling his arms around her fanned the flame. She thought she'd never feel this way again. Alive. Hot. Sexy as hell.

She opened her lips, sucking his bottom lip into her mouth, touching it with her tongue. He held her against him, the water rushing around them while all else stood still. He withdrew his mouth for a moment, looking into her eyes. That look. So damn sexy. Hungry. His hunger for her like a beacon. She looked back. Her gaze was bold. Holding her against him he lowered his head and kissed her thoroughly, taking possession of her mouth. She felt small in his arms, yet strong. One arm around her back, his other hand came up to hold the back of her head. His mouth trailed along her jawbone, nibbling as he went, before kissing her neck and collarbone. His head dipped lower.

Eyes closed, she threw her head back, giving up to the sensation of his mouth against her tender skin. She wrapped an arm around his back, tugging him closer. Drum paused, lifted his mouth from hers and she opened her eyes, breathing hard. He was frowning. Harriet breathed out in a rush. He let her go and stepped away and she almost sank below the water, before gathering herself, her feet firm on the riverbed. She tried to read the emotions that flitted across his face as he glanced away, then back at her. The expression in his eyes had changed from lust to something else. Anger?

'What are you playing at Harriet? What sort of woman are you?' He glowered at her.

Her own anger rose quickly. How dare he! What the hell was this about? 'What do you mean by that? What *sort* of woman am I? **You** kissed me!'

'I did!' he growled the words. 'You're as sexy as hell. But I don't share Harriet. With anyone.' He moved away to the deeper water.

'What the fuck? Are you kidding me?' She was shouting. Totally pissed off now. 'What's wrong with you?'

He spun around. 'Ben is a mate. I've seen you with him. That's fine. He's a good bloke. So, stick with that. Don't put it out to anyone else. I won't betray a mate. All right!'

She wanted to slap him. His words cut her deeply. Her voice

was pure ice when she spoke. 'What did you see Drum? Friends laughing together. Having a chat. Sharing a hug? Really? How old are you?' She started toward the riverbank, intending to get out. She didn't have to explain herself to anyone. Certainly not to Drummond Murray.

'You looked pretty cosy, from where I stood.' He was quieter now, doubt creeping into his voice. He folded his arms across his chest.

'Get your facts straight before you start accusing people. Accusing me. Of what? Being a slut? Putting out all over town?' She stopped, sadness replacing her anger. She shook her head and waded toward the bank.

'No! Wait Harriet. Harri. Please.' His tone was urgent. She turned. He looked confused, his eyes now questioning hers.

'What is you want Drum?'

He spoke quietly, walking toward her in the water. 'I'm sorry. I'm asking Harri. Are you involved with Ben? I need to know.'

'Why do you need to know?'

His eyes darkened. 'Just tell me Harri. Be honest!'

Her anger reignited. 'I'm always honest, Drum!' She took a step toward him. 'No. I'm not involved with Ben. But we are friends. Good friends. And I wouldn't change that for anything. Or anyone.'

He stood silently, looking at her, his eyes dark, but no longer angry. She could feel herself leaning toward him again. This man. Damn his arrogance!

'Good.' He reached for her. She began to turn away, didn't want to make it easy for him, but his mouth came down on hers. Gently this time. She felt herself melting into him. Willed herself to pull away. Walk away. 'Harriet.' His voice was raspy, full of need. She leaned into him, her head against his shoulder, breathing hard, not quite ready to form words. He wanted her. For himself. A buzz of happiness left her shaking.

'Harri.' He looked over her head, then down into her eyes. 'I'm sorry. I had to know. The thought of you with someone else …' He shook his head, then smiled at her, warmth back in his voice. 'We should talk, I think, before we, uh, go any further.'

More in control, Harriet spoke quietly. 'Well. Now you know Drum. Don't ever question me like that again. You want to talk? Of course. Yes. Talk.' Standing on her toes, she reached up, kissed his neck then breathing against his throat, she murmured, 'When would you like to do this, uh, talking, Drum?'

He chuckled, then laughed loudly. 'Your pal, my daughter Billie, is staying at Tiffany's until tomorrow. You know, new puppy and all.'

'Ah! Yes. The puppy.' Harriet moved out of his grasp. Lowered her body completely under the water, coming back up quickly, pushing her wet hair back from her face. 'I owe you a meal. Dinner at my place tonight? I'll cook for you.' She felt powerful. Strong and in control. And damn the man could kiss. Surprised at the strength of her own reaction she wondered what else he could do.

'Think about it for a moment Harri. Yes, I'd love to come over for dinner. Will come over for dinner. But think about this. I'm married, for the moment and we are each other's closest neighbours. We've barely become friends. Don't get me wrong, I want this. Want you. But maybe we should, ah, cool our jets? I can, you know. I can come for dinner, we can talk. Get to know each other.'

He was right. Of course, he was right. Why jeopardise their fragile friendship, her developing relationship with Billie? And they are neighbours. Rushing in would be foolish. Of course, it would.

'If that's what you want Drum. Yes.' Moving toward the riverbank, she threw a sexy look over her shoulder. 'Dinner at seven. See you then.'

Drum moved quickly, right behind her before she reached dry land. His large hand on her shoulder, he turned her. Covering his mouth with hers he kissed her deeply. Half turned in his arms, she almost fell, but he held her steady, deepening the kiss as she returned it with abandon.

Lifting his head he kissed her lightly on the nose, then the top of her head. 'Oh yeah. I'll come to dinner tonight and we'll *talk*.'

Laughing, they almost fell on to the grassy bank together. Drum handed her a towel, before vigorously drying himself. Heart racing, Harriet tried to act nonchalant as she wrapped her towel around herself, scooped up her clothes and almost ran to her car. His sexy chuckles echoing in her ears.

46

Back in the cottage Harriet rushed to the kitchen. What to cook? Rummaging around, she decided to keep it simple. Teriyaki chicken and rice. She had two bottles of Tyrrells Semillon in the fridge. That would go nicely with Asian food. She spent a few minutes cutting the chicken, making the marinade and put it together in a covered glass dish in the fridge.

Taking a breath, she looked around the cottage again. It felt homely, but stylish. Her furniture suited the little house and her art created interesting pops of colour on the walls. Having the paintings up, and books on the bookshelves, somehow stamped her personality on the place.

Glancing at her watch, it was already after six. Drum would be here in less than an hour. A quick tidy up and she was standing in the bathroom, looking at herself in the full-length mirror. Trying to be objective, she touched the scars on her lower abdomen gently. They had lost the red, angry look, but remained pink and puckered. A longer, neater scar led from the original knife entry wound up to just under her navel. The surgeons had operated again, after peritonitis set in from the original wound and subsequent surgery. She drew in her breath. The counsellor at the hospital advised she needed to learn to love her scars, as a sign of her survival. Her triumph over near death. It sounded logical, but she found it difficult to embrace. She'd lost so much. Not her life of course. But almost certainly the ability to create a life.

Shaking her head, she stepped into the shower, letting the water run over her. What had she been told about having children? That she couldn't? Or shouldn't? The internal scarring, and damage to her fallopian tube on the right side diminished her chances of pregnancy. But more than that, her ability to carry to full term, if she was able to fall pregnant, was unlikely. Better to delete the option of pregnancy and childbirth altogether, she'd been told. Consider other options when the time came. She'd left Sydney, believing she would remain single. Focus on her business, her career.

Washing her hair, she thought about Drum. Was he looking for a relationship? Or a lover? He was still married, needed to get through the financial maze a marriage breakdown caused. She'd been though the settlement part herself. But there had been no children involved, or extensive property. Their house and business had been relatively easy to untangle and reach agreement. Drum's situation, with his generational property, was more complicated. And he had Billie to think of. Clearly, he was now her primary carer. He may be looking for a lover. Someone discreet, trustworthy. Harriet admitted to herself it was unlikely he would marry again and further risk the property. So, a lover then? Could they be friends too? She admitted her physical reaction to him was strong. But she liked him too. Really liked him.

'Face it Harri, Drum sets you on fire.' Saying it aloud somehow cemented her thought process. Dinner with Drum tonight, and if they picked up where they left off at the river this afternoon, she'd go with it. Enjoy it. Biting her lower lip, she grinned wickedly at her own image in the mirror. The pash sesh with Drum in the river had lit a flame, and Harriet knew it wouldn't need much oxygen to turn into a fireball. Glancing down at her scars, she frowned. She would tell him, over dinner, about the stabbing. Prepare him. Give him a chance to re-think it too.

Ten minutes to seven, Harriet dressed in matching, lacy underwear. Sheer. Underwear she hadn't worn since before the accident. Before her life changed. Over the top she pulled on a knee length shift, loose and floaty, in palest blue. Hair loose, a touch of mascara and lip gloss, and she was ready. Pushing her feet, now quite tanned, into flat sandals she drew her breath in when she heard a quiet rap on the front door.

*D*rum stood on the front porch, frowning. A couple of the veranda floorboards were more than a little bit spongy. He'd come over tomorrow and repair them. He paced along the veranda, roughly measuring the length of the boards with his stride. Two boards, maybe three. He was sure he had at least a half dozen of the right length and width stored in the tractor shed.

The front door opened, a pool of light spilling out. Although not fully dark, evening was swiftly approaching.

Wordlessly he stepped across the threshold, leant down and brushed his lips lightly over Harriet's. She smelt so good. Chanel, he thought, happy it wasn't a fragrance Annabelle favoured.

Closing the door behind him, she leaned her back against it, looking up at him.

'Drum.' The way she said his name, softly, full of promise, stopped him in his tracks. He wanted to take her in his arms so badly. But he held himself slightly straighter. He also wanted to talk to her, get to know her. Let her know he liked her for more than this sizzling connection he'd felt at the river. He knew she felt it too. She'd let her guard down. But he wanted to know her too. Her story. Needed to know.

'Harri.' He raked his eyes over her. She looked beautiful. Luminous. The dress she was wearing was light, floating. He could sense her curves beneath it. Returning his gaze to her face, he looked into her eyes. She breathed out quickly. Had she been holding her breath? He set the bottle of wine he was holding on the hall stand and stepping toward her he gathered her in his arms. She melted into him. He kissed the top of her head, holding her close for a moment.

Her heart was racing. Was she nervous? Taking a half step back, his hands still on her shoulders, he looked down at her.

'Let's have some wine, talk a little. I'd like to get to know you. We don't have to rush this. I don't want to rush this.' She nodded. Turning, he took her hand in his, picked up the bottle with the other hand and led her through to the living areas.

'I hope you like Asian food Drum. Teriyaki chicken?' Harriet moved past him, into the kitchen. Ignoring the wine he deposited on the bench, she opened the fridge and drew out one of hers. She handed him the bottle to open and placed two glasses on the bench.

He watched her move around the kitchen. She was comfortable. 'I eat everything Harri. Love Asian food. I'm not good at cooking it though.'

Glancing into the living area, the vivid paintings on the wall caught his attention. 'You've hung your art. These are stunning. May I take a closer look?'

She beamed at him and walked out to the dining area. 'The rice needs a few minutes, I'll show you around.' Leading him from painting to painting, he watched her face as she explained the provenance of each piece. Where it came from, its meaning to her. She was lit from inside, so expressive. Animated and even more gorgeous if that was possible. Her love of her art, and enthusiastic telling of the stories captivated him. He followed her from piece to piece, asking questions, chuckling at some of her answers.

He was about to move back into the hall, he had noticed a number of watercolours as he walked through earlier. Knowing now that each piece had meaning for her, he'd love to see them more closely.

Smiling up at him, Harriet stepped into the hallway, before turning suddenly and pushing past him, almost running back to the kitchen. 'The rice!' Following her, he saw the saucepan bubbling over. Turning the heat off first, she grabbed a potholder and lifted the saucepan to one side, muttering under her breath.

'Um … need a hand?' Not sure if she was going to be angry at herself, or take it in her stride, he waited, leaning against the kitchen bench, one eyebrow cocked. With her back to him, she stirred the rice a bit, muttering to herself again. He thought she said 'who can't cook bloody rice. Bloody first year home economics.'

Sauntering to the fridge, he reached in for the wine, intending to top up their glasses. Glancing back, he saw the heat was back on, although less flame this time. Harriet turned to him, potholder in one hand, tea towel over her shoulder and her empty wine glass in the other hand, extended to him, both eyebrows raised.

He laughed out loud, delighted that she chuckled with him. Peering toward the offending saucepan, he asked, 'can it be saved?'

Harriet snorted, mid sip of wine, spluttering a little. Wiping her mouth with the back of her hand, exaggerating the action, she replied, drily. 'It can. Five minutes on low and I'll start the teriyaki. Not enough time for a guided tour of the paintings in the hallway, but more than enough to set the table.'

'Right. I'll do that. Tell me where everything is.' He rallied, liking her attitude to the cooking hiccup. No dramatics and a dry sense of humour. Annabelle slipped into his thoughts. She had rarely cooked, but something like this would have sent her into a rage, crying and angry, and would have ended with her throwing everything in the sink and sulking in her room, leaving him to clean up the mess. He heard Laura's words in his head. 'Chalk and cheese Drum. Chalk and cheese.'

Five minutes was all it took. Fragrant, light teriyaki chicken, on a bed of rice was in front of them in record time. Harriet handed him the second bottle of wine. He wanted to ask where she grew up, went to school. He assumed Sydney and was keen to hear the details. The way she spoke and dressed he thought she was a north shore girl. Classy. Well-educated.

But Harriet got her questions in first. Asking him about his family, their history in the region. He found himself sharing his great grand-father's story, her eyes fixed on him, nodding for him to continue after a sip of wine or mouthful of chicken. Somehow, they got through the whole meal, and second bottle of wine, and were still discussing his family. His brother Fergus, their other property in Armidale.

Leaning back, his plate empty, he lifted his glass to his lips, draining the last mouthful. 'Enough about me Harriet. What about you? What's your story?'

Getting up, she picked up their plates and started toward the kitchen, saying over her shoulder. 'Not much to tell. I'll just put these in the sink and then we can sit on the back veranda and chat. We can open your bottle of wine if you like, or maybe a glass of tawny port? The port is in the dining room dresser.'

Feeling relaxed by the wine and the effortless conversation, he opened the cabinet, lifting out the nearest bottle of tawny port. There were several. Good ones too. The woman had taste. All class but no artificial airs and graces. He was liking her more and more. A silver tray with four small port glasses sat on top of the dresser. He poured a nip in two glasses, carrying them back to the kitchen.

Harriet walked toward him, tendrils of thick honey hair curling around her face. The night was warm. She took the glass he offered, sipped, then tossed the rest back in one gulp. She set the glass firmly on the counter-top, moving closer to him. He threw back the port and almost slammed his glass down next to hers. As one they moved together. She walked into the circle of his arms, lifting her face to be kissed. He did. Thoroughly. Wordlessly. All thought of more conversation left his mind, as his blood quickened.

Taking his hand, she led him down the darkened hall to her room. Moonlight from the partly open curtains dappled across the bed. Holding her tightly, he kissed her again, tasting the port on her tongue, nibling her bottom lip before sucking it into his mouth. She gasped, her arms around his waist, nails digging into his back. He lowered her gently to the bed, lying beside her, one leg thrown across hers, holding her face in his hands.

'Harri? Really? We can slow down. Fool around a little.' He was rock hard and wanted her. Badly. But he also sensed a vulnerability about her, despite her show of sexy confidence. He could stop. Untangling himself, he lay on his side, gently stroking her face, her hair.

She lowered her eyes for a moment, then looked back at him. 'I have scars. Horrible scars. I'm afraid… afraid when you see them, you'll change your mind.'

Drum didn't know what she was going to say but telling him she had scars wasn't one of them. He frowned momentarily. 'It's okay Harri. Tell me about your scars. What happened to you?' He continued stroking her hair for a moment, then put his hand over hers. Bringing it to his lips. He turned her hand over and kissed her palm, gently. Her vulnerability was real. He could wait. Wait for her to tell him about it.

She took a deep breath. 'I was stabbed, in Sydney. On the train. Getting on the train. It was a bag snatch gone wrong. My own fault. I tried to grab it back, my bag. Didn't realise he stabbed me to begin with. It all happened so quickly.' She held his hand, lowering it to her waist, then gently moved it lower, almost over her hip. He felt a small bump. Barely there, through her dress and underwear. Still holding his hand, Harriet moved it away from her wound.

'When did this happen Harri?' he was gentle, he could see tears in her eyes. The memories were painful. Perhaps her wound was too. He recalled the first time he met her, when she hit the kangaroo. How slowly she got out of her car. She must have been still healing then. And other times, at the river, when she tried to cover up. He thought she was modest, or body sensitive. He had no idea she had been through such trauma.

'Almost a year ago. But there were additional surgeries. Infection, a drain bag.' She shuddered, and he lowered his head, kissing her cheek gently, then brushing her lips with his. 'I'm not a victim.' She said this with more conviction. 'I made a poor decision. Trying to pull my bag back from him. One really bad decision, which changed my life.'

He wasn't sure how it had changed her life. He waited. 'My husband… ex-husband now. He turned from me, said the scars are ugly. That hurt at first. But now, well, we weren't doing that well at the time. I knew it, just wouldn't admit it. He wasn't faithful. I'm … I'm trying to see this as the catalyst to move on. To have a better life, even if it is on my own.' She looked at him for a moment. 'I want you to see me. The scars. See my body. No one has. Not like this. I need to know….' She was crying now, and he kissed her gently. 'I need to know if it matters. I feel so sexy with you. This afternoon, at the river, I almost forgot. But you need to know, I wanted to warn you.'

4 8

Harriet's heart was thumping. Drum was gentle, caring, but she hadn't missed the flicker of surprise in his eyes when she told him, and again when she let his hand move across her wound. And that was with her clothes on.

'Emotional scars are far worse than physical ones Harri. Trust me. Relax, you're beautiful. Inside and out.' He looked up at her. A tear slid down her cheek when he added, 'stop me if you're uncomfortable. Stop me anytime.'

Pulling his head back down to hers she focussed on the kiss. Deep, sexy. The fire he'd lit down at the river burned more fiercely. She pulled him over her, tugging his shirt up. He sat back on his haunches, pulling it over his head in one swift movement, tossing it to one side. Leaning down he kissed her mouth, her cheek, nibbled his way to her collarbone where he sucked on the delicate skin there. She arched her back, allowing him to drag her dress higher, his hand sliding up underneath, to her ribs. Higher. Cupping her breasts. She wanted him. Drum. It had to be him. She raised herself slightly, enough for him to pull the dress all the way off. It joined his shirt on the floor.

Drum rolled off her, leaving her bereft for a moment. He tugged the curtains further open, letting more moonlight in. He returned to the bed, his erection straining against his jeans. Lying beside her on his side he trailed his hand down her body. She knew her sheer underwear didn't hide much and gasped when he bent his head to her breasts, first one then the other. He reached beneath her, deftly unclipping her bra with one hand, before removing it. Reaching down, he touched the top of her undies. She raised her bottom off the bed, allowing him to pull them all the way down.

Now he could see her, all of her. Completely naked, moonlight streaming in. She watched his face. Needed to see his reaction to her body. The scars completely exposed. He kissed his way down her torso, flicked his tongue around her belly button, then stopped at her hips. He raised his head and looked into her eyes. She held her breath as he gazed at her body, ran his fingers over her wound, then lower. She gasped when he bent his head to her scar and tenderly kissed the length of it. Kissed all around it, before moving back up her body.

'Harriet. You're lovely. All of you. The scars are a part of you, of your story. You wouldn't be here without them, wouldn't have come looking for a place to start over.' He kissed her gently. 'I'm keen on your scars. Very keen. They brought you to me. Don't hate them Harri, thank them.' Surprised and touched by his words, she didn't respond for a moment. He moved back down her body, ran his tongue across her lower abdomen, murmuring, 'thank you little scar, and you, and you.' Harriet giggled, then gasped as his kisses headed further south.

He raised himself over her, met her eyes. 'I don't want to stop, but I will if you're not sure.' She held his gaze for a moment, then reached between them, touching his erection through his jeans, before dragging his zip down, releasing the length of him into her hand. He returned his attention to her mouth, kissed her deeply, then stood and removed his jeans. She raised her eyebrows. No underwear. The man had come to her house for dinner with no underwear. So damn sexy. He covered her body with his and she gave herself up to the heat.

4 9

The week flew by, Harriet caught up with Drum and Billie at the river on two very warm afternoons. Drum touched her surreptitiously in the water when Billie was practising her swimming stroke. They had spoken, on Sunday morning about how they might manage things with Billie around. Drum told Harriet he had been to Sydney to check some information about Annabelle, as he was in negotiations to settle their divorce.

Drum spoke quietly, while keeping an eye on Billie as she swam. 'We have more information now. About Annabelle. The divorce. It's good news for me. But maybe not for Billie. Not only is she seeing an international businessman, quite a bit older than herself, but if my source is correct, she's pregnant and keen to marry him soon. He has a large home in Sydney's eastern suburbs and another in London. Word is, they plan to marry as soon as our divorce is finalised and return to London.' He glanced over at Billie.

'Her lawyers advised she would seek custody of Billie and take her to London with them unless I increase my settlement offer. But it was a bluff. Barlow countered that we would draw out the settlement and divorce, with the likely result that her baby, their baby, would be born before they can marry. We offered a reasonable settlement with a quick outcome, more if she relinquished any custodial rights to Billie.' He looked at his daughter, who had climbed out on to the far bank and was preparing to jump back in, shouting for them to watch her. They did, clapping when she surfaced and swam back to the bank to do it again.

'The speed with which she agreed to give up Billie was breathtaking.' Drum looked at Harriet, they were sitting side by side on the rocks in the middle of the river, the water washing over them. 'But it's sad for Billie that she will have little or no contact with her mother. I can send her for a stay in the holidays when she's older, but I fear Annabelle, and maybe her husband, may not care to encourage that.'

'Oh Drum.' Harriet leaned against him for a moment. 'She has you, this community, so many people who care for her. Truly care for her. She won't miss out. Maybe she won't have Annabelle, but she can call and zoom with her. What you're offering her here. This life. This place. It's better Drum. She'll have a good life.' She gazed at Billie as she waved and jumped back into the water. A lump rose in her throat. In her mind she added, 'And me. Billie has me and I love her so much already.'

Billie joined them on the rock. 'Did you see me Daddy? Did you see me Harri? I jumped right in on the deep side. Way over my head.'

Drum pulled her close for a moment. 'We did see you, Billie. Your swimming is really improving.' Harriet nodded too. 'It's good you swim so well Billie.'

'And Tiffany is coming to stay on Saturday night. It's a sleepover. Daddy said we can sleep in the big bed in the guest room together. And I'm going to give her a riding lesson, on Chippy.

Daddy says I can ride another horse, a little mare called Lady. He's been riding her himself for ages to make sure she's quiet enough for me.' Billie was squirming with excitement and Harriet felt a glow of happiness at her enthusiasm.

'May I come and watch the riding lesson?' Harriet nudged Drum with her foot.

'Oh yes Harri. We can get another horse ready, and you can have a riding lesson too.' Billie pulled at her father's arm. 'We can, can't we Daddy. We can get another horse in and teach Harri to ride. Oh, I can't wait! Then Harri can come with us to check the cattle sometimes Daddy!'

Drum looked at Harriet. 'Would you like that, Harri? A riding lesson with Billie and Tiffany?' He grinned at her. 'And come with us to check the heifers sometimes?'

Laughing on the inside, Harriet nibbled her bottom lip. 'Yes. Okay. I'd really like that.'

'It's okay Harri, you don't have to be scared. We'll look after you, won't we Daddy?'

Drum looked at his daughter's happy face, then at Harriet. Quietly, he said, 'There's nothing I'd like better.'

Saturday dawned, very warm but with a chance of rain in the afternoon. Harriet was sitting on the front veranda, drinking an early morning cup of tea when she saw Drum drive out with Billie in the back seat. Going to pick up Tiffany, no doubt. Drum raised his hand in a wave, while Billie wound her window down, her little hand waving madly as they went by.

Half an hour later they were back, Tiffany in the car too. Harriet saw them from her bedroom as she pulled on jeans and boots. She knew the plan was to have a riding lesson in the morning before possible rain. She was keen to join them, not have a riding lesson herself, but to watch Billie, and Drum, in action.

Strolling toward the stables and yards, past the homestead and tennis court, she stopped and looked to the west. Clouds were gathering in the distance, a bit high and could still be blown off course, but she crossed her fingers for some drenching rain later in the day or overnight.

The girls ran to her when she arrived. Billie wrapped her arms around Harriet's waist and raised her face for a kiss. Harriet planted a kiss on her nose, while Tiffany grinned, almost bouncing on the spot, while she explained she was going to learn to ride.

'Hey Harri!' Drum called a greeting as he led Chippy and Lady into the round yard together and tied them to the fence rail. He called the girls over, watching and nodding as Billie explained to Tiffany how she greeted each horse with a pat, then brushed them down. Drum produced two small apples and stood back as the girls fed their horses.

He sauntered over to Harriet. 'If you're keen, you can try either horse once the girls are done. I have several others,' he jerked his head toward a nearby paddock, 'but most of them haven't been ridden much lately. Could be a bit fresh for you to begin with.'

Harriet glanced away, slightly flushed. She should probably tell Drum. About her background. Now would be a good time. About to speak, she paused as Drum stepped toward the girls. 'Not near their back legs Tiff. They may kick if startled.' Tiffany nodded and moved back to Chippy's withers, brushing and chatting with the horse and Billie.

Drum moved back to the gate and whistled. Jack, his large bay stallion cantered up from the paddock. Drum opened the gate, Jack following, nudging his back as he walked. Reaching over the fence, Drum picked up a bridle and placed it over Jack's head. He tied his horse to the fence, leaving him with a nosebag of grain, happily munching away.

'Okay girls let's get the saddles on. They followed him into the tack room, returning with Tiffany carrying the bridles, Billie carrying her little stock saddle and Drum carrying a larger one. Drum decided they would put Billie's little saddle on Chippy for Tiffany. Billie could ride Lady using the regular stock saddle.

Harriet moved into the yard, patting the horses, rubbing their noses. Drum winked at her. 'Good. They don't frighten you.'

Narrowing her eyes slightly, Harriet responded. 'No, they don't frighten me.' She had been about to share something, but the arrogance and assumption of his remark annoyed her.

Billie attended to Tiffany first, helping her mount Chippy before leading her around the yard in a walk and trot. Tiffany seemed relaxed and Drum nodded approval. He held Chippy while Billie mounted Lady. She had trouble reaching the stirrup to get on, Lady was taller than Chippy, but before Drum could assist, she led the mare to the side of the yard and climbed on to her from the fence. Harriet laughed and clapped her hands. 'Well done, Billie. You're a born problem solver.'

Drum instructed both girls to walk their horses around the yard while he saddled Jack. He planned to take them out into the nearest paddock; he would lead Tiffany on Chippy and Billie could ride Lady. Harriet could see Drum was being careful, making sure both girls were confident as despite Billie's experience, she wasn't used to the slightly bigger mare and larger saddle.

'I'll head home for a while, I need to put some washing on. I'm going to make something for afternoon tea, so I'll see you later.' Harriet waved them off, before walking back to Bellbird Cottage.

5 0

After an hour on the horses, riding around the home paddock, the girls chose to head inside to make lunch. Drum was pleased they had been eager to help unsaddle their horses, brush, feed and water them before turning them out into the small house paddock that he thought of as Chippy's.

Tiffany had done really well, had a good seat and listened carefully to his, and Billie's instructions. Drum smiled to himself. He'd talk to Melanie, see if Tiffany was interested in a regular riding lesson with Billie. He could move Billie up to Lady permanently and keep Chippy for Tiff to ride. It would be great for the girls to share the interest and improve their riding together.

Drum smiled as they ran back to the homestead, reminding them to wash their hands and change out of their riding clothes before starting in the kitchen. Closing the gate, he watched Chippy and Lady trot into the paddock, shaking their heads, before kicking up their heels and cantering down to the hay rack.

He kept Jack in a smaller side paddock with a high post and rail fence all around. His grandfather had strongly advocated for any stallions to be kept separately. They could be unpredictable if one of the mares came in season. Drum's father had agreed.

His mind turned to Harriet. He wondered if she really did want to learn to ride. Billie would love it. He thought he might too. They hadn't had a chance to be together since last Saturday night, but images and thoughts of her had been on his mind. But he'd had to go to Sydney, speak to Annabelle himself. Ensure he was doing the right thing for Billie, but also for Annabelle. That she was happy moving on.

Drum believed there was more to Harriet than she let on, and looked forward to spending time with her, getting to know her. They would need to talk. He wasn't going to rush into it. And he had Billie to think of. He wanted to talk to her about that, see what she wanted. Expected. What she was looking for. Would she be happy to wait while he managed the settlement with Annabelle? He didn't want anything to unsettle Billie, yet he felt instinctively that Harriet knew that. Would always put Billie first.

He looked to the west. Dark clouds hung over the Barrington Tops, up over the National Park area. It looked like it was raining up there and may move this way. Good. They need rain. A flash caught his eye. Lightning up over the Tops. It looked like it was a decent storm. He hurried into the house.

'We're making toasted ham and cheese sandwiches Daddy. And you can have tomato in yours too if you like.' He smiled at them. They had set up the sandwich maker, buttered several slices of bread and had the ham and cheese ready to go and a tomato and sharp knife on the cutting board. He had asked Billie not to use the sharp knife unless he was there.

'Great job, thank you.' He sliced the tomato and watched as Billie expertly laid the fixings in the sandwich maker. 'What would you like to do this afternoon?'

Billie looked at Tiffany, they nodded and said in unison. 'Go to see Harri and help her make afternoon tea.'

'Really?'

'We were going to ask if we could swim, but it looks like the storm will be here soon. So, we thought we could go to Harri's and cook. And maybe look at her books or watch a movie with her. She has Netflix.' They nodded in unison.

'Alright. I'll give her a call and see if that's okay with her.' Drum picked up his phone.

'Umm. You don't need to do that Daddy. I already called her from the house phone. Harri said she'd love to have us come over.' Billie looked a bit sheepish.

'I'm sure she would Billie.' Drum looked at her sternly. 'But you know you should have checked with me first?'

'Yes.' Billie looked down for a moment. Drum couldn't bear to see her disappointment and didn't want to chastise her too much in front of Tiffany.

'Well, I will just call her now and double-check.'

'Thank you, Daddy.' Billie beamed at him, before lifting the lid of the sandwich maker with potholders on her hands, using an egg flip to get the first two out. 'Why don't you put yours on Daddy, then it will cook while you talk to Harri.'

'Good idea, little Miss Practical.' He did as she suggested, then walked into his study and called Harriet.

'Hi Drum.'

'Hi Harri. I believe my daughter has already arranged a visit with you after lunch.' He smiled as he spoke.

He could hear the humour in her voice when she answered. 'Oh, she did. It's great. I thought they might want to. We're going to make chocolate crackles and scones.'

'Okay. I'll walk them over in a half hour.'

'Perfect. Oh, Drum?'

'Yes.' He was grinning now, he could sense she was having fun with him.

'You can stay and bake too if you'd like.'

'Hmm. Lovely offer. I couldn't think of anything I'd enjoy more, getting hot in the kitchen with you Harri.' He lowered his voice, his meaning clear. 'But not while my girl is there.'

'Ha! You got me.'

'But I'll take a rain check.' He ended the call, adoring the laughter in her voice. Despite all she'd been through, Harri had an easy-going humour, but she'd also shown she wasn't a pushover. He grinned. He had Billie with him permanently, and he had an interesting neighbour to get to know. He thought for a moment of the way she'd fired up at him at the river. She had a keen sense of justice and was, he thought, very forthright and honest. But not a walkover, and he liked that. In fact, her temper, once raised, almost matched his. Chuckling to himself, he decided the future looked interesting, and maybe a bit challenging, at the very least.

Humming, he stepped back into the kitchen. Billie had just served his sandwich on to a plate. 'Thank you, Billie.' He looked at Tiffany. 'Would you like anything else Tiffany? Another sandwich?'

'No thank you Mr Murray.' Drum raised his eyebrows. Of course, that's what she'd call him, he's the father of her school pal. He wondered if he should ask her to call him Drum but thought he would check with Melanie first.

'We're going to have a *feast* at Harri's Daddy, we don't need anything else.' The way she emphasised feast made him laugh.

'Alright. How about you go and set up everything in the spare room for later tonight, then I'll walk you across to Harri's.'

'Okayyy!' they chorused as they got down from their chairs, taking their plates to the sink.

'I'll wash up. You go and do girl-stuff now.' Drum chuckled as Billie flew into his arms for a quick hug before racing from the room, Tiffany right behind her.

5 1

*H*arriet had all the ingredients ready in the kitchen for cooking with the girls. She was really excited about it. Every time she saw Billie her affection for her grew. And Tiffany was gorgeous. She seemed quiet at times, but when she was comfortable, she was as quirky and independent as Billie. Harriet remembered being served by her on her first day in town. She could see how the girls had become friends. Perhaps like Rose and Debbie were from the same age.

Stepping out to the back veranda, she looked toward the mountain range, the Barrington Tops. Dark, low clouds hung there, most likely raining already and slowly heading toward them. A bolt of lightning lit up the sky. Harriet shivered. She wasn't keen on electrical storms. Hearing voices, she glanced toward the main homestead. Drum was walking the girls over, but he was leading Jack.

Hurrying through to the front door, she opened it and met the girls at her garden gate.

'Harri! Are you ready for us?' Billie and Tiffany stood side by side, looking up at her expectantly.

'I sure am. Go on in and check I have everything ready for the chocolate crackles, the recipe is on the bench.'

'Okay!' they ran up the path, kicking their shoes off at the door, then disappeared inside the cottage.

Drum stepped forward, looked over Harri's shoulder, probably to ensure the girls had gone in, then leaned down and kissed her gently on the mouth.

'Hmm. You taste good. Did you start without them?'

Harriet laughed and kissed him back. 'I may have tried a piece of chocolate, you know, just to check it's okay.' She looked at Jack, then back at Drum. 'Checking the cattle?'

He glanced west. The clouds had edged closer. 'It's not just rain Harri. It's quite a storm. And unless it blows out before it gets here in the next hour or so, I'd say we're in for a drenching. And that's all good, we need it. But the electrical activity, well, it scares the stock. I've got the good bulls and heifers for the sale in paddocks up on those ridges.' He pointed. 'But it's heavily forested and if a tree goes down, it could startle them. They'll head for home and won't care about fences. I don't want them injured.'

Frowning, Harriet looked where he pointed. 'Of course. Are you moving them closer?' His two working dogs sat at his feet.

'I'll bring them down to paddocks on the other side of your creek there. If you don't mind, I'll take Jack through your back garden and head out over the creek. I'll open the gates as I go up and when I get behind them, with the help of the dogs, we'll just walk them back down. You'll probably see us down here in a couple of hours.'

Stepping back, Harriet opened the gate to her garden. 'Come on through, I'll open the back gate. I won't keep you.' She hurried ahead, opening the rear gate. Drum nodded his thanks as he walked through. Harriet was conscious that the girls were now on the back veranda. She knew he would have kissed her otherwise.

In the saddle in one fluid movement, he turned Jack, waved to his daughter, then cantered to the creek, jumped it and continued up the slope into the trees. The dogs followed, swimming across the creek, then ran along behind the horse.

As Harriet walked up the back steps, a few large drops of rain splashed in front of her. the clouds were moving quickly now, rolling and dark. She shivered again, an uncomfortable sensation sending the hairs on the back of her neck standing straight up. It's the electrical activity, she thought.

Moving into the kitchen, she let the feeling go as she helped the girls mix up the first batch of chocolate crackles. Harriet didn't do much herself, letting the girls have their way in the kitchen. They were both quite organised and followed the recipe carefully. Bits of chocolate powder found its way on to their faces, and even in their hair, but they were having fun and she was happy watching them, answering their questions and making suggestions.

The rain was coming down steadily, so heavy that at times they had to raise their voices to hear over the noise it made on the tin roof.

More than an hour later, they had also mixed the scones and she was heating the oven for them. Hearing hoofbeats she walked out the back. A few heifers had made their way down to the creek and more were walking out of the trees further up the slope. No sign of Drum, but he was likely bringing the heifers down first, then going back for the bulls as he'd surely put them into a different paddock.

The rain was heavy now, the sky dark. Lightning crackled every few minutes, some of it seemed really close. Harriet felt uneasy. She had expected to see Drum behind the heifers before he went back up.

Her phone rang. She pulled it out of her pocket. Laura.

'Hi Harri. Big storm, good rain.'

'Yes, it's really coming down now.'

'I've moved my stock close to the house. Nothing I can do now but watch it soak in and my grass start to grow.' She laughed. 'Wondered if you'd be interested in a visitor. Thought I might drop over and watch the storm with you.'

'Yes, come over. I've got Billie and Tiffany here, just putting some scones in the oven.'

'Righto, I'm on my way.'

LAURA RAN UP THE PATH, A RAINCOAT OVER HER HEAD. THE RAIN was really bucketing down. Harriet let her in, and they sat in the kitchen with a cup of tea, chatting with the girls. Laura tried a chocolate crackle and swore it was the best she'd ever had. The girls giggled.

Harriet glanced out the back a few times. It looked like most of the heifers were down. No sign of Drum, but perhaps he'd been and gone while they chatted in the kitchen. Unfazed by the thunder and lightning, Billie and Tiffany went out to the laundry to wash their hands.

A scream ripped through the air. Billie. 'Harri! Harri!' She ran out, Laura behind her. Billie was pointing across the creek, now crying out, 'Daddy! Where's Daddy?'

Harriet saw Jack, riderless, his reins dragging in the mud on the other side of the creek where the hooves of the heifers had churned it up.

Laura and Harriet looked at each other for a split second, then Harriet jumped into action. 'Laura, call Rose, find Angus, let them know we think Drum may have fallen off Jack. Get someone up here with a motorbike or quad to help search.'

Billie was crying. Harriet wrapped her arms around her. 'Be brave now Billie. Your Dad is smart, and a good rider. He may have come off and Jack got scared and came down behind the heifers. Dad may just be walking down now. But you know we have to be sure. So, we'll go and find him.' Billie stopped crying and nodded. Tiffany stepped close and held Billie's hand.

Harriet could hear Laura speaking to Rose. She ran to her room, threw on the jeans and boots she'd had on earlier at the horse yards. She looked at her watch, less than three minutes since Billie had raised the alarm.

'Angus and Jamie are on their way. They've got motorbikes on the back of the Ute. They'll be about fifteen minutes.' Laura spoke normally, trying not to alarm Billie and Tiffany.

'Good. Wait here for them Laura. Look after the girls.' Harriet ran down the back steps and into the rain before Laura had a chance to answer. She'd jammed an old Akubra hat on to keep the rain off her face, at least. She looked at Jack on the other side of the creek. The creek had risen, the water noisy as it made its way higher, swirling and gushing against the dry banks. Harriet whistled, like she'd heard Angus do. Jack lifted his head. She whistled again. He lunged into the creek, heading straight for her. As he came up the bank he stopped in front of her, tossing his head about.

Patting him, she spoke softly, and he seemed to settle. Grabbing the left stirrup, she pulled the leather down, measured it against her arm and shortened it by six notches. Moving under his neck, she did the same on the other side. Back under his neck and already wet through, she stood on her toes, securing her left foot in the stirrup, she was up in the saddle in a moment. Gathering the reins up, she patted Jack on the neck and leaning forward spoke to him encouragingly.

Pulling the Akubra more firmly onto her head, she trotted Jack back a few metres, then turned and dug her heels in. He bounded into a canter and jumped the creek with room to spare, Harriet firm in the saddle, cantered up the slope on the other side. She cut through the cattle, moving out of their way quickly. Harriet could see the hoof marks of the herd in front of her and cantered up the slope and into the cover of the trees. Lightning crackled and a loud clap of thunder startled Jack. He shied, but she kept her seat, urging him on. She managed to close the gate to the creek paddock without dismounting, locking the heifers in securely. Urging Jack back into a trot, they climbed higher. Harriet cast around looking for signs of the mob of bulls, or Drum. Thinking the dogs must have stayed with him, she kept going. Her instinct told her he was injured.

A movement to one side caught her eye. Peering through the rain she saw the bulls, Black Angus, blending with the trees. They were standing together near a gate. It was closed but not latched. Harriet felt this was the one Drum had opened, but the wind must have blown it closed. She slowed Jack, then dismounted, leading him quietly along the fence line to the gate. She opened it and immediately the bulls began to move through it, some of them jostling the others. Harriet tried to count them. She knew there should be about forty. She counted thirty-eight. Close enough. It was likely they were all there. She closed the gate and remounted Jack, heading further west.

What had Drum been wearing? Dark jeans. And his shirt? She closed her eyes for a moment. Dark blue check. The tree cover kept the rain off her to an extent, but the low dark clouds made it difficult to see too far in any direction. She loosened the reins and gave Jack his head. He trotted steadily west, his long stride covering a lot of ground quickly.

A bark alerted her. The two dogs ran towards Jack, tails wagging, tongues lolling. Now she knew Drum must be hurt and not far away. The dogs wouldn't leave him. She was surprised Jack hadn't stayed with him too.

The dogs ran south a few metres, then ran back to her. Harriet followed them. She saw him. Drum. Propped up against a tree. His shirt was torn, or maybe half off. He looked at her. Pain and surprise, and relief, on his face. Quickly dismounting, Harriet threw Jack's reins over a tree branch and in two strides was beside Drum. Now she could see his shirt. Tied around his right arm like a sling.

'Harri.' He leaned back against the tree.

'It's okay Drum, Angus and Jamie are coming with bikes, we'll get you down to the house. Do you think your arm's broken?' She looked into his eyes. He was in pain and seemed to be struggling for breath.

'Collarbone, I think. Lightning struck a tree.' He wheezed, struggling for breath. 'Jack reared. Rolled on me. Didn't get out of the saddle. Quickly. Enough.' The effort to speak left him breathless and Harriet frowned as he tipped his head back, leaning against the tree trunk.

'Okay. Don't try to speak. Save your energy. We know what we're dealing with then.' She hoped it was just the collarbone, and his shortness of breath was due to pain and nothing more sinister, like internal injuries.

Beyond the trees, the rain was still heavy. Harriet bit her lip. The motorbikes would have trouble getting traction up here, it was steep. Too much rain to get a chopper in either. She looked at Jack, then back at Drum.

'Jack came down to the creek. Billie saw him.' Harriet frowned. 'I'm really surprised he left you. Thought he'd stay, like the dogs.'

Gritting his teeth, Drum tried to smile. 'I made him go. I sent him home, slapped him on the rump. He took off.' He paused, catching his breath. 'I wasn't sure whether he'd follow the heifers to you. Or return to the homestead. I knew you'd raise the alarm.' He gasped and leaned back.

'Don't speak anymore.' She knelt beside him. 'I didn't bring anything. Bandages. Pain relief. I'm sorry. My only thought was to find you.' Harriet berated herself. She should have grabbed some bloody Aspirin, at least.

'Billie? Tiffany?' Drum looked worried.

'Laura's with them.' Harriet pulled her phone out. 'I'm going to try to call her. I don't think the bikes will get up here.'

No signal. Too many trees. She'd need to move him down to the cleared areas. She looked again at Drum, too pale, breathing shallowly. She had to get him down to flatter ground. She glanced at Jack. His head was up, ears twitching in the heavy rain, but not prancing around. Probably as calm as a horse could be in these conditions.

'We need to get you down to the flats, meet up with Angus and Jamie. I'm going to help you on to Jack, lead you down.' Harriet spoke firmly.

Drum looked from her to his horse. He gritted his teeth and nodded. Harriet helped him sit up straight, then got his feet under him, leveraging his back against the tree truck he stood, his face creased in pain, struggling for air.

'I'm going to adjust this sling, make it firmer. Hold on, this will hurt.' She worked quickly, but his arm was more stable now. Apart from letting his breath out, he made no sound. He just nodded at her, his face a pale mask of pain.

Jack stood still, turning once to watch, as she got Drum's left foot in the stirrup. 'Use your left hand to hold the saddle, I'll steady you.'

It took two attempts, but he was in the saddle. Despite the rain filtering through the trees, she could see sweat on his brow from the effort. He nodded to her. Taking Jack's reins Harriet started leading the horse down. She slipped a few times herself, and her old injury was sore, but she pushed on. Drum didn't speak, just held on. It was slow going, but they made it to the paddock she'd locked the bulls into. Only a couple of them stood near the gate, most had moved down to lower ground.

5 2

Gritting his teeth, Drum hung on to the saddle, willing himself not to fall. He watched Harriet, slipping and sliding in the mud and torrential rain in front of him. Despite slipping over, she didn't stop. Just got back on her feet and pushed on. He was grateful. And impressed

So bloody determined. He'd known she'd raise the alarm if Jack turned up without him, but he hadn't expected her to come looking for him herself.

He frowned. How the hell did she find him? And she rode Jack? Really? He was a good horse but spirited. He'd believed only an experienced rider could manage him.

He looked at the closed gate. The bulls. His prize stud bulls. 'Harri!' She didn't hear him over the rain. He tried again. 'Harri!' She stopped, stepped back to his side.

Nodding toward the gate, all he could manage was, 'The bulls?'

'I counted thirty-eight!' She had to shout over the rain. 'I knew there should be about forty, and maybe I miscounted. But I think I got them all through.'

'You? By yourself?' He shook his head. 'How?'

'Not by myself. I had Jack.' She turned and continued walking, leading the horse.

Drum clung on with his legs. His head was spinning, the pain intense. He focussed on Harriet. He had so many questions. It seemed like hours but must have been about forty minutes, and they broke through the tree cover. Drum could see her cottage down the slope and over the creek, which was up to the top of its banks now. He squinted through the rain. Billie was waving from the veranda. He wanted to wave back but couldn't lift his arm. Harriet waved and called out to them.

Movement to the side caught his attention. Jamie on a motorbike, Angus at the creek, wading through the quickly flowing water.

The rest was a blur, the men helping him off the horse, carrying him over the creek. There was an ambulance, Billie hugged him before they closed the door. He looked for Harriet but couldn't see her. The paramedics had given him something for the pain.

Drum woke in Barrington Hospital. He looked around, tried to speak. The nurse came to him. 'Ahh, Drum. Back with us, Good. Doctor will be in shortly.'

Closing his eyes, he nodded. Hours later, or maybe minutes, he was woken by the Doctor. 'Drum. How's the pain?'

His mouth dry, Drum rasped. 'Okay.'

'You've had surgery. Broken scapula and collarbone. We've put a plate in there. And you have two broken ribs, one punctured your right lung. We've reinflated the lung. You'll be all right, but it will take some time. Questions?'

'Billie?' Drum breathed in. Punctured lung. That explained a lot. 'Where's Billie? And Harriet? Is Harriet all right?' He had a strange image in his mind of Harriet mounting Jack like a stockman as he was lifted over the creek. He must have dreamt it. She'd cantered back up the slope, heading south toward the homestead.

'They're all here if you'd like to see them. Harriet and Billie stayed here all night. Melanie took Tiffany home, wanted to take Billie, but she wouldn't leave you, so they stayed. We made them comfortable in the visitors room.' The doctor glanced up. 'Ahh. Billie. Come in, your dad's awake.

Billie walked quickly to the bed. He tried to lean over, give her a kiss. 'Don't Daddy. Don't move. You've had an operation.' He could see she'd been crying, but she was smiling now. He smiled back. Bless his sweet girl. She took his hand and climbed on to the edge of the bed, away from his bandaged shoulder.

'Harri saved you Daddy. I saw Jack without you and screamed. I knew you must have fallen off. Harri just shortened the stirrups, then she got him to jump the creek.' Billie frowned for a moment. 'The creek was up very high too. Then she galloped up the hill and into the trees. Like Norah of Billabong.'

Billie looked toward the door. 'Harri! He's awake. Daddy's awake Harri.' Billie beckoned her in. Harriet walked in slowly. Drum narrowed his eyes. She was in pain, he could tell by the way she walked.

Before he could speak, Rose, Angus with little Charlie in his arms, and Laura appeared in the doorway. Angus strode forward. 'Mate. Good to see you awake.'

Drum nodded. Billie squeezed his hand and he smiled at her. She beamed back.

Looking at Angus, Drum spoke. 'The stock?'

'We checked them all last night, and again this morning. The storm passed just after dark, headed across to the coast. The river and creeks are up, but not over their banks. We'll have good feed for the summer.' He grinned at this. 'I did a head count against your listings for the sale. All accounted for. It was good you got them all into the lower paddocks before your fall.'

Drum noticed Harriet had moved back, now beside Laura. 'I didn't. I fell before I got the bulls in. Harriet found them, got them into the paddock and closed the gate. On her way to me.'

'Well, what do you know. You didn't mention that last night Harriet Russell.' Rose had her hands on her hips, but she was smiling as she looked at Harriet. She turned back to Drum. 'Billie raised the alarm. She saw Jack. Then Harriet and Laura sprang into action.' Drum looked at his daughter with pride.

'Good girl, thank you.' He squeezed her hand for a moment, tried to catch Harriet's eye.

'But it was Harri, Daddy, who found you. Harri was on Jack so fast I couldn't believe it.' Billie looked at Harriet, screwing up her nose as she spoke. 'I don't think she needs riding lessons. I think she already knows how.'

All eyes turned to Harriet. Drum didn't miss the blush to her cheeks and as he looked around the room, neither did the others.

'You didn't tell me you could ride Harri.' Billie, still slightly bemused, looked across at her.

'You didn't ask, Billie.' As Harriet answered, Drum could see she was uncomfortable.

'But Daddy said you're a city girl.' He chuckled inwardly as his daughter persisted.

Drum tried to smile as he looked at Harriet. 'Yes Harri. While some city girls may ride, in my experience they're not usually comfortable on a spirited stallion, galloping about fearlessly in a violent storm.'

Rose moved to Harriet's side. 'Well done, Harri.'

'Yes. Well done Harri.' This from Laura, grinning madly. Harriet shook her head, tried to step back, but Drum beckoned her closer.

'Harri was just about to tell us where she learned to ride like that.' He was enjoying himself, despite his physical discomfort.

'Um.' Harriet looked at Laura, who nodded. Drum thought she sounded a bit defensive as she answered. 'No one asked me. Except Laura.' Her voice rose, and she pointed her finger at Drum. 'You kept referring to me as a city girl.'

'Yes, I did. Alfa Romeo, city clothes, plenty of style. I did assume that.' Drum was chuckling now, although it hurt his ribs when he did. 'So, what's the truth of it Harri? I'm so bloody grateful, whatever it is.' He tousled Billie's hair with his left hand as he spoke.

'I've been living in the city for ten years, it's true. But I grew up on a farm. A large dairy farm, down in southern New South Wales.'

'Really? A dairy farm. And your horse-riding skill?' Drum wheezed a little as he laughed, then winced. Laura chuckled at his words.

'And the rest Harri. Tell him the rest.' Laura was laughing harder. Drum stared at her for a moment, then looked again at Harriet. It seemed everyone in the room was waiting for her answer.

She mumbled something.

'I beg your pardon, Harriet. I didn't quite catch that?' Drum again.

'I said. My father is a horse breaker.' She looked at each of them in turn. 'Gordy Russell. You may have heard of him.'

Drum laughed out loud, his left hand on his ribs, but he wheezed his words out. 'Gordy Russell! Are you kidding? He's the horse whisperer himself! Bloody hell Harri, why keep this to yourself?'

'I don't know. I almost told you yesterday at the horse yards. But your assumptions about me, um, annoyed me.' Harriet raised her chin in half-hearted defiance, before continuing. 'I love the country. Love horses, cattle. But I wanted city life, I was keen on business. But now, coming here, I'm back in the country. Buying Bellbird Cottage, well, I had thought to ask you if I could keep a horse, later on, you know. In one of your horse paddocks.' Billie was bouncing up and down in delight. 'Um, my dad was going to send me one of his, when I'm ready.'

'Oh! You can Harri. And we can go riding together! Can't we Daddy?' Drum raised his good arm, beckoned Harriet closer. She stepped to the side of the bed.

'Sit, please Harri.' He patted the bed as Billie scooted back to make room. He whispered to her, 'Come closer, I want to tell you something.' Although she glanced at the others, Drum was ready when she turned back to him, leaning closer. With his good hand he turned her chin toward him and kissed her hard, and loudly, on the lips.

'Thank you, Harri.' He murmured softly. 'For everything you've brought to us all.' Somewhat louder, he added, 'You can keep ten bloody horses if you want!'

Smiling, Harriet leaned in again, kissing him gently on the lips, before turning to the others, her face flushed. 'Don't thank me. It's you.' She looked at each of them. 'All of you. From the night I hit the kangaroo driving into town. I've found my place. My place to start over. It's here. In Barrington. Right here.'

Drum leaned back against the pillows, aching and tired, but happy, as his sweet daughter climbed on to Harriet's lap. He looked at Billie. 'Oh, we need to do some shopping Billie. I want to bake a chocolate cake for someone.' He grinned at Harriet. 'From scratch.'

THE END

AFTERWORD

While the town of Barrington does exist, it is little more than a village with a general store.

I've imagined elements of nearby larger towns, such as Gloucester, to create my version of the township of Barrington for this story.

Any similarities to people living or deceased, are purely coincidental and a product of my imagination.

The Barrington Tops, Bucketts Mountain, Rocky Crossing and Barrington and Gloucester rivers do exist – and it is a stunning region to visit.

ACKNOWLEDGMENTS

Huge thanks to Bloke, for support, encouragement, the cooking of many fine meals and for keeping my life filled with music and laughter. And to my girls, Jas and Emi, for your positive support and great marketing and design advice.

A huge thank you to my fellow authors and beta readers Emma Powell and Louise Forster. Your comments and guidance helped me produce a better manuscript. Thank you also to Rhonda Forrest and Leanne Lovegrove, who along with Emma and Louise, worked with me to create the Sunburnt Land anthology. What started as a one-off project has turned into a fabulous author support group. Watch this space for more offerings from the five of us.

The beautiful cover art was created by my dear friend Fiona Hayes @fionahayesart.

Thank you for the many chats and movie dates during the creation of this book.

∾

If you have enjoyed this book, I'd love you to take a moment to rate and/or review. Ratings, reviews and social media mentions are such an important part of the marketing mix for independent authors. Reader support is what keeps me writing. Thank you.

ABOUT THE AUTHOR

Susan Mackie is first and foremost a farmer's daughter. Her career as a journalist, small business owner, tourist resort developer, real estate agent and government employee created a wealth of experience from which to develop characters and storylines. Susan has two daughters, two grandchildren, and lives in a country town in southern Queensland with Bloke. A Place to Start Over is the second novel in her Barrington series, although they can be read as stand-alone's.

https://www.susanmackie.com/